THE EDGE OF DESIRE

Tuhin A. Sinha is a best-selling author, a columnist and the scriptwriter of several popular TV shows. His three previous books – *That Thing Called Love*, *The Captain* (formerly *22 Yards*) and *Of Love And Politics* are widely acknowledged for breaking new ground in terms of subject and treatment. Apart from writing fiction and scripts, Tuhin is a keen political observer. His columns on Indian politics appear often in India's leading dailies. Tuhin also has a regular blog on ibnlive.com. When he finds time from all of these, you might catch him on a news channel, debating politics or cricket.

THE EDGE OF DESIRE

Tuhin A.Sinha

First published by Hachette India
(Registered name: Hachette Book Publishing India Pvt. Ltd)
An Hachette UK company
www.hachetteindia.com

1

Copyright © Tuhin A. Sinha 2012

Tuhin A. Sinha asserts the moral right to be identified
as the author of this work

All rights reserved. No part of the publication may be reproduced,
stored in a retrieval system (including but not limited to computers,
disks, external drives, electronic or digital devices, e-readers, websites),
or transmitted in any form or by any means (including but not limited to
cyclostyling, photocopying, docutech or other reprographic reproductions,
mechanical, recording, electronic, digital versions) without the prior
written permission of the publisher, nor be otherwise circulated in any
form of binding or cover other than that in which it is published and
without a similar condition being imposed on the subsequent purchaser.

This is a work of fiction. Any resemblance to real persons, living or dead,
or actual events or locales is purely coincidental.

ISBN 978-93-5009-443-3

Hachette Book Publishing India Pvt Ltd
4th/5th Floors, Corporate Centre, Plot no. 94,
Sector 44, Gurgaon 122003, India

Typeset in Adobe Jenson Pro 11/14.3
by RECTO Graphics, Delhi

Printed and bound in India by
Gopsons Papers Ltd., Noida

To every woman who has been a victim of gender crimes in this country that deifies umpteen goddesses.

PROLOGUE

In Delhi's Tihar Jail, a corridor leads you past a row of dingy cells to a slightly more spacious 'VIP' cell. Seated inside this confinement, with her back against the wall, her dusky, dark-eyed face resting on her knees, her long hair dishevelled, is politician Shruti Ranjan. At 33, she is petite and slim but looks older than her years. She glances up. Her face reveals nothing.

Amidst drizzle, in a Connaught Place bookstore window, a more cheerful image of Shruti is visible on the cover of a book that is selling like hot cakes. *The Edge of Desire* is what she calls her memoirs. The owner of the store proudly announces that the book has sold over 2000 copies from his shop in just two days – a record of sorts. The book has become something of a craze with everyone trying to get an inside into Shruti's tumultuous rise and fall from power.

In his official Boring Canal Road residence in Patna, State Cabinet Secretary Rohit Verma sits watching India News, along with his wife, Shyamlee. It is raining here as well. On the news channel, anchor Abhay Sarkar talks about the political fallout of the revelations made by Shruti in her book. Rohit quietly lights a cigarette. His wife can sense Rohit's awkwardness. Rohit walks up to the window.

Broadcast live from Humayun Road in Lutyens' Delhi, two prominent national leaders rave about Shruti's guts on Sarkar's show. Shruti has written in her book that while she had known that not all of Home Minister Sharad Malviya's decisions were completely above board, she had purposely decided to kowtow to him as Malviya was promoting her and opposing him would have jeopardized her career.

One of the two leaders, who has known Shruti for several years, simply says, 'If Shruti had realized that she had played into Malviya's hands, she would never have done this.' The other nods sagely.

Back in Patna, Rohit feels increasingly uncomfortable as Abhay begins to dissect each section of the book with his guests. Seeing his discomfiture, his wife turns off the TV and places a hand on his shoulder but Rohit can't keep his eyes off the book, a copy of which lies on the table in front of him.

The mild rains give way to violent thunder-showers...

PART ONE

PART ONE

1

KISHANGANJ, BIHAR, 1997

Sporadic thundershowers greeted us as our car entered the district on the morning of second July, after an excruciating sixteen-hour journey from the state capital. Rohit and I had been married two days ago in Patna but our marriage had not not yet been consummated. Nor did the long journey give much scope for romance, considering there was a gun-toting guard on the front seat who didn't miss any opportunity to peer back at us, gauge our proximity to each other, and exchange sly glances with the driver. I'm not sure if I felt particularly romantic, anyway. After all, ours was a conventional arranged marriage.

Dad had put out a standard ad in the newspapers. You know, the kind that says, '*High status, IAS/ IIT/IIM groom for professionally qualified, beautiful, modern yet traditional, 25/5'5 bride from decent, well-educated family of doctors. Dowry seekers excuse.*'

This ad is what had brought Rohit Verma into my life.

Government servants, I've realized, attach a lot of significance to terms that hold their worth only for effect. Rohit wanted a beautiful bride, as any prize government official would. More importantly, even though he would not explicitly say so, he wanted someone who would willingly play second fiddle to him. I have a strong feeling the inclusion of the word 'traditional' may have influenced his liking. No, the *Veronicas* of the world did not excite him. After all, as the wife of an IAS officer, I'd be expected to accompany him to social dos of all kinds, from flag-hoisting ceremonies on Republic and Independence Day, to undertaking some social work of my own, to being his arm candy when he assumed more important responsibilities in the state capital. Anyhow, that's how he had explained the responsibilities of an 'IAS wife' to me on one of our arranged, pre-marriage dates.

❖

When our car entered Kishanganj town its speed had to be reduced to a crawl – about ten kilometres an hour – so bad was the flood situation. The nullahs were overflowing. River water had, in fact, entered several parts of the town. At one point, we were compelled to stay put for two hours on a small stretch of road till the water receded.

As we sat staring at the rising water, I looked at Rohit glumly. He was my husband. I was going to spend the rest of my life with him. Why did he then still seem a stranger to me? Why couldn't he just hold my hand and act more like my man?

Or was I, perhaps, expecting him to be like Abhay, the guy I had once been in love with?

Rohit and I had met just three months ago. I was in Patna staying with my parents. I had quit my job as a correspondent with one of the first private Indian news channels in Delhi and had taken a sabbatical from work. I guess I was trying to find meaning in things – to understand why stuff that I had not anticipated was happening to me.

Being ditched by Abhay after five years of living together had taken the sheen off my existence. After all, we had been a couple right from our second year in college. We had done our Mass Comm. together. Abhay was lanky and dark and by no means good looking, but he exuded a confidence that made him appear quite cool. And in college – when most guys are a bit unsure of what the future holds for them – the swagger he displayed attracted a number of girls. That he, discounting their advances, showed his preference for me, naturally flattered me. It was only later that I realized he was not what he seemed to be.

Living with him I so enjoyed the comfort zone that his company provided that I never realized we were growing apart. We had our differences, sure, but by then my emotional attachment to him was so strong that it didn't matter what kind of man he really was; I would still have happily continued living with him. We were both quite content in our careers; we were both being noticed by our bosses and moving smoothly up the ladder. Abhay Sarkar had joined the print media; I, the electronic.

Sometimes, it takes a jolt to acquaint you with the truth. Mine was the discovery that Antara, my best buddy and colleague, whom I had introduced to Abhay, was secretly having an affair with my guy.

I'm not sure how many other women have experienced what I did that fateful night: the sight of my boyfriend and my best friend entwined in an unclad and passionate embrace. They weren't expecting me home that early; I had a late-night reporting assignment that was cancelled at the last moment.

Strangely, when I was subjected to this horrid sight, my mind focused on the bedspread. It was the violet velvet one that I loved so much and which I had bought after much searching, to make our nights together more dreamy. The same sheet now draped Abhay and Antara as they stood in front of me trying to conceal what little they could.

I'm not sure how I would have reacted to an apology from Abhay. But the fact is that Abhay did not apologize; nor did Antara. In fact, Abhay tried to justify his actions by telling me that ours was a 'confused, overstretched college romance that had outlived its life'.

His words shattered my self-belief. I found it virtually impossible to get a hold on myself. When I moved out and rented a single room apartment, I felt such a sense of forlornness that it killed me from within. How could a man dismiss three years of courtship and another two of living-in together as a *confused, over-stretched college romance*? And how could I have not seen it coming? How could I have been in such denial of the state of our relationship?

The sight of them together did not cease to haunt me. I desperately tried to erase the last five years from my life, forgetting that human existence hadn't yet found a way to do that. The image of them together would not let me forget anything. My mental state was that of a dead woman walking.

My parents, both of whom were doctors, knew as much about my romance as one could share with educated Bihari parents of the generation who like to believe they are progressive and communicate well with their children. I had thus, without divulging the intensity of our bond, told them about my 'special friendship' with Abhay. It was even implied that we'd get married one day. When I subsequently informed them about my break-up, it was only natural for them to press the panic button. After resisting their persuasion for nearly six months, I finally gave in. I took a sabbatical from work and came back to Patna, the city where I had gone to school.

Leaving Delhi, which I'd begun to feel would be my home for the rest of my life, wasn't easy. But then, at that point, my journey with the city too seemed to have reached an impasse. Professionally, I'd been covering the same stories over and over – a young French Embassy official molested in the heart of Lutyens' Delhi; the exploits of Delhi's infamous Red-Line buses; stories of the various protests that Jantar Mantar had become synonymous with. None of these stories contained the fodder to excite me. About the only assignment I remember with some sense of satisfaction was a press conference convened by the young and dynamic leader of the Opposition, Sharad Malviya. Those were the days when the PM's post seemed to be decided by a game of musical chairs, what with two of the most unlikely people – Deve Gowda and I.K.Gujral – suddenly occupying the top post thanks to them somehow getting the required numbers on their side. Sharad, in his press conference, had been scathing about the tenets of 'Westminsters' democracy' that enabled any combination of parties to cobble together a government at the Centre if they managed to conjure the required numbers. He called for a massive overhaul of our democratic process.

I'm not sure if Sharad's party subscribed to his views. That, of course, never deterred him from saying what in his opinion served the country's interest the best. In hindsight, I sometimes feel that had I got more assignments like Sharad's press conference maybe I would have sustained my interest in my profession and not quit it as abruptly as I had when Abhay dumped me.

To be honest though, the main reason for leaving Delhi went beyond my profession. I'd got to know the city with Abhay. Without his company, the city and its roads and lanes seemed to leer at me; the landscape turned unfamiliar – alien, unknown and hostile. What was worse was when I chanced upon Abhay and Antara holding hands as they walked past me through the buzzing Connaught Place market. Yes, they were officially a couple now. After seeing them in public together once, I'd get paranoid about spotting them again whenever I visited the India Gate area or North Campus.

I realized the streets of the city had begun to taunt me.

Once back in Patna, Dad convinced me that the best way to move on was to get married. I scoffed at the thought. My first reaction was like – *with a stranger?* That night however I pondered over how people whom you think you know well can suddenly seem strangers. Who then *is* a stranger? A week later, one evening when Dad broached the issue again, I relented. My sudden change of heart, though, was triggered by something else; Abhay had called that morning. His call had taken me by surprise. There was still some faint hope in me that he would repent.

Instead he said, 'Shruti, Antara and I are getting married next month. and we'd like you to come...'

I froze. For an hour or two after talking to him I felt sick to my stomach. My head throbbed and I felt waves of nausea assault me. Luckily, both my parents were not at home and I managed to compose myself before they came.

My parents were relieved by my decision. The next Sunday, the TOI matrimonials' page carried the familiarly-worded ad. Ten days after that, Rohit, whose parents lived in the same Kankerbagh locality of Patna as us, met me when he came home on a short Holi break.

❖

The thundershowers had cleared; only a mild and lovely drizzle remained. Slowly the water levels receded and the driver got ready to start the ten-kilometre drive to the Collector's bungalow, my new home in Kishanganj.

'Chai?' an old, fragile woman enquired rapping on the car window.

I didn't mind the luxury at all. But where would she get it from?

I was explained that the poor, in difficult situations like these, often made money by offering small services to the rich. So, while they weren't professional tea-vendors, they'd double as them to make money. Similarly, people sold food and even provided shelter in their homes for a fee. Rohit asked her for four cups.

'I quite love the rains. In fact, when it rained in Delhi like this, I'd spend the whole day moving around from one place to the other. It's romantic, isn't it?' I said, trying to lift our spirits and relax the strained formality between us.

Rohit's response was strange. 'Moved all *alone?*' was all he asked. Before I replied he added, 'Rains in these parts are such a dampener. They ruin your day.'

I nodded, still hoping that I would fall in love with him, sooner than later, as Dad had assured me I would. As we sipped our tea, I couldn't help thinking back to our first meeting.

❖

It was the day after Holi. The venue was a restaurant in Hotel Samrat. We were both nervous; I, because I found it strange to go through the process of an arranged marriage after having been 'mentally married' to someone else; Rohit, because he hadn't really been in a serious relationship before. As such, he was a bit inexperienced in 'handling women'.

That inexperience revealed itself more prominently in his oblique queries about my past.

'So have you been in love before?' he asked me with sudden, bluff confidence.

'Yes,' was my terse response, while my expression clearly said – *you'd be abnormal if you haven't.*

'Was it a long relationship?'

'Yes.' My responses to both of Rohit's questions were so cryptic that they cut short any further queries.

Rohit was a decent looking chap of average height – 5ft 8 inches, average build, fair skin, a neatly trimmed moustache and a formal disposition; just the sort you'd imagine a character artist playing an upright sarkari officer in a Bollywood movie would look like. He spoke slowly; his words were always guarded and carefully emphasized. This obviously impeded impulsive reactions on my behalf and often had me wonder, especially in our early days of courtship, whether everything that he spoke was considered and weighed before it was uttered.

Rohit was happiest talking about his job. I discovered he was a diligent worker and had a mission plan for his district, which was famous for all the wrong reasons. He was driven by an urge to bring about real change in the quality of people's lives. He was really bugged by corruption at all levels; yet was pragmatic enough to know he could not wish it away. He had a strong point of view on almost every social or political issue; yet knew when to put these aside lest they become a hindrance in the discharge of his job responsibilities. Rohit was clear about his role – he was a catalyst between the government and the people; moreover, he was an instrument of the government, at the service of the people. He was a workaholic and a proud one.

Rohit wasn't quite into music or the arts. He did like watching movies though; his preferences were confined to Madhuri Dixit Hindi films or international action flicks. And like most Indian small-town men, he feasted on cricket.

Our first date can't be called romantic by any stretch of the imagination. I guess Rohit had some apprehensions in his mind; worries that I might not like him. This had probably prevented him from being more expressive of his sentiments to me. Perhaps I just liked to think that Rohit was not the sort of guy who demonstrated his feelings. But when we parted he did mention to me that he'd had a great evening, perhaps the best in many years.

That still did not prepare me for what happened two days later. Rohit's mom called up my dad to say that Rohit wanted to marry me. It took us all by surprise. I mean, things were happening far too suddenly; my meeting with Rohit two days ago hadn't given me the vaguest idea that he would be so prompt with decision-making. Rohit was supposed to leave for Kishanganj the day after and said he wished to meet me once again before he left.

This time round we met for dinner. Rohit surprised me once again with the suddenness of a question that I hadn't anticipated. 'So, how far did you tread in the relationship that you were in?'

'Sorry?'

'I mean, was it a *physical* relationship?'

I paused, uncertain how to feel about this query. Was he probing, inquisitive, or just plain envious?

'Yes. We lived together as a couple.'

He took a long pause to absorb this. 'And why did it break?'

'Because he lost interest in me, while I kept thinking love is eternal,' I said bitterly. I found it hard to hold back my emotions. 'One part of me still loves him as much as I hate him. Because that part of me belongs to him. A close relationship often moulds you in a certain way without your realizing it.'

What I said was heart-felt; I couldn't stop myself from saying it. I was certain Rohit would not want a future with me after hearing me out.

'Will you allow me a part of you?' he asked unexpectedly. 'A part to begin with, and then, maybe if we do fall in love, we could belong to each other completely?'

I was completely bowled over by Rohit's words. Sure, he was less fun; a bit of a chauvinist too. But he seemed like a nice, honest bloke. He did have a sensitive side, which was often camouflaged by some of his more mundane preoccupations. Maybe this was due to the largely administrative nature of his work and the fact that his job required him to deal with boring, lesser evolved, junior-level government employees.

I was emboldened enough to ask him how come he hadn't been in a serious relationship yet.

He shook his head. 'I guess relationships are destined. I've been meaning to experience one, but never quite felt as inspired as I do now... there is something about you that makes me want to spend the days – and nights – with you.'

When Rohit said this he seemed less a stranger to me than Abhay had these last few months. If anything, Rohit was a *positive* stranger, who meant well. That was the subconscious trigger that made me want to go for him at that point.

I had experienced the perfunctory existence of a big city. I now felt a craving to live in the far-flung interiors. Besides, I would have a doting husband for company. To my surprise I did not feel any aversion towards an arranged marriage.

❖

By the time we entered the Collector's bungalow in Kishanganj town, the rain had ceased. Looking around my new home I saw that the bungalow was quite modest. Even though Rohit had invested in new furniture and curtains, they did little to lift my spirits. I wondered why Rohit's favourite colour had to be violet. The vivid brightness of the curtains took me back to the day I'd bought the same shade of fabric with Abhay after a whole day of searching and shopping.

'What's happened, Shruti? Are you alright?' Rohit said, looking at my suddenly pale face.

'Y… ye… yeah. I'm fine. I'm fine.'

After a pause, I asked hesitantly, 'Rohit, can we change the curtains?'

'Sure,' he responded casually.

I wondered at that point if Rohit was aloof and oblivious to some things because he was insensitive, or because he was way more mature – comprehending things without articulating them?

I was to realize later that he was a bit of both.

Our first night was expectedly unexceptional. New things had to be learnt and a lot of things I knew had to be unlearnt. After all, Rohit and I had to achieve a certain synchronicity between us to make things work. We ended up merely embracing each other. A laboured peck on the lips is all that it led to. The restraint was mutual. My fatigue notwithstanding, I fell asleep only in the wee hours of the morning as strange thoughts floated through my mind.

The next day I was up in time to see the sun rise, which in itself was pretty amazing considering that the sun was making an appearance after almost a week of heavy, unyielding clouds. I went out into the garden to watch the sun's luminous glow fall upon the drops of water on the plants and leaves. The sight wasn't new, yet its surrealism seemed reiterated. I basked in the morning sun and for a moment felt so charged that I felt I could indeed fall in love with the world all over again.

I felt a tap on my shoulder. It was Rohit. He seemed amused to see me so excited. 'It's nice to see that small things can make you so happy,' he chuckled and drew me close.

On an impulse, I reached up and kissed him on the lips. I guess I wanted to know if I could kiss him with the same passion I had felt for Abhay. His surprise notwithstanding, my kiss was reciprocated well. That we had the beatific rays of the morning sun bathe us, made the moment so special that sometimes I yearn to live it again.

Soon after, Rohit left for work. As I started to arrange stuff inside the house, I remembered Rohit's words – *It's nice to see small things can make you so happy.*

At that point, I didn't know that small things did not necessarily make *him* happy.

❖

Later that day, I went to the market to do some shopping. Fish, I'd been told, was Rohit's favourite dish. But even before I bought the fish, I wanted to buy new curtain fabric and give it for stitching. That I had to make do with inferior material was okay, as long as it was another colour.

Talking to Rohit's driver, Harish, who was remarkably well-informed about the area, I learnt that nearly 70 per cent of Kishanganj's population comprised of Muslims. Burqa-clad women and bearded men with 'tagiyahs', could be seen all around. I was to learn that inter-religion marriages were also pretty common here with many couples following both faiths. The ex-journalist in me revelled in these details.

Even though I hear that commendable development has taken place of late, in those days the roads were deplorable: a minefield of pot-holes, uncovered man-holes, piles of rubble, open drains and other accident-inviting disasters. It goes without saying that travelling on them in the rains was worse than a nightmare.

Another interesting aspect about Kishanganj was its location. It borders Nepal to its north, whereas only a very narrow portion of West Bengal separates it from Bangladesh on its east. It was therefore only natural that the influx of illegal migrants and criminals were issues of concern.

It was in the fish market that I had my first brush with the underlying anarchy in the town. A bunch of men were abusing a fish vendor. The abuse was about to escalate to physical assault. As the drama unfolded, all the other vendors fled from the scene. The attackers cautiously steered clear of me, realizing who I was, but even so I had to return without buying any fish.

As we drove back, the driver, Harish, explained to me who the goons were. '*Rangdari*… that's what it is called in the local lingo. Extortion is the biggest menace in this place,' Harish said to me.

'But why doesn't the administration stop it?'

'It's tough. The kingpin here is a man called Salim Yadav; he is related to the State Revenue Minister.'

'Ah, so he does his own revenue collection,' I reacted, sarcastically.

That evening Rohit and I had a lengthy talk on the issue – an unusual evening conversation for a newly-wed couple.

'It's a vicious circle, Shruti,' said Rohit. 'A year ago, when I was first posted here, the situation was far worse. I suspected even the local Superintendent of Police had a nexus. I've finally had him transferred. But extortion and embezzlement is simply all-pervasive. Even major government funds that had been given to contain the kala azar outbreaks have fallen into the hands of these goons.'

'And what's the solution?' I queried.

'Support from locals. I've tried to involve some prominent local citizens in our drive against crime. These include a respected cleric of the local mosque, Maulana Ashar, the principal of the local college, Dayanand Tiwari and Dr Nusrat Khan – a prominent doctor and social worker. They have been asked to counsel people to take a stand against crime and inform the police of the slightest disturbance. Moreover, the informer network is being strengthened. Whenever Salim Yadav or his men are seen headed for a tamasha, we expect the locals to inform us immediately so that we take pre-emptive action.'

I sighed. 'Well, I really hope your measures work. What I saw today frightened me.'

In answer, Rohit hugged me tight.

❖

A few days later, we went to see an evening show of *Yes Boss*, which had recently released. I am a total Shah Rukh Khan fan. Two years ago, I'd seen *DDLJ* all of seven times – once every day on the first week of its release! There had been two drastic and distinct changes in my cinema experience since then. One was the venue, the other the company.

From the plush Chanakya Cinema in Delhi, it was now the downmarket Iqbal Talkies in Kishanganj town. From the indulgent Abhay, it was now the somewhat phlegmatic and propriety-conscious Rohit who sat on the seat beside mine. The cinema hall, supposedly the best in Kishanganj, was like a seedy cinema hall in far-flung Azadpur in north Delhi.

I wasn't complaining, though. I had this ability to find happiness in simple things. And this time round, I did so by enjoying some of the delightful comments from the spontaneous, happy-go-lucky crowd that whistled and cheered and threw coins at the screen every time they loved a scene! They were oblivious to the presence of us 'VIPs' in the top row; not that it would have mattered to them had they been aware of us.

That night Rohit and I exchanged notes on the movie.

'You liked the movie?' he asked me, sounding as though I was expected to say no.

'Yeah… it was good fun,' I said.

'Nowadays four good jokes coupled with Shah Rukh's hamming passes as a film…'

'Come on, Rohit, didn't you find it entertaining?'

'It was a bore.'

I suspected he was a little jealous of my fondness for Shah Rukh. Or maybe he believed Shah Rukh had got more success than he deserved.

❖

Two days later, we threw a small party at our place. The party was meant to be our marriage reception for Rohit's friends in Kishanganj. Our house could accommodate about twenty people and that's how many we had over that evening. Among those whom I met that day were the local SP, Samarkant, and his pretty wife, Ritu; the Deputy SP; the Asst. DC Anwar Khan; Maulana Ashar; Dayanand Tiwari; Dr Nusrat Khan and some other prominent locals including an eighty-year-old freedom fighter, Kamleshwar Dubey, who blessed me and gifted me with a shawl in the colours of our tricolour. In fact,

Dubeyji was particularly upbeat that day as he had just received news that the government was going to bestow a special honour upon him and several others on our 50th Independence Day, which was barely a few weeks away.

I mingled with all the guests, making them feel at ease as best I could. I figured that was what Rohit would have expected his IAS wife to do. And I could see he wasn't disappointed. I noticed him keeping a tab on me with oblique glances; I'm not sure whether he was being watchful of my demeanour or whether it was his chauvinist streak that made him do so.

I particularly enjoyed talking to the affable Maulana. He told me an interesting anecdote of how Kishanganj got its name. Settling back on the sofa he recounted the tale:

'During the period of Khagada Nawab, a Hindu saint is said to have arrived at this place. He was exhausted and wanted to rest, but when he heard that this place was called "Alamganj", the river "Ramzan" and the landlord "Fakiruddin", he refused to enter. When the benevolent Nawab got to know of this, he renamed the portion of land from Kishanganj Gudri to Ramzan pool "Krishna-Kunj". Over time the name got converted to "Kishanganj".'

Hmm, interesting bit of local folklore, I thought.

When the Maulana learnt that I used to be a journalist, he affectionately extended an invitation to me to teach in one of the madrasas in my free time.

I also enjoyed talking to Ritu, the wife of the SP. I have to confess that Ritu was far more attractive than I was and seemed completely at ease being an 'IPS wife'. She taught science in the local Kendriya Vidyalaya. I'm sure she was able to effortlessly command the attention of her students.

When it was time to serve dinner, Rohit and I cut the cake that I had ordered from Altaf Bakery – the only bakery in town back then. Though the cake was no match to the ones that I'd had at Nirula's in Delhi I realized I was truly enjoying the evening and liking my new world. Were I to compare the people here with those I'd interacted with in Delhi, they'd have seemed to belong to another planet. This planet though was far less complicated. These people didn't worry about speaking faultless English. There was a certain honesty to their speech and intentions, which I had found increasingly hard to come by in my big city friends. Kishanganj seemed a very interesting place and I decided I wouldn't mind plunging into it.

My optimism was shortlived.

The bonhomie of the evening was disrupted by the entry of a guard who walked in and informed us that Salim Yadav was at the gate insisting that he be allowed in. Before he could be stopped, Salim actually barged in carrying a huge bouquet of roses and ignoring the protests of the guards. I gathered from his name that he was the same person of whose exploits I had heard from Harish, the driver.

Salim was bearded and big built. Both his eyes and his smile had something distinctly lecherous about them. He sported a white khadi kurta-pyjama with a dark green gamcha thrown rakishly around his neck. From the reactions of the other guests, I could tell he was detested by them all.

Salim swaggered up to Rohit. 'Collector sahib, it's a happy moment for you. Even though I was not invited I couldn't resist coming and wishing you. That's how happy I am for you and your beautiful wife.'

I admired Rohit for the restraint he showed. He acknowledged the remark with a curt nod and then turned to talk to someone else.

'Won't you introduce me to my beautiful Bhabhiji?' Salim persisted brazenly. He came and stood in front of me. I must say that every time he called me beautiful, my skin crawled.

'Namaste, Bhabhiji. Myself Salim Yadav, social worker.' He introduced himself in his rustic insult of the English language and added, 'Both of you look so nice together. I pray to God to keep you both happy forever.'

Even as Salim uttered these supposedly well-intentioned words there was something evil about his expression that shadowed everything else. I could not decipher what it was. He left soon after, leaving us all bewildered by his abrupt entry and exit.

That night Rohit and I made love for the first time. I was allowing a man to make love to me after almost a year. Frankly, I had some apprehensions before it happened. What if it would remind me of the man whom I'd thought I'd be making love to all my life? Would that mean I'm not faithful to my present partner? I've always believed the nuances of morality are purely subjective; that infidelity need not always be physical. Many a times it is purely psychological. This is precisely the reason why I'd delayed our love-making, first citing adjustment issues and then saying I'd got my periods.

When Rohit and I finally consummated our relationship, I was glad the experience was a lot more mystical than I'd imagined. My apprehensions were allayed. About the only thing that jarred, if at all, was an image that perturbed me. It was the memory of Salim Yadav sitting in my living room and leering at me.

2

Kala azar is a chronic and potentially fatal parasitic disease that damages the spleen, the bone marrow, the liver and lymph-glands. It is transmitted by a seemingly innocuous breed of sand-fly. That we seldom hear about the disease despite it affecting several thousand every year in Bihar, Jharkhand and West Bengal is testament to how inured urban India is to the real problems the country faces.

You would wonder what makes me talk about the disease. That's because the disease in its own un-suspecting way filled the void between Rohit and me. Despite our increased communication and sexual engagement, a certain unfamiliarity persisted between us and was hard to overcome. There were moments when we had nothing much to say to each other. That is when the kala azar menace broke out in the district. Hundreds were afflicted by the disease. Rohit dealt with it with a crusading zeal that sharpened my respect for him and inspired me to contribute my bit. Shared motive and passion did our marriage a lot of good, as I was to realize later.

It started with news reaching us that the disease had struck with vengeance in one of the low-lying villages called Majhua in the far-flung Thakurganj block. Some three hundred people had reported sick in the last two weeks. Rohit was headed for a visit to the affected region when I asked him if I could accompany him.

What I saw there will remain one of the most disturbing images that I've ever seen in my life. Nearly a hundred children, all afflicted by the disease, lay in a large emptied cowshed, whimpering feebly. The enlargement of the spleens and intestines of many of them had resulted in a grotesque distortion of their bodies. Most of them had been down with high fever for many days and were extremely weak.

In Kishanganj the victims of the disease had to deal with three demons – one was the disease itself; the other was the ignorance attached to it; and the third and most disturbing demon was the total collapse of the government machinery in dealing with the menace.

I must tell you here that, for all its deadly implications, the mortality rate from the disease is quite low. The disease is treatable provided the rigorous medication schedule is strictly adhered to. But the only government hospital in Kishanganj had exhausted its medical supplies. This was particularly shocking considering the government had sanctioned Rs 50 crore to twelve of the worst-affected districts for the purchase of drugs only the year before. So where did the funds allocated to Kishanganj go?

Initial investigations pointed to embezzlement. These medicines were being sneaked out of government hospitals and sold to private hospitals in some of the better-off districts at exorbitant prices. And the kingpin behind this was once again speculated to be that swine, Salim Yadav.

I had never seen Rohit as furious as he seemed that day. He ordered SP Samarkant to raid all possible warehouses and hideouts of Salim Yadav. Rohit personally accompanied the SP on two of the raids; and indeed huge quantities of drugs were recovered from at least four places.

Salim was arrested but instantly obtained bail, thanks to his connections in the government. He managed to convincingly plead innocent by disowning his own goons. Thanks to the vast clout he enjoyed, he portrayed himself as the victim instead of the culprit. So while cases against Salim's men were filed, he simply hired new goons and continued to make merry, albeit, on lesser crimes.

Rohit subsequently retaliated with a cornered attack on Salim. Thus, in one week, more than a hundred of his extortionists were arrested. As there was sufficient evidence from those taken into custody to prove that they were working at Salim's behest, there was little that Salim could do to avoid arrest this time round.

So he went underground.

Rohit had to subsequently tone down his drive on instructions from the State Chief Secretary. He was told that there were several complaints of bias against him for 'torturing innocents'. I still shudder to think how any state administration could be so callous, and shudder even more to think that the State government always got away with it.

The truth was the government at the Centre was critically dependent on the support of the Bihar Lok Morcha that ruled the state. Thus for its survival, the Central government invariably pretended ignorance on the issue of the misdeeds of the State government.

Salim's disappearance spelt a victory of sorts for Rohit. The law and order situation in the district marginally improved; new funds were organized to combat the kala azar epidemic. Rohit was viewed as some kind of hero, gaining overwhelming respect in the district.

❖

I vividly remember our fiftieth Independence Day. Our marriage had completed a month-and-a-half. I accompanied Rohit to the flag-hoisting ceremony at the municipal grounds, where he unfurled the national flag. I have to admit the occasion made me feel important; more important than I had ever felt in public until then. And yet for the first time it sort of made me feel guilty. What business did I have basking in a ceremony of which I was part merely by virtue of being the DC's wife?

That evening I felt awful.

Ironically, our Independence Day made me feel more bound down than ever: to my home, my husband, and to the incumbent situation. It reminded me with a sense of loss of all the career aspirations I'd once had: had they all died with Abhay?

That night over dinner, I spoke my heart out to Rohit. Rohit was as understanding as a staid stickler for logic can be. He suggested I apply for the job of teacher in the local Kendriya Vidyalaya.

So I met the principal of the Kendriya Vidyalaya the very next day. He was an overly rule-bound old man who told me there were no vacancies for permanent teachers as they were in the middle of the session. However, I could substitute for two months for a teacher who was on leave. Walking out despondently from his office I happened to bump into Ritu, who taught at the same school.

'Arrey chill yaar… perhaps the principal did not pay attention to your resumé. Had he realized you are the DC's wife, he'd have taken you in. Just ask Rohit to call him up,' Ritu advised me casually.

I wasn't sure if I wanted to do that. After all, I had called up the school myself, like any other applicant would, not wanting to use my connections. Being seen as the DC's wife was okay at the flag-hoisting ceremony; it was not okay when it usurped my identity.

A week later, my desperation to get out of home made me think differently. Rohit was pretty exhausted that night. I told him about the favour I needed from him. His indifference to my plight, though unintended, took me by surprise. 'There are many other schools. Try to get in to one of those,' he said dismissively.

I could not tell at that point if Rohit was annoyed with me for expecting him to do something he wasn't comfortable doing, or if this indifference was a behavioural trait. I was to discover it was the latter, which in turn made me more realistic about the level of empathy that I could expect from him. In a marriage, one has to learn to ignore certain things. I chose to ignore his aloofness.

I took up the part-time assignment offered at the Kendriya Vidyalaya. Once a week, I would also visit the madrasa and help Maulana Ashar with his teaching. Off and on, I'd also visit the local hospital and check on the kala azar patients to make sure they were being treated properly. Rohit, on the other hand, was completely tied up with his assignments, which often made him leave early and return only late at night. Rohit and I thus ended up talking less.

I was happy, in a way, with the space I got. I wasn't prepared to bare every bit of my soul to him yet. We were both largely happy not getting too close for comfort.

In October that year, when the situation in the district had begun to look up and Rohit was in a position to take four days' leave, we went on a much-belated honeymoon to Darjeeling.

After watching the sun rise at Tiger Hill, the highest point in Darjeeling, even as we basked in the beautiful weather, something in me made me veer the conversation. 'Rohit, I've been feeling a void. I want to do more in life,' I said, apropos of nothing.

I'm not sure if another man would have taken what I said differently, but I sensed that Rohit inter-preted my sentence as a failure on his part. 'Why aren't you happy, Shruti?' he asked me pointedly.

'I'm not sure.' There was a long pause before I explained, 'Sometimes, I desperately feel like getting back to journalism. And that's not possible here.'

'Wait for some time. Maybe the next district to which I get transferred will have more opportunities.'

I did not respond. How could I tell Rohit that at one time I'd aspired to be among the country's top journalists? And how that was impossible unless I was based in Delhi. I mean, what would I report on in these districts – floods, disease, extortion, that's it? Who cared about all that at the Centre? The real stories, the ones that had the press buzzing, were of political intrigue and scandal. But was it at all possible for me to shift back to Delhi? Besides, did

I really want to get back to the world I had abruptly abandoned?

I was conflicted. There were many questions in my mind but no answers. I did not know what was really bothering me or what I really wanted. Was I already battling an acute identity crisis? Was it the hunger for an independent professional existence that bugged me?

There are times when your partner rubs you the wrong way by not being adequately sensitive. And then there are times when you bug your partner with expectations that are clearly exaggerated. It dawned on me that I was perhaps doing the latter. More than empathizing with Rohit for all the stress that his work gave him, I was indirectly exerting pressure on him by expecting unrealistic concessions. After all, I had known well enough what I was getting into when I had agreed to marry him.

I decided at that point to be a good wife. I thought raising a child is not all that unimportant a thing. For the first time in my life, I felt I might want to have a baby. The last two days of our holiday were much better. The reason: I gave up my expectations and tried fulfilling his. With this transformation, I sensed a positive shift in our happiness quotient.

❖

The Diwali of 1997 will remain my most memorable ever. As a kid, I remember constructing a Diwali ghar with bricks every year outside our house along with my younger brother. This time around I decorated our house so that it actually looked like the Diwali ghars from my childhood. As they had at our reception party, a host of guests dropped in for the Diwali party too. However I could sense a difference in my attitude this time. I craved an intimate evening with Rohit; I wanted some one-on-one time with my husband and was impatient for the guests to leave so that it would be only Rohit and me, amid the glitter of the diyas.

That night, after the guests left, Rohit and I sat in the veranda holding hands. In the majestic light of a few diyas burning around us, we felt an unprecedented equanimity. That we could sit like that for hours and without much conversation reassured me I could indeed fall in love again. I was truly happy.

❖

Two days later, I went to the hospital to take stock of the situation. Luckily, now there was no problem with the medicine supply. The patients too seemed to have responded well to proper treatment. Their bodies no longer looked as disproportionate and scary. On an impulse, I bought 500 bucks worth of fruits for them. I was just so happy; and I guess my happiness had to do with my new-found love for my husband.

On my way back, I saw a commotion in the Pothia market area that had brought traffic to a halt. I asked Harish what it was.

'Perhaps a fight has broken out,' he conjectured.

When we reached closer to the spot, I saw three men abusing a girl. I could tell from one glance at her that she was mentally handicapped. A passerby informed us that the girl had stolen a couple of apples from a roadside vendor. Harish added that the people who were supposedly doling out justice were Salim Yadav's henchmen.

As I watched, one of the three men suddenly grabbed the girl's hair and dragged her to the other side of the road, even as he kept abusing and slapping her and forcing her to confess her 'crime'. There he suddenly banged her head against the wall. Instantly, the girl's head started bleeding. I was numbed; it was a nauseating sight. As the girl collapsed, the man ripped off the sleeve of her blouse. I couldn't bear this savagery anymore and plunged into the centre of things. 'Will you stop this?' I screamed hysterically and pulled the girl away, my hand getting all bloody in the process.

I heard one of the men bark behind me: 'Now who is this *vilayeti kutiya*?'

The man came in front of me and tried pulling the girl away.

'Leave her, you bastard. Just get lost!' I screamed furiously.

He smiled insolently, staring right at my bosom.

'Get lost,' I said. 'Go sleep with your sister if you're that desperate.'

The man raised his hand, perhaps to hit me the way they had the girl, when another one shouted from behind, 'Stop it! She is the DC's wife.'

The men exchanged glances and perhaps concluded that it would be best to leave. Just then a battered Maruti Esteem drove up with Salim grinning at the wheel. He waved to me as his goons climbed into the car and drove off with him.

Harish and I picked up the bleeding girl and put her in our car. She was dazed and trembling with fright. After admitting her to the local hospital, I went straight to meet Rohit. We didn't carry cellphones in those days; Rohit learned of the incident only two hours later.

Surprising as it sounds, the police chowki of the area chose not to report the incident, despite it having taken place barely 200 metres away from the police station. The solitary telephone line in the police chowki, I was informed, had been dead for months.

❖

When Rohit heard of my run-in with Salim and his henchmen he was understandably aghast. Raids were carried out through the night to find Salim Yadav. They didn't meet with any success. It goes without saying that the administration really had no means of verifying which of the police stations in the district were on Salim's payroll.

The Pothia incident made me very cautious. I knew that one could not depend on the police here. Kishanganj manifested the existence of what we call the 'Jungle Raj'. Meanwhile, there was speculation that Rohit would be transferred to another district because of his 'interference' in local matters. Actually, he would have been transferred out a long time ago had the Home Minister not had a falling out with the CM, thanks largely to the Opposition going on overdrive against the Home Minister and accusing the CM of being hand-in-glove with the former. The Home Minister had been asked to put all new appointments and transfers on hold. He was subsequently shifted out of the ministry and awarded the resoundingly unimportant Fisheries Ministry.

A fortnight went by. The scars of Pothia had begun to gradually subside. At least in the seven days since, no untoward incident, even of extortion was reported from any part of the district. It was safely assumed that Salim Yadav had fled Kishanganj and had decided to shift his nefarious operations elsewhere.

How I wish that pest could have been exterminated that easily.

❖

One day, just as I was leaving for school, there was a knock at the door. I thought it would be Harish and was stunned to see Salim standing in front of me, right inside our veranda! I was even more shocked to see four of his goons holding our two guards hostages. Salim had his devil smile writ large on his face.

'Namaste, Bhabhiji,' he greeted me with his lecherous smile and walked right inside before I could protest.

At first I was too startled to react. Then I shouted, 'Will you just get the hell out of here?'

He looked around the house audaciously. 'Very nice décor. I'm impressed, Bhabhiji,' he said and clapped his hands like the shady villain of an eighties Hindi film.

'What do you want?' I muttered between clenched teeth.

'A cup of tea, Bhabhiji,' he retorted with a sly smile. 'Prepared by your soft, beautiful hands. After all, my business has been destroyed by your husband and you. I've been running around like a nomad with no place to call my own. A cup of tea made by your attractive hands is surely a very small price in exchange for not killing your husband, isn't it?'

I was aghast. I rushed towards the phone. But Salim had pulled out the plug and flashed his wicked grin again.

He walked up to me and took hold of my hands, caressing them: 'Come on, Bhabhiji. Be a good host. Get me a cup of tea,' he drawled.

I don't think I had an option. I was going crazy with fear. If this could happen to the DC's wife, I wondered, what was the fate of ordinary women living in the district? I pulled my hands away and rushed into the kitchen.

I gave him the tea and he sipped it leisurely, ogling at me suggestively, in my own house. After that the bastard went off. I was completely shaken.

❖

This time round, when I narrated the incident to Rohit, I could not help breaking down. By now, my confidence was shattered.

'Rohit, can I request something?' I made a defeatist suggestion through my tears.

Rohit nodded quietly.

'For God's sake, can you try and get a transfer to another district?'

In another situation, Rohit would have retaliated to my suggestion with anger. This time round, he just hugged me tight.

That night, we indulged in our most prolonged love-making. Stress and tragedy often precipitate the drive for sex, it is said. That may have held true in our case. The truth is neither of us could sleep and not having sex meant the same sombre thoughts haunting us.

About three weeks later, I experienced some unusual symptoms – terrible fatigue, nausea and the absence of my period, which was a week overdue. I spoke to my cousin Rashmi who said these were the symptoms of pregnancy. Two days later, a medical test confirmed the same.

It is strange how the prospect of parenthood can sometimes act as a panacea to all evils. It almost mitigated the impact of the negative thoughts that we were fighting day in and day out. Salim Yadav receded to a thing of the past. Every evening Rohit would try and return home early. We'd spend long hours just holding each other's hand and chatting and sharing our anxieties about the new addition. After a few weeks of morning sickness, I was without any symptoms except a ravenous appetite and an upbeat view of life.

On the second Sunday of January, Kamleshwar Dubey paid us a surprise visit. He had dropped in to invite us to the wedding of his granddaughter, Rachna on the 18th of January.

Oh, how I wish I could blot out that inauspicious date.

❖

The wedding was to be held at Dighalbank block, which was quite some distance from where we stayed. However, there was no way that Rohit could turn down the invitation. I knew he respected Kamleshwarji a lot. His respect had to do with the fact that Kamleshwarji had been a genuine freedom fighter unlike many others who, lately, had been faking their role in the nationalist struggle in order to avail of government largesse.

The day before, on the 17th, an SOS from the state's CM called for Rohit's presence in Patna to evaluate the efficacy of the development schemes that the government had initiated in six of the most backward districts (Kishanganj included). As Kamleshwarji had called up Rohit once again to confirm if we were coming, there was no way Rohit could refuse, so I was deputed to represent him. Rohit assured me that SP Samarkant and Ritu were expected to attend the marriage too and asked me to leave Dighalbank latest by 7:30 p.m. so that I would be home an hour after that.

I found it odd to attend the marriage alone. For a good part of the day, I debated whether to attend it or not. Finally by evening I decided to be a bit more proactive. Besides, I suppose, I was curious to see what a Kishanganj marriage was like.

Once there, I had a great time. As we waited for the baraat to arrive, the women started to dance. And in no time, Ritu and I were dragged onto the floor. At first I was conscious and awkward, what with my three-month baby-bulge, but then I let myself go. We danced to some of the more bombastic Hindi film item numbers, interspersed generously with foot-tapping Bhojpuri folk songs. I didn't understand the words of the Bhojpuri songs, but that didn't lessen my enthusiasm.

The festivities were so engaging that in no time I was past the deadline that Rohit had set for me. The baraat had not yet arrived, which meant I was pestered to stay on till it showed up. Eventually, I managed to leave only by 10 p.m.

I had no idea when I left how traumatic my return journey was going to be.

❖

It was my bad luck that the car broke down at the most inappropriate of places – an uninhabited area called Tulshia. Right in the middle of that desolate stretch Harish stopped the car, inspected the front tyres, and reported a puncture. That's when the spare tyre was reported unusable too. Harish flagged down a motorist who was crossing the area and requested him for a lift to a garage some three kilometres away, so that he could get the tyre fixed.

I waited for Harish's return with two guards for company. They occupied the front seat while I sat in the rear. I was hoping that the SP's car would cross mine, but I guess they'd decided to stay back longer. The night had turned chilly and the cold was unbearable. A thick fog enshrouded us. We rolled up the car windows and waited for Harish to return. A long while later I glimpsed a jeep cross in the opposite direction. But then frost covered our windows and the night turned an impenetrable pitch-black.

I shut my eyes momentarily, and was rudely woken by a loud rapping on the car window. One of the guards opened the door and before he could react, he was pulled out by two men who snatched away his gun. The other guard tried to ready the ancient rifle that he carried, but even before he could, his colleague had been shot through the head. Horrified, I shrank further into the back seat. Even as the second guard battled the assailants a few feet away, a hand snaked in through the front door and unlocked the back. A torchlight was flashed in my face. I've never experienced a more terrifying moment in my life. The limited visibility was enough for me to identify the debauched face of the most villainous man I knew.

Yes, it was Salim Yadav. From his astonishment, I gathered that he hadn't really expected me to be there. On seeing me, his expression changed. His face looked like a hungry tiger's when its prey walks right into its den.

He reached in and stroked my arm with his filthy fingers. 'Bha-biji...' he slurred, looking at me lecherously. He was completely drunk. 'Arrey, idiots, see who's here,' he laughed raucously, calling his men, who were busy savagely kicking the guard. 'Oh ho, leave that poor chutiya nandan aside. Come on, let's have a good time with Bhabhiji.'

One of Salim's henchmen smashed the other guard hard on his head and, as he slid to the ground, he shot him in the chest. I screamed in fear, shivering and trembling as Salim gagged my mouth with his hand and forcibly dragged me with him into the back of his jeep. When I tried to resist he punched me in the face. His men climbed into the front.

Thereafter, Salim pinned me down in the back, one hand on my thigh and the other groping inside my blouse. The foul smell of country liquor suffocated me. I begged for mercy on the grounds that I was pregnant. Of course this meant nothing to those goons. Even as I screamed and cried myself hoarse, Salim told his men to take the jeep to a place whose name I don't remember. All I remember is that it was a bumpy, unpaved road. All along the journey, the swine kissed me and felt me up forcibly.

I was finally dragged into a small empty hut. What happened there was a haze of unending humiliation and unbearable pain. Even now when I think of it, it makes me physically sick; I can the feel the nausea ride up my gut and my head ready to explode. My clothes were ripped off and Salim's men pinned me down. Even as I pleaded and begged with him, even as I kicked, threatened and swore, my fate was sealed.

I was brutally raped; not by one but three men who took turns on me. First Salim. And when he had his fill, he let his goons make merry.

I was a piece of meat thrown in front of three wild dogs. I was ravaged until the wee hours of the morning, when I lost consciousness.

3

Raavan's abduction of Sita in the Ramayana, was indisputably an act of revenge for the insult that Ram and Laxman had heaped upon his sister Surpanakha. Smitten by Laxman, the ugly Surpanakha had tried to seduce him. Outraged by Surpanakha's brazen behaviour, the brothers taught her a lesson by chopping off her nose. Raavan retaliated by usurping Sita's honour. He took Ram's wife hostage – an act that was to irreversibly change the course of history.

It leaves me wondering if permanently scarring a woman closely related to the enemy is the most satisfying revenge that man can think of.

Sex is a sacred act when performed with the man you love. But when the same act is forced violently on you by a savage, dissolute animal, you end up hating every part of yourself that has been desecrated. I was filled with a self-repugnance that I couldn't understand; I wanted to blank out the act perpetrated on me by effacing my very existence.

In my case, apart from suffusing me with feelings of death on an emotional level, the rape also caused the physical death of life within me – I suffered a miscarriage.

I lost the child I had nursed in my womb for three months.

❖

I wonder how many of you have been raped? I ask this to know if you can even begin to understand how hollow I felt that night, and every night for several years, after this macabre incident.

On the face of it my question may seem callous and bitter. I will, nonetheless, repeat it: *How many of you have been raped?* I ask this also because you will be shocked if I tell you that in our country only 1 out of 50 rape cases is reported. Moreover, in only 1 out of 5 reported rapes cases is the accused convicted. In most rape cases the culprit and the victim are known to each other. Does that carry an indication of how commonplace the practice really is?

During my years as a journalist I had reported on rape victims many a time and had been outraged by their suffering; but I had never quite understood the extent of their humiliation. Now I struggled to understand my situation with the same journalistic detachment.

Almost all cultures have a history of rape. Indian history is replete with such dastardly instances. Have you wondered why people living in our northern parts look so different from those in the south?

History will tell you that the Dravidians who were the original inhabitants of our land were pushed back by the invading Aryans. The early foreign invaders enslaved thousands of our women who would then be carried back to be used as sex slaves.

Never has an event in history resulted in more rapes than the Partition. While Muslims in Pakistan settled scores with their Hindu counterparts by kidnapping their women, usurping their houses and raping the women in those same usurped houses, Hindus retaliated by raping Muslim women on the Indian side. Hundreds of women were encouraged to commit suicide in order to avoid the ignominy of rape.

The resort to rape as a device to settle scores went on way beyond Partition. So if Hindu women were raped in the run-up and aftermath of the mass exodus of Kashmiri Pandits from Kashmir in January 1990, Hindus raped Muslim women at will in the post-Godhra riots of 2002. Rape is a perverse custom that has dotted the history of conflict around the world.

It makes me retch to think that this is the most honourable means of revenge that the male species knows.

The vengeful act perpetrated on me evoked an odious rising of bile against all men. One, it brought home to me the fact that the male species has dominated its female counterpart through the ages because of its physical advantage; two, that men have openly revelled in the sadistic joy of the forced nakedness and humiliation of women. I mean, a woman being raped must be the equivalent of a dethroned king being paraded naked through the streets of his kingdom. What makes the position of the female worse is her susceptibility to violence.

If I were to think of my fate in the context of history, my husband's enemies resorted to the ultimate humiliation that one male can heap on another: raping his wife. They were attacking him by usurping the rights to a certain privilege, which by virtue of him being my husband, were solely his.

There is another fundamental reason why men rape women: to control or discipline them. Most men rape women whom they think 'need to be disciplined'. Hence the rapist uses sexual assault to punish women who are not subservient enough. Or in retaliation to an affront that the woman has inflicted upon him. Rape, therefore, is not about sex, but power. The use of sexual force or violence is only incidental – to exercise control over the victim.

Anyway, to say that the incident devastated me would be an understatement. While I could see and understand all that was happening around me, the shock rendered me virtually speechless for a week. I could only speak in monosyllables; any recollection of the incident would make me so frightened and sick that I would freeze halfway through what I was saying.

❖

After my night-long ordeal, I was brought back to consciousness in the morning by the feel of water being splashed on my face. Two men and a woman, who were supposedly a part of the village panchayat, stood in front of me, as aghast as I was at my bare, bruised and bleeding state. A bigger crowd stood behind them, gawping at me. One among them had recognized me as the Collector Sahib's wife. I was taken to the nearby nursing home from where SP Samarkant was phoned and informed of my ordeal. The doctors there confirmed a miscarriage.

The SP and Ritu personally came and took me to their home that evening. We did not file an FIR then as I was too dazed to talk. The SP called up Rohit, and told him that I had had a fall in the bath. Then he sent his men back to the spot where the two dead guards lay. Harish, who had not been able to find a mechanic, had managed to find his way back, only to be shot dead too.

It was only 36 hours later that my husband finally sat in front of me and learned of the actual circumstances of the fate that had befallen me. I lay bruised and traumatized in a room in the SP's house and communicated to him in short instalments of words, gestures, sobs and written notes till I broke down completely and eventually passed out.

An FIR was lodged that evening.

That night the police team killed four criminals in an encounter that I doubt was genuine. But then the police had to do something to show it was effective. The version we got to hear was that four gangsters owing allegiance to the Salim Yadav group were fleeing in a jeep and that the police had a strong suspicion that Salim Yadav was among them.

❖

In a sense, my rape was Rohit's first crucial test as a husband. In good or ordinary times a lot of mediocrity gets through, but not so in crisis situations. Rohit's reaction was on expected lines: shock, despair, indignation and then stoic resignation – that was how his graph went. As much as I find it silly now, at that point I'd wonder what disturbed Rohit more – my rape or my miscarriage.

Rohit's guarded way of showing his feelings left me confused. He stroked my forehead reassuringly or held my hand in his, but I so wished he'd *say* something, that he'd hug me tight, give vent to his anger and frustration; oh why did I always forget he was not Abhay?

While the local press behaved as expected, thronging my doorstep, hoping to get first-hand grabs of the victim; a victim from their own fraternity, the attitude of the government was truly shocking. My rape was a heinous crime. But what was even more distressing was the government's frivolous attitude to it and its sheer apathy.

The death of four petty criminals unrelated to the crime in question was a travesty of justice. But the government, to suit its convenience, wanted it to be believed that the killed four were indeed my rapists. So the State Home Secretary even went on record saying that 'prima facie evidence suggests that the rapists are dead'. What better way to kill the case!

I knew the men who had attacked me were still stalking the streets. They weren't dead. I knew that in the dark alleys of the district and our society, they'd still be perpetrating rapes that would never get reported.

My parents and parents-in-law were sympathetic but kept urging me to forget the incident and look ahead. *Look ahead at what?* I wanted to scream at them. In a strange way, the government's stonewalling and my parents' fear made me more determined to fight the injustice that had happened with me; the energy that I had seemed completely drained of came back to fire me in the form of a primeval and unrestrained anger. I was empowered by an overwhelming sense of rage. I was not going to let the government bullshit on a matter as critical to one's identity as this!

I was a journalist after all, damn it.

I knew how to take on the establishment.

I was going to fight back.

❖

For the next week, Rohit and I did everything that we possibly could. We met the state CM, who assured us that 'action' would be taken. He sounded as plastic as a polythene bag.

For a week after that, nothing happened. On the contrary, the SP was transferred to another district and replaced by a stooge who went by the name of Devnath Pandey. The new SP dropped several old cases of extortion, loot and other petty crimes that were pending against Salim Yadav and his men. He refused outright to take instructions from Rohit, making it amply clear that he had been sent with a clear agenda. The next day, when the state CM was questioned by media persons on the state's inaction, he said: 'I can't be looking after every small incident. Ask the concerned department...'

The incidents of the past week only added salt to my wounds. We knew that justice would be at a premium if we went the ordinary way. 'I've decided we'll approach the Central government for help,' Rohit told me as we watched the CM's insensitive comments on TV.

'But, Rohit, you might have to pay with your job,' I cautioned him.

'I don't care. This incident will become the state government's Watergate. It will make this government fall.'

I did not expect much from the central government as it was dependent on the support extended by the ruling party in Bihar for its survival. But I must say I've never admired Rohit more than when he said this.

Rohit and I went to Delhi and met the Union Home Minister. I utilized my media contacts to give as many interviews as I could. I felt sheepish and awkward reaching out to my old friends in a situation as hopeless as this. I, once a hotshot journalist, was now a hapless victim.

Among the many scribes who came to interview me was Abhay who now worked with a news channel. I was stunned to see him. It was the first time I was seeing him after that hurtful encounter when I had seen him canoodling with Ananya in Connaught Place. It was weird that we had to meet in this manner. But what was even more bizarre was to see him behave the way he did.

'Assuming what you say is true, do you by any chance blame *yourself* for what happened?' he asked in the course of the interview.

I was appalled by his insensitivity. 'What do you mean – *assuming what you say is true?* Salim's men were openly abusing and beating up a mentally-challenged woman on the streets when I stopped them. If I'd not intervened, that woman might have met the same fate,' I shot back.

'What I'm trying to say is, do you think your husband was targeting Salim Yadav for reasons other than those we know?'

'What are you trying to say? Are you trying to *justify* my rape?'

Abhay paused and then uttered something that numbed me. 'No. The point here is whether it was a rape at all.'

I couldn't believe he was saying this. *'What?'*

'Well, we've just got news that Salim has courted arrest in a Patna police station. However he has a different version to what happened.'

'And what's that?'

'That the two of you were having an affair...'

I couldn't believe my ears. 'What? Are you insane?'

'He has produced pictures of the two of you in a compromising position inside your house.'

I was aghast.

❖

That evening as Rohit and I watched TV in our hotel room, I could sense a strange awkwardness between us. Salim, the swine, had managed to turn the case around. TV news-grabs displayed at least half-a-dozen pictures of Salim and me together. The proximity between us in those pictures ranged from Salim having tea in my living room, to Salim and I locked in greater intimacy. It goes without saying that the pictures had been doctored.

But, yes, the case had been successfully sabotaged. I was up against the odds now. According to Salim, he and I were having an affair and my husband and I had irreconcilable differences.

More than Salim I was upset that Abhay – with whom I'd shared five years of my life – had sided with the devil who'd reduced my life to nothing.

When your fate is as demonic as mine, it doesn't take much time for abject despondency to take hold of you. For the first time that night I could sense my biggest pillar of support beginning to crumble. Rohit was completely shaken by what he saw on TV. Besides, I could feel what Rohit did not explicitly say – Salim's version of events and Abhay's gleeful acceptance of them had sown the first seeds of scepticism in his mind.

❖

Five weeks went by. All hopes of my ever getting any redressal were virtually dead by now. I was beginning to resign myself to the inevitable; that I would have to spend the rest of my life quietly like my parents wanted – praying my terrible shame was never revealed and tacitly swallowing the un-avenged insult to my person as just another male slight to my ego.

In these five weeks, Rohit and I never even tried making love. Perhaps that was only normal considering the scar that forced sex had left on me. On one occasion, Rohit and I did come close to having sex but then Rohit pulled back. I thought he was being protective. Perhaps he did not mean to thrust sex on me when I was not psychologically ready for it.

I was wrong. I realized this rather cruelly when I picked up the phone extension in the living room and happened to overhear him talking to his childhood pal in Patna.

'Raj, yaar, I don't think I can ever make love to her. Every time I come close to her, I am reminded that she has been abused by three strangers.'

'Listen, buddy, you need to be practical. Just get her examined to make sure she is not carrying a disease – you know what sort of people raped her. If she's alright, forget what happened and get back to normal life.'

'That's not the only thing, Raj. I've realized I'm not such a broadminded man, after all. I just can't come to terms with the fact that my wife has had sex with three bloody strangers.'

'She didn't have sex with Salim.'

'Whatever. I will never know the truth.'

'What? You mean you believe Salim's story?'

'No, of course not... not really... well... I don't know... it just doesn't get out of my mind. God, why did this have to happen with me?'

I did not find it necessary to hear the full version of my husband's views on my rape. Overhearing this, was no less a discovery of what sort of mentality he possessed. Was he suffering from amnesia? Had he forgotten that I had been involved in a physical relationship with Abhay for three years before I met him? Did he indeed consider the rape my doing? Was all his show of support a sham?

I wanted to ask him all these questions. But I just couldn't. In a strange way, I realized the power equation between us had shifted. Thanks to my ordeal and his support for me through my initial helplessness, I didn't have many options now.

I couldn't afford to confront him; so I went back into my shell.

Clearly things hadn't changed much since the days of the Ramayana. Wasn't it a mere washerman, a dhobi, whose words had sown the seeds of doubt in Ram's mind and had him demand that Sita undertake a second test of purity? Obviously, there are two ways to interpret Ram's behaviour – one inference is that the dhobi merely touched a raw nerve. The other is that Ram the king triumphed over Ram the husband. In his attempt to be fair towards the sentiments of every citizen of his kingdom, Ram chose to put his wife on an unfair trial. In the end, all he wanted to convey was that, for him, all citizens, Sita included, were equal. That Sita was wronged in the process, however, is indisputable.

I wondered if Rohit was in a similar predicament. Or was he simply what I sometimes perceived him to be – a weak character?

I kept brooding about Rohit's attitude towards me for the next few weeks. We were not yet *in* love.

Sure, we loved each other as husband and wife but the trust factor, which can often be a long-drawn-out process in arrangements such as ours, was yet to build up. We'd known each other for less than a year. Was it expected of him to trust me blindly just because I was his wife? Even Lord Ram did not provide Sita that immunity; Rohit was a much lesser mortal.

Then one day, some measure of physical chemistry ignited between us again. Rohit wanted to go all the way. There seemed some amount of preparation in his mind for what he was doing; as if he were willing himself to make love to me. I can say this with certainty because I was the passive partner this time around. At the penultimate moment, Rohit once again abruptly withdrew. His expression clearly reflected the dilemma confronting him.

'You don't have to force yourself, Rohit. It's okay if you don't feel comfortable,' I said.

There was a long silence in which I sensed something going on furiously in Rohit's mind. And then he looked into my eyes in a way he'd never done before: 'Shruti, can't you just swear on me once and say that everything that Salim has said is a lie?'

I looked at him, completely distraught.

He was already regretting what he had said. 'Don't get me wrong, Shruti... I... I just want you to say it once. I mean you... you did entertain him inside our house once.'

A sob caught in my throat and I ran out of the room. To be let down by Rohit, my lawfully wedded husband, was far, far worse than being ravaged by Salim who was only an animal guided by his bestial instincts.

Rohit followed me, calling my name. I locked myself in another room and wept the whole night. At some point, driven to despair, I consumed several sleeping pills – prescribed to me after the rape assault – without even realizing that my action amounted to an attempt at suicide.

I was just so desperate to escape.

When I regained consciousness, I was in hospital. Rohit was by my side. His face reflected a gamut of emotions that were difficult to understand. Mostly, he was livid; this time though he was angered at his own doing: 'Shruti, I'm really, really sorry. I don't know what came over me. I swear I'm never going to behave like that again. I swear on you... For God's sake, please forgive me...'

I could sense Rohit was genuinely sorry. What I was not aware of at that point was just how critical my condition had been prior to my regaining my senses. Rohit's contrite words were perhaps those of a husband who had nearly lost his wife to an act for which he could never have stopped blaming himself.

My death would have made him a murderer.

Another week went by. Rohit did everything he could to compensate for his failing earlier. It made me wonder about how many different personalities there could be to a character. There are people who are outright corrupt and then there are those who aren't corrupt, but simply fragile. This catastrophe was a test of character as much for Rohit as it was for me. We did get through it eventually, even though I have to confess Rohit's condition was very often more precarious than mine.

4

Yada yada hi dharmasya
glanir bhavati bharata
abhyutthanam adharmasya
tadatmanam srjamy aham
(Whenever righteousness falls and the unrighteous rule
The Almighty reveals His presence
Though unborn and undying He manifests in
human form
To overthrow the forces of ignorance and
selfishness.)

It is strange, but people whom you are very fond of and those whom you detest often find ways to re-enter your lives. This time it was the turn of a man whom I'd met only once two-and-a-half years ago and who had left me wanting to meet him again – Sharad Malviya.

Sharad will go down in history as one of the finest Opposition leaders that the country has ever produced. His dynamic, effervescent persona and his no-holds-barred persistence became instrumental in bringing the first Nationalist League-led coalition to power. A pan-Indian appeal of zero-compromise on national security and the nation's self dignity, were what elevated him to this rare high pedestal. He was a brilliant orator and a superb motivational speaker.

I have to add, though, that he somehow seemed to belong to the wrong party. The demarcation between the Left, Right and the Centre can be quite fuzzy in a democracy like ours. It requires great skill to walk the tightrope and come out projecting yourself as nothing but a nationalist. While Sharad did manage to do this successfully, his party invariably failed him and would often get drubbed for being 'hawkish'. Moreover, the 51-year-old, good-looking Sharad was only rooting for an older septuagenarian leader to be the PM.

With a month left for the Lok Sabha elections, parties had begun to campaign aggressively. Almost every other day, some political heavyweight would come into the district and Rohit would be involved with the administrative supervision. Loudspeakers and mikes would blaze all day, at times playing out political speeches and at other times crooning cleverly reworded popular Hindi songs for the campaign. In Kishanganj, the Opposition party leaders, would at some point during their speech bring up my rape to drive home the message of lawlessness. By now, the constant reference did not evoke any response in anyone nor even surprise me.

On the evening of 26th February, Sharad Malviya came to the district for a rally. The elections were shaping up into a close fight. The ruling Indian Democratic Party at the Centre was naturally jittery. And if there was one person who could make a crucial difference to the election results, it was Malviya. These elections had catapulted him into being the most charismatic campaigner around, what with even his smaller rallies recording a turnout of no less than 20,000 people.

There was an unprecedented buzz in town on the day of the rally. Even though I was engulfed in gloom I could sense the energy that his persona could enthuse in the masses. I thought briefly of attending one of his rallies – perhaps he could help me. But it was a passing thought, which I soon disbanded, my desolation taking grip of me again. It was so unreal, considering what I'd been through. I had lost all faith in the electoral process, in democracy and the state.

At around 7 p.m. that evening, Rohit called me. 'Listen, Shruti, Sharad Malviya wants to meet you. He would like to drop in at home in the next half hour.'

❖

There are situations that are thrust upon you, where the onus to decide is not on you. I'd have said no, had it been any another politician. After all, every politician wanted to exploit my situation. And quite frankly, I was beginning to feel like a commodity. But some intuitive undercurrent in me wanted to have this meeting.

In 45 minutes, Sharad Malviya was sitting in front of me; Rohit by my side. He looked as smart as an Indian politician could. He'd dispensed with the traditional khadi-kurta garb at the very start of his career and wore a regular pant and shirt. Clean shaven, and with a pair of thin-rimmed specs, his countenance carried a boyish appeal that was both charming and deceptive; it masked his true substance and the missionary zeal with which he went about his 'karma'.

'Sir, I attended one of your press conferences two years ago,' I told him, not wanting to talk about my cause for fame. 'The one which became controversial due to your radical take on our model of Westminsters' democracy.'

Sharad smiled, trying to recall the event. One who is at the centre of all the attention, invariably does not remember those he gets the attention from. But Sharad surprised me when he said: 'Are you the young girl who pinned me down to clarify whether my views were those of my party or my personal views?'

I smiled sheepishly, for a moment forgetting my ordeal, the reason that had brought Sharad to my home. A few minutes of polite conversation later, Sharad got down to business and spoke of what he had in mind. 'Shrutiji, I have been following your case. The whole country knows what happened that night. The state government's non co-operation makes it the most shameful incident that I can think of.'

I listened. There was nothing new that he'd said so far, except that he was not done.

'The state government can get away with all this simply because the Indian Democratic Party government at the Centre survives on the support of the Bihar Lok Morcha. It's an utterly hopeless situation.'

There was still nothing new that he'd said except that his face exuded promise. And then it came:

'In as much as I can empathize with you, as a rape victim who is also an ex TV-journo and an IAS officer's wife, you have slight advantage over other rape victims.'

I looked on, astounded, as he continued, 'There is a burning fire in you to fight your case and get justice.'

Both Rohit and I were now looking attentively at him.

'My party would like to give you the Lok Sabha ticket from the Kishanganj constituency.'

'Just for being raped?' I asked in shock.

'No. To empower you to fight your own case,' he said, exuding his customary reassurance. He added, 'Lest you don't already know it, the Bihar

Lok Morcha is planning to field Salim Yadav from the constituency. Once he wins, your case, which has already been spoilt, will be closed forever. This Lok Sabha ticket is your ammunition to fight your own case and get justice.'

Sharad Malviya was clearly a hugely inspirational personality. I think there was something magnetic about his eyes. Intense and passionate, they had more life than any other eyes I'd seen. When he looked at me directly, something happened to me. I'm not sure whether this is how most women felt about him or whether my tryst with him was pre-ordained. But much after he had left, his words ricocheted in the dark confines of our bedroom, even as a tense silence prevailed between Rohit and me. We were still to come to terms with what the situation implied.

Finally Rohit broke the silence. 'I think you must go for it,' he said.

'Rohit, do you realize I will get sucked into another world? What will happen to our plans of starting a family?'

'Don't think about that right now. Once you set this case straight you can put it behind you. You can always quit politics and come back to start a family. I think it will just be a matter of a year or two,' he reassured me.

That night, Rohit slept holding my hand, while sleep eluded me yet again.

By the time sleep finally got the better of my thoughts, I felt greatly unburdened, perhaps for the first time in several weeks.

There was some sort of assurance inside me; a ray of hope that promised that tomorrow wouldn't be just another day.

5

Nominations to the Lok Sabha are filed in the office of the Deputy Commissioner. I had the unusual experience of walking into my own husband's office and filing my papers in his presence. I wondered how much more bizarre my story could get. I mean, my husband took me through the formalities with a sense of personal detachment, which, little did I suspect at that point, would soon become the norm between us. Onlookers and the media gave me the kind of attention that I was getting used to. Yes, I had become a celebrity of sorts, not in the least for reasons I could appreciate.

Just as I stepped out of the office and was about to get into my car, I turned and saw Salim Yadav standing a few feet away from me. A that very moment, two jeeps full of his supporters drew up as well. I was given to understand Salim was scheduled to file his papers later that day but on hearing about my presence, his priorities had changed. He flashed his lecherous smile at me. Then, all of a sudden, he rushed towards me and fell at my feet.

'Durga Mai, pranam,' he shouted.

I was stunned by Salim's antics.

He got up and looked melodramatically at the people all around him: 'What are you all staring for? Look at her. Here is a re-incarnation of Goddess Durga herself, who has come down to earth to fight evils like yours truly! Hey, Tiwari, come here and perform aarti on the Goddess.'

In no time, a puny pandit materialized from somewhere and started performing an aarti around me. I watched, bemused. I was being mocked but I was totally calm.

'Goddess Durga will fight the elections against this rakshas,' the swine laughed derisively, before turning towards me in anger. 'Aren't you ashamed of your existence?'

Luckily, at that point, the police came and took charge of the situation.

Salim's antics had become so commonplace now that Rohit and I did not even talk about them. Our focus was on something bigger – the elections. Winning them was the only answer to our plight.

❖

In one of my speeches at Dumaria Gram Panchayat in the Thankurganj block I said, 'Brothers and sisters, unlike others who have been harping on my rape, I shall not do so. I've come to you with a humble prayer and with a promise. Please vote for me and I will eradicate the menace of crime and lawlessness. I will put a tab on illegal migrants and the fake ration card scams that thrive with them and rob you of the government resources meant for you. Please vote for me.'

Afterwards, my party-workers told me candidly that my speeches were 'staid and unnecessarily intellectual'. I wondered what that meant. At the end of the third week of my campaign I was still pretty clueless about which way the elections and my fate were headed.

The local MLA who belonged to the same party as mine was thoroughly disappointed with my performance. 'Melodrama, Shrutiji… melodrama…' he exhorted, sitting behind me.

Quite frankly, I was dissatisfied with my performance too. I had attended enough political rallies during my time as a reporter to know that the thing about a good campaigner is that, election results notwithstanding, you evoke an instant rapport with your audience. I could see that this was not happening in my case.

I didn't speak the local dialect; I couldn't connect with them on their terms. Their worldview was different. A sense of belonging, thus, was hard to achieve. In a situation like this, the villagers were inclined to trust Salim Yadav's antics more than my boring pleas.

It goes without saying that my first few days of campaigning were of no consequence. Salim Yadav was predictably at his slimy best. He wouldn't directly talk about the rape incident. Instead he only made oblique references to it and then quickly changed the topic. He thus aroused the villagers' curiosity with his insinuations and just when the villagers wanted to know more, he'd not say a thing, implying there were things about my character and conduct, which he – *out of his respect for women* – could not go into.

I hated every bit of everything that was happening around me. I was filled with revulsion for all men and mankind. I loathed the Almighty in front of whom I had been taught to bow every morning.

In my saner moments, I wondered what it was about this vile Salim that allowed him to get away with so much rubbish. Forget his protectors in the government, what was it about *him* that allowed him to deceive people like this? It goes without saying that Salim had the upper hand in the elections and was the candidate more favoured to win.

❖

By a strange coincidence, the name *Salim Yadav* symbolized the coming together of two communities that were both critical in determining Bihar's electoral fortunes in the nineties. And the MY (Muslim–Yadav) vote was all that mattered in Bihar's politics in those years. Yadav, in a broader sense, implied the backward castes. If you had these two sections voting for you then losing an election was extremely difficult. I had no idea at that stage of the laws of nomenclature that had been employed to give Salim Yadav this double advantage.

Salim had assiduously nurtured what continued to be his core constituents – the illegal migrants. Thus, he had fake ration and voting cards issued to nearly 50,000 such migrants, out of whom 50 per cent had been provided ration cards under two or three different identities. It goes without saying that the state administration, with obvious ulterior motives, had looked the other way on the issue. After all, when you don't officially exist as per the records of the state, then you might as well exist in several avatars, in innumerable fake entities. I have to say that being an illegal migrant in our country is quite a privilege.

Salim, by his machinations, had thus manufactured at least one lakh extra votes, which, in a constituency that has ten lakh official voters and where the voting percentage seldom exceeded 50 per cent, was crucial.

In addition to this, despite the Election Commission acting tough, booth-capturing was pretty commonplace in the Bihar of those days. It was quite methodical too: the ruling party would capture booths in areas where it was unlikely to do well. Hence in the present situation, Maulana Ashar's campaign against Salim was likely to affect his votes in the areas around the madrasa. Those areas were therefore likely to witness heavy rigging.

As against Salim, I had to grapple with critical handicaps. My biggest disadvantage was that I did not belong to either of the two sought-after communities. I was a Kayastha – the upwardly mobile, educated community that constitutes just 1 per cent of the population of Bihar. It's another thing that the bureaucracy of the state is full of them. Kayasthas are traditionally supposed to study engineering or medicine or appear for the civil services exam. A Kayastha female fighting elections in the manner in which I was, in a constituency such as Kishanganj, was next to unimaginable.

❖

In my first brush with electoral politics itself I figured out that religion and caste, no matter how much one might want to wish them away, were inextricably tied to our electoral system. That I was educated and did not speak the local dialect was another disadvantage. In the politics of these parts, if a woman has treaded far, she has invariably been the daughter or wife of an important politician and existed merely as a rubber-stamp substitute. My poor husband, unfortunately, was only an IAS officer!

One good thing to happen however was that Maulana Ashar came out openly in my support.

One day, he met Rohit and me over breakfast. 'Shrutiji, I do understand your dilemma. If someone from my family had been in the position that you are in, I'd have not allowed them to cry out their sob story and plead for sympathy votes. It's just so demeaning.'

'But what is the solution, Maulana sahib?'

'Have you heard of the fatwa?'

I nodded, and he continued. 'I've never issued one despite political parties always pressurizing me for it. The reason is that they want to use religion to get votes.'

We listened to him intently.

'But today, I will use religion to protect its followers from that devil, who by virtue of belonging to this community is wilfully getting away with all his nonsense. I will issue a fatwa that will ensure that no true Muslim votes for Salim.'

And the Maulana remained true to his word. He virtually abandoned his job till the end of my campaign and accompanied me to all my election meetings.

'...Islam teaches you to *protect* women. The one, who plays with their respect, can never be a Muslim. Salim must thank his stars that the law of Shariat has no place in our society, for if it had, I'd have had Salim caned to death! He is a criminal, an extortionist, a rapist, everything *but* a Muslim. If anyone of you does vote for him, you dare not visit the mosque again!' the Maulana thundered.

I was surprised to find how vitriolic the Maulana could get for me. I was even more amazed to see the impact it had on the listeners. From a mere hundred-odd the audience swelled to way beyond a couple of thousand in no time. Moreover, the crowd heard out the formidable Maulana with a dual sense of reverence and fear. This duality of reverence and fear is what actually makes followers 'God-fearing'. I felt hopeful now that the God-fearing would support me.

Salim Yadav, however, retorted by distributing even more outrageously doctored pictures of mine. I wasn't able to lay my hands on any of them, but I'm told that they were so filthy that a good section of the villagers were inclined to be taken in by them, and even questioned the Maulana's motives in backing me. What weakened the Maulana's position further was a counter-fatwa issued in Patna by another renowned cleric, Maulana Taufiq, asking Muslims to support the ruling party in the state as they had been good to the community.

So with just over three days of campaigning left, it was back to square one for me with the odds tilting marginally in Salim's favour.

❖

I was very agitated as I drank my morning tea with Rohit. 'Rohit, I really don't know what's going to happen. What if I lose?' The thought of a smug Salim wearing a victory garland and strutting through the streets made me sick to the stomach.

Rohit just patted my hand reassuringly. I knew instantly how wrong it was for me to be talking like this at this stage.

At that point, the telephone rang in the other room. Rohit went to answer it. He returned a moment later and looked at me with an inscrutable expression on his face: 'Sharad Malviya wants to meet you in Patna in the next two hours.'

'What?' I asked, shocked.

'He is on a visit to the state capital. He has sent a helicopter for you that will be reaching the municipal grounds any moment now. He wants to review your election campaign.'

I was stunned.

Rohit's expression was difficult to fathom. Today when I look back on that day, I feel that his suspicion of Sharad Malviya was already taking seed in his mind.

I took the copter to Patna. To my surprise I had Maulana Ashar for company. It just showed that Sharad had indeed been following my campaign closely.

Sharad took stock of the campaign from us. Understandably enough, there was little in our feedback that could make him feel positive. He took a deep breath and thought hard before he finally spoke. 'Have you heard of Lucretia?' he asked me.

'Yes, I have. But there's not much that I can recollect of her,' I said defensively.

'A legendary figure in the history of the Roman Republic, Lucretia was raped by the then king, Lucius Tarquinius Superbus's son. This led to her suicide, which was directly responsible for the events that triggered the revolution that overthrew the tyrannical monarchy and established the Roman Republic,' Sharad explained.

The Maulana and I exchanged glances trying to guess what Sharad might be getting at.

Sharad then looked at me. 'It's strange how everything that happens in the present day has a precedent in the past. Shruti, you are the present-day Lucretia. You don't realize that the unfortunate incident that happened with you will help us throw out the present government in the country and will lead to our coalition forming the next government at the Centre.'

Sharad truly had huge motivational powers. But what he said right now seemed grossly exaggerated. 'How?' I asked, hoping he wasn't going to ask *me* to commit suicide.

'The Kishanganj contest is being followed closely by the whole country. Kishanganj goes to the polls in the very first phase of polling. Just wait till the result of the exit polls come out on TV that night. A victory prediction for you will impact voters favourably for us in every other constituency that goes to the polls in the second and third phases! Let us not forget, after all, that yours is an extraordinary battle – that of victim against rapist! Rationalized on a national scale it's a battle between a coalition that represents criminals and one that represents the suppressed majority.'

I was yet to absorb the magnitude of what Sharad had said.

'So be positive and prepare yourself for your very own tryst with history,' Sharad finished with a chuckle.

However his words of inspiration could not instantly dispel the pessimism that had marked our copter journey to the state capital. With some hesitation in mind, I blurted out my fears: 'But, Sharadji, I'm not too sure if I really stand that good a chance. I mean, every day I hear that bastard Salim stoop to a new low – sometimes with concocted stories that malign my character, at other times with morphed pictures and videos. And you know that the state administration supports him?'

Sharad thought for a moment. 'What if I hand you a weapon that will most certainly destroy your enemy?' A shrewd smile crossed Sharad's face as he took out a file from his bag. 'Here, take this and read it.'

'What is it?'

'Think, Shruti, doesn't a name like "Salim Yadav" intrigue you, as much as it makes your blood boil?' He put the file in my hands: 'This file tells you the history behind its creation.'

I looked through the contents.

Salim Yadav, the file said, was a child born out of rape. Salim's father, Govardhan Yadav, a small-time political activist had raped his East Pakistani (Bangladesh hadn't come into being then) refugee maid when his wife was away. When Salim's mother became pregnant, she was shunted out of the house. Salim's mother gave birth to him and brought him up with the help of some relatives in the Doligunj village, which was now a part of the neighbouring Purnia district. Salim's mother subsequently married a younger guy called Anwar. Anwar tried hard to discipline Salim, but Salim was always an aggressive and uncaring child.

Govardhan Yadav did not have any offspring from his wife. Twelve years after Salim was born, he was called by Govardhan, who was then on his deathbed, battling the last stages of lung cancer. Govardhan bequeathed all his properties, including forty-odd buffaloes, a prosperous milk business, and a decent-sized haveli, to Salim.

The day he inherited this, Salim who hated his stepfather, turned his back on the mother who had struggled to bring him up. In fact, when Salim started his extortionist activities, he made sure that his goons gave his stepfather a tough time for the ill-treatment that he had given him.

To settle scores with Anwar, Salim had his own teenaged stepsister molested by a friend of his. His mother never forgave him for the misery he caused her daughter. After that shameful episode, the family shifted to Danapur near Patna, just to ensure that Salim did not know about their whereabouts. Salim's mother disowned him and cursed herself for giving birth to such a criminal character.

'This story will win you the elections if you use it the way I tell you to,' said Sharad, calmness personified, when I looked up after reading the file.

Before I could respond, he turned on the intercom and asked a peon outside to send someone in. In no time, a frail, elderly lady walked in. 'Zahida Bano is Salim's mother. She will campaign with you,' Sharad said.

I looked at the old woman not knowing what to say. She wasn't as old as she looked; perhaps she had aged prematurely from the scars that life had inflicted upon her. I could understand her pain.

I turned to Sharad, completely stunned, even as Sharad continued to talk: 'Take her along to all your meetings for the next three days. She will tell the truth about her son to the world. And *then* let the voters decide whether they will still believe Salim's story.' Sharad's smile got broader.

I couldn't believe what was happening! In the space of three hours the situation had reversed itself. From the sense of dreariness that I had experienced when I opened my eyes that morning, I was beginning to exude definite optimism. But that part of me that makes the educated middle-class a stickler for ethics was still somewhat sceptical. 'But, Sharadji, will this be ethical? I mean dragging his poor mother into all this?'

Sharad laughed, and this time it was a much more assertive laugh: 'I can hear Lord Krishna tell me – it's the call of duty. If the attainment of the larger good is impossible without this supposed "unethical act" then go ahead and do it. It's your karma, my dear.'

Sharad left soon after as he was supposed to reach Delhi for an important meeting and Rohit and I made our way back to the war zone with Salim's mother in tow.

❖

Zahida Bano had a riveting story to tell, and she told it with all her heart: 'I have nurtured Salim for nine months in my womb and know him better than anybody else. You will not find a more evil creature on this earth than him. And there's a reason for that – he was not born out of love, but out of sinful violence…'

As Zahida Bano addressed the gathering that had assembled for Friday evening namaaz outside the mosque, the difference in crowd reaction became clearly visible. They were rapt, seething in silent fury at her pain. I mean, a mother instigating the masses against her own demonic son and supporting the victim of her son's cruelty was bound to have a revolutionary impact.

'Decades after his father inflicted the torture on me that was to lead to Salim's birth, he responded to the calling of his blood by repeating that dastardly crime on his hapless sister. No incident can shame a mother more than her offspring outraging a woman's modesty. My tragedy is that being a mother I can't even pray to Allah to curse Salim. All I can do is pray to you all to support this child, Shruti, and help her win.' As Zahida Bano said this, she burst into tears. I could sense the crowd quietly weeping with her – so moving was her outburst.

The Maulana, however, just about managed to conceal his delight. Yes, what we had been finding so hard to achieve had been accomplished by Sharad's masterstroke! By the time the meeting ended, a section of the crowd was so agitated that it was shouting abuses against Salim.

For the next two days, I turned a silent spectator and let the Maulana and Zahida Bano do most of the talking. Their speeches were so vitriolic – Maulana's employing religious fervour and Zahida utilizing emotional angst – that all I needed to do at the end of their rousing speech was to fold my hands and stand on the dais like a woman wronged. By the time, the campaign ended, I could sense that things had changed drastically in just the last two days. A group of people had actually ransacked and burnt a couple of benami properties that Salim supposedly owned.

The only fear on our minds now was that Salim Yadav would resort to heavy booth-capturing. Luckily our regular appeals to the Election Commission bore fruit. The new Chief Election Commissioner, who was remarkably apolitical unlike his predecessors, provided security of an unprecedented scale. In fact, the entire town looked like it had been seized by the armed forces.

To our surprise, barring a couple of glitches, the election process was largely smooth.

❖

That night, after the votes had been cast, Rohit and I stayed awake till late despite there being no apparent reason for it. I guess we were both trying to gaze pensively into what seemed like a tense future. 'Rohit, I really don't know what's going to happen. What if I win?' I said.

Rohit looked at me for a long moment, before breaking into a smile. 'Just three nights ago, you were worried about losing. And now you're worried about winning? Not bad,' he observed.

I took a deep breath. 'I don't know why, but tonight, the prospect of winning seems just as scary,' I confessed.

❖

A month later, I found myself sticking out like a sore thumb in the jam-packed central hall of Parliament, among the MPs elected to the 13th Lok Sabha. As I waited for my turn to take the oath of office, my eyes wandered impatiently, trying to locate my husband who was seated just metres away in the visitors' gallery. At that moment that small distance between us suddenly seemed liked an unbridgeable gap. I felt a shiver of fear down my spine.

And then my name was being called out. I got up and walked the last few steps, each step as tentative and hesitant as it could get.

'*I, Shruti Ranjan Verma, do… uh…swear in the name of God that I will faithfully execute the office of… Member of Parliament of the Republic of India, and will to… uh… the best of my ability preserve, protect and defend the Constitution and the law… and that I will devote myself to the service and well-being of the people of the Republic of India...*'

I fumbled many times over that short paragraph – and distinctly recall registering Sharad Malviya, sitting in the front row, taking note of my unease.

❖

Later that night, Rohit and I made love. I could sense he was very relieved. It showed in his unhindered movements and domination of the way he wanted our love-making to go. For some strange reason, I was left cold.

Much after we had finished making love there was a lingering image that loomed in my mind: the punctuated content of my oath and Sharad Malviya intently observing me as I fumbled through the oath.

6

The best part about democracy is that it spares nobody. Even the Mahatma had to face the flak of the people on numerous occasions. The electoral process has also been ruthless on stalwarts like Indira Gandhi and Atal Bihari Vajpayee, who were made to bite the dust at the hustings.

The Lok Sabha elections that year were a watershed in Indian politics. A corrupt and crime-patronizing Indian Democratic Party-led coalition was unseated. This obviously meant bad news for the Bihar Lok Morcha government in Bihar, which was a part of the previous coalition. I doubt if I came anywhere close to being Lucretia, but, looking back, Sharad's pep talk in the middle of my election campaign had been the turning point for me.

Sharad went on to become Home Minister in the new government headed by Yashwant Modi as Prime Minister. In many ways, it was a dream come true for Sharad. He had always championed the cause of internal security, as he felt that the fruits of economic development would be nullified if the increasing law and order problems were not addressed immediately.

'You see, the very idea of India is under attack,' he would say and then elaborate: 'In the north-east, there is infiltration from Bangladesh. Right from Nepal to Andhra Pradesh runs a Maoist corridor that is waiting to explode. Then there are the terrorist sleeper cells sponsored by Pakistan. Besides, none of our neighbours can be trusted. If we don't deal with the problem with an iron hand, then I doubt our succeeding generations will be lucky to see India in this shape.'

Sharad's contemporaries would laugh off his concerns and dismiss them as unwarranted. He definitely had a penchant for exaggeration, as was evident in his drawing a parallel between me and Lucretia. But what remained unquestionable were his rare foresight and tact – qualities that he had probably imbibed from his devotion of Krishna; the same qualities had led him to discover the strength and electoral worth in a hapless rape victim.

My first few days in the Parliament were marked by confusion. Once again there were many questions and few answers. The good thing, though, was that this time around, the confusion wasn't the kind that could bog me down. I was simply puzzled by the sheer magnitude of everything around me. It sometimes made me feel completely inadequate and at other times gave me an elevated sense of self-worth. Every time I thought of the topsy-turvy ride that my life had been since Abhay cheated on me, I felt surer that my destiny had been marked out for some of life's more volatile experiments. For instance, Rohit's life seemed so uneventful compared to mine. Of course, I had no idea at that point that the vicissitudes of fate would deeply mark his life as well.

The changes in my life meant reviving my association with the city that until recently had haunted me. Being back in Delhi meant I'd have to make an extra effort to keep away from certain people and places.

As a new Member of Parliament I was completely taken by the grandeur of two massive structures. The first was the Parliament building – the ultimate seat of power where the legislature formulated laws that affected the ordinary. I wondered if the size of this building was indicative of its vast authority. In the early days, I would feel most insignificant inside its imposing walls. That was when I missed Rohit the most – even breaking down on one occasion when the loneliness became difficult to cope with.

The other structure that I found special was North Block, which housed the office of Sharad Malviya. Built on Raisina Hill, on either side of Rajpath, North and South Block, also known as the Secretariat Buildings are among the most impressive state office buildings in the world. North Block houses the Ministry of Home Affairs.

The gateway of North Block has an inscription which reads: *'Liberty will not descend to a people: a people must raise themselves to liberty. It is a blessing that must be earned before it can be enjoyed'.*

Sharad had put up this inscription in his office too. When I first went to Sharad's room to congratulate him on assuming office, his watchful eyes caught mine reading it. True to his style, he dwelt at length upon the essence of what the inscription meant.

My distraction with the enormity of things around me notwithstanding, I was always heedful of the larger battle of my own; my need to settle scores with that bastard, Salim Yadav.

And I quickly got down to it, with some able guidance from Sharad.

❖

After the most important business of the passing of the Union Budget and some other Bills had been carried out, it was decided to let me raise the issue of my rape towards the end of our first session of Parliament.

All of it went pretty much according to plan. The idea was that when I spoke of the sexual assault on me I was to speak so convincingly that the House, where we had a majority now, would go up in clamour, and demand the imposition of President's rule in Bihar.

I acted pretty much according to the script. I worked up the melodrama and much against my own wish, re-lived every morbid detail of that dreadful night. I surprised myself by the actual depth of my own anguish, which I thought I had been careful to suppress. After silencing the House with a detailed description of that inauspicious night, I then went on to talk about the necessity for the speedy trial of such cases:

'Honourable Speaker sir, the rate at which crimes against women have risen in our country in the last three decades or so makes me wonder in shame if this is still the country of umpteen female goddesses, many of whom, including Durga and Kali are revered for their physical strength…

'Various factors, both social and legal contribute to the menace. One, in 97 per cent cases the culprit is known to the victim. In many cases it's a relative or neighbour who attacks them. Hence, often the victim does not even convey what has happened to her family members. In cases where she does confide it is she who is blamed for being "loose". There are still other cases where the culprit emotionally blackmails the victim by telling her, "Don't tell me you didn't enjoy it…" Sexual deprivation and the taboo associated with having a "male friend", especially in rural areas, makes the victim silently succumb to being raped.

'Of course, there's the legal aspect too. Only 1 out of 50 cases is actually reported. Of these less than 25 per

cent lead to conviction. There are two main reasons for this. One, in our legal system, the onus for proving she has been raped lies on the victim and not on the culprit to prove his innocence. Two, in court, the defence lawyer often derives great mirth in asking the victim outrageous questions that are no less hurtful than the assault itself. There is a concerted effort to prove the woman is of loose character and that sex was consensual.

'Honourable Speaker sir, the sex ratio of our society only fuels the problem. In some states the sex ratio disparity is so stark and unhealthy that it almost invites such crimes. Therefore, if this menace has to end, we will have to arrest the problem from ground zero. First and foremost, female foeticide will have to be conclusively checked. I propose therefore, sir, that female foeticide be included under Section 300 of the Indian Penal Code under which culpable homicide is murder. After all, the sex of the foetus can normally not be detected until the 15th week. Abortion, in such cases, has no reason not be seen as a killing.

'Sir, we need to initiate a massive campaign to ensure that rape cases are reported. Police officials, especially in rural areas, who hush up these cases, ought to be sacked. The police is a protector. If it becomes the broker, then it abets such crimes with its complicity. Police officials who have shielded rapists or not lodged an FIR should be made co-accused.

'Sir, my rape has proved that anybody can become a victim of this heinous crime. I would think I am *reasonably well-educated. As the wife of an IAS officer, as much as I may not have acknowledged it, I think I enjoy a reasonable clout. Yet I met a fate that was no different from what thousands of women, especially in our rural regions suffer in silence.*

'Sir, as a victim and sufferer I know what it means to be a rape victim. I can thus feel the physical and emotional trauma of every woman who has suffered the crime. I find it absolutely despicable that men who worship a Durga or a Lakshmi at home do not blink before subjecting the embodiments of the same goddesses to this act of ultimate cruelty. Since our society has failed to fix the problem, honourable sir, I would hereby propose a radical legal solution.

'Sir, India today needs fast-track or tatkaal courts specifically and solely to deal with crimes against women. Each of the 626 districts of the country ought to have a tatkaal court that clears cases pertaining to crime against women. These courts should settle each case not later than six months from the date of start of trial. That, to the best of my opinion and knowledge, sir, is the only way the massive backlog of millions of pending cases of crimes against women can be fixed. That is the only way India can change her unsavoury reputation of being the most unsafe country in the world for the girl-child.'

❖

The hysteria that my speech generated took me by surprise. Over 200 MPs rose up in murderous zeal, all shouting slogans against Salim Yadav and the Bihar government. Luckily, the Bihar Lok Morcha had now been reduced to just about half-a-dozen seats in the Lok Sabha. And the Indian Democratic Party, now occupying the Opposition benches, could not afford to be seen siding with them on this shameful incident.

The culmination of this high drama was the Home Minister Sharad Malviya stepping in and assuring the house that the culprit would be meted the severest possible punishment.

'I would like to assure the House that the culprit Salim Yadav will not be able to hoodwink the system and get away with this heinous crime. I will personally urge the PM to write to the Bihar CM advising him to seek a CBI enquiry into the incident. The government is committed to protect women and will leave no stone unturned in ensuring that the culprit gets maximum punishment.'

A week later, a CBI enquiry was ordered to probe my rape attack. Among the other things that the CBI was required to do was to prove whether there was a nexus between Salim Yadav and some ministers in the Bihar government that had allowed Salim Yadav to carry out his illegal activities with impunity. It was asked to determine if this nexus had shielded him in my rape case and if Salim Yadav had been running a human-trafficking scandal where some of these ministers were interested parties.

The CBI was asked to complete its investigation on a priority basis and submit its report within 90 days.

❖

The constitution of a CBI inquiry came as a big relief to me. Yes, it was only a partial battle won. But had I not been an MP, the battle might never have begun. My fate would not have been dissimilar from that of the 4 other women out of 5 who are never able to get their rapists convicted. Salim's conviction was still a long distance away but I felt a positive undercurrent that told me that all would be well. I would attribute that optimism to Sharad Malviya, whom I felt deeply indebted to.

The setting up of the CBI enquiry reminded me once again of the inscription 'Liberty will not descend to a people….' I guess this was a truism, going by the way that the situation had unfolded for me in the last few weeks. I was developing an even deeper respect for Sharad Malviya; a respect borne out of him walking his talk.

When I walked out of the Parliament that evening, I was greeted by a huge group of media persons. This time round, I did not feel like hiding myself. Their eyes beamed their admiration for me. They had come to congratulate me.

'Shrutiji, it takes immense courage to stand up for the truth like you did. How does it feel?' a woman scribe asked me.

It took me just that extra moment to think how I'd like to respond to her question. 'Well, on balance, I'd still have been better off if such a thing had never happened to me,' I said.

The obviousness of what I said left everybody silent for a moment. Journalists, after all, ask you such unintelligent questions sometimes.

'My journey from the time that my modesty was outraged till this moment has been an arduous one. And it's still not over. It won't be over till devils like Salim Yadav lurk in our small towns and abuse our women at will. My fight will continue till justice is meted out to every woman who has ever been raped.'

I spoke with as much honesty as was there in me, hardly realizing that the unassuming sound bite would catapult me into being seen as a messiah of all womanhood.

That evening, beyond the clutter of intrusive journalists, stood a familiar face, shorn of the smug confidence that he normally exuded. Abhay stood at a distance quietly observing my interaction with the media, even as a junior from his channel threw questions at me. After most of the journalists had left, I saw Abhay still hanging around.

'I'm happy for you, Shruti,' he said, finally coming up to me. 'I can understand the pain you must have gone through.'

Where was this guy coming from? I wondered. How could he so conveniently forget that he'd added to my pain? After all, wasn't he the first journalist to insinuate that my rape might not after all be rape at all? By saying this he had made Salim's escape route much easier. And Abhay, my boyfriend of three years, had done so most unabashedly on national television.

He knew I was seething with anger.

'Shrutiji, can you give me two minutes?' he said, the additional *ji* from him adding insult to injury.

I could not create a scene, lest the other people found out that Abhay and I knew each other from before. I composed myself and walked with him a little distance off, away from the other journos. Protected from the attention of his colleagues and fellow scribes, he revealed a side of his that I didn't know: 'Look, Shruti, I'm really sorry about that interview. I mean, I was left with no option.'

'There is always an option,' I retorted coldly.

'You know the electronic media can be so damn cruel at times. My boss felt I didn't have it in me to grill people in my interviews. I'd been given an ultimatum that day – if that interview did not increase viewership…' His words trailed off uncomfortably. The look of stunned disgust on my face prevented

Abhay from completing his sentence. 'But Shruti, I... I repent it. I'm really sorry.'

As perfidy of that nature and scale is simply indefensible, I just walked away.

❖

That night, much of the sense of relief that I should have felt was eroded by the deep disgust I felt for Abhay. My thoughts only underlined the fact that he'd probably always been this shallow and self-occupied and that it was my blind love, my inability to judge character, which had failed to recognize his real self. After all, my apparent disapproval hadn't prevented him from keeping uncomfortably close contacts with several female friends even during our courtship days. For all I know, I'd always been an instrument at his service, to exploit easily and at will.

While his meanness was perhaps not a shock to me, what was a little strange was the candour with which he had confessed to doing what he did. Why would he do that to me? I mean I was merely his ditched ex-girlfriend. What interest would it serve him to acquaint me with his vice?

After a while I wondered why I was thinking about him in the first place. I mean, it's strange, isn't it, that we often spend more time thinking about those who hurt us rather than those who help us heal? That could also be because those who heal often don't keep talking about all they've done for you.

I could safely say at that stage that my world revolved around my healer. Some hiccups notwithstanding, my husband deserved all the credit for standing by me through a phase that could have seen many lesser men fail.

❖

'Shruti, I miss you,' Rohit's voice was choked with emotion. These were simple words that any well-meaning husband would say to his wife. What made them special was that Rohit had said them to me for the first time. He said them to me when he came down to see me in Delhi after the CBI enquiry had been instituted.

'I miss you too, Rohit,' I said, not knowing for sure if I'd have said those three words had Rohit not said them to me first.

Yes, my new role as an MP had resulted in some kind of distance setting into our personal lives. No longer could we meet at the dinner table every night and chat away our anxieties. No longer could we rest assured on tense nights that we'd have each other to sleep beside. And both of us felt somewhat guilty for not being able to stand by the other's side in our respective everyday battles.

Even though I spent most of the time when Parliament was not in session with Rohit in Kishanganj, I knew my husband craved for more time from me.

'Shruti, how long do you think it will take for the entire thing to get over – the CBI enquiry and then the court trial?' he asked me.

'I have no idea, Rohit. I hope it happens fast.'

He looked a bit disoriented, his apprehension a marked contrast from that decisive night when he'd reassured me – *Once you set this straight, you can always quit politics and come back to start a family. I think the trouble will be just for a year or two.*

All wasn't quite well with him; this time it was he who seemed in need of reassurance. Knowing Rohit, I could understand that much of his woes had to do with the reactions of people around him, mainly his parents. And knowing his parents' mindset, if the party seat had not happened for me, they would have exhorted Rohit to divorce his raped wife.

Anyway, at that point, they seemed to be in a dilemma over whether to bask in the glory of their bahu having become a political leader or to feel ashamed that she was a damaged woman who had blatantly exploited her rape to attain this position.

My own parents were only slightly more supportive; but they were also dead clear that, first and foremost, I ought to be sensitive to my in-laws' position.

On my part, I really didn't have much to choose from. I was living a day at a time.

❖

A week later, I participated in what was a much-belated victory march held for me at Kishanganj. This march, organized by my party, was not something I personally favoured. But, as a newly-elected political leader, I realized that sometimes you need to do things for people who've selflessly worked for you.

I knew my victory wouldn't have been possible without the hard work and prayers of the thousands of invisible men and women who had supported me. If it made them happy to see me thank them publicly with folded hands, I wasn't the sort who'd deprive them of the joy. It was another thing that the effort was a rather painstaking one. For, what I had been told would be a two-hour affair, extended to a whole day. There were so many stories that the janta wanted to share with me. And for some strange reason, I wanted to hear them all – least of all because it was a professional obligation.

'My victory is a victory for the oppressed and victimized. I take this opportunity to extend an offer to all of you. All those who feel you have suffered in the Bihar Lok Morcha regime and your tales of woe have fallen on deaf ears, can meet me tomorrow morning at my residence. My staff will study each grievance personally and ensure that you get justice as quickly as possible.'

The security for my victory march was the responsibility of the DC's office. Even though Rohit was personally present only for a short while, I could sense some discomfort in him on seeing me mobbed by unknown people. By the time I finished meeting them and went to see him, he was gone.

The next day I was surprised to see some 500 'victims' land up at our place in response to my offer to help them out. A long queue had to be organized outside the house to ensure that the crowd did not go berserk. Rohit, who had a headache the previous night, woke up late and was understandably annoyed to see the commotion outside.

Some of the stories of extortion were so morbid that the people would go hysterical narrating them. It was while this was on that Rohit walked in there and lost his cool. 'Shruti, I want to talk to you,' he said in a gruff tone. Before I could react, he reiterated his urgency. 'Now.' He took me inside and said, 'Shruti, this is our home, not an orphanage.'

'But, Rohit, it's only a matter of time. You know I'm renting an office for meeting people soon,' I protested.

Luckily, Rohit immediately realized his mistake. He held my arms and explained what was on his mind. 'Listen, Shruti, I'm sorry, don't get me wrong. I just miss spending time with you.'

I was still reeling from the unfairness of Rohit's 'orphanage' remark and so did not quite react to his unmeant apology. From the expression on Rohit's visage, I knew there was a deeper angst that he was battling.

'Shruti, when you meet Sharad Malviya next, will you please discuss your plan of quitting your seat? Your agenda in this game is over. Once the CBI indicts Salim Yadav, there is no way he won't get convicted. You will have your revenge.'

He knew his words had taken me aback but clearly he had thought out what he wanted to say to me. 'Look Shruti, being an elected representative is no joke. You don't have a private life. Just look at the people outside. What do you have to do with *any* of them?'

❖

After a long time, that day, I once again felt alienated from Rohit's thought process. No, I certainly wasn't reaching out to these illiterate, dirty people just because my role as an elected representative *demanded* it. And weren't they the same people for whom Rohit had gone out of his way, when they were battling the menace of kala azar? I knew now that there was something deeper that was bothering Rohit. I had no clue what it was. I therefore agreed to his demands.

'Fair enough. I'll do as you wish. In any case, I'd not have got this far without your support.'

I could see some relief on his face when he heard this. The only request that I made was to give me some more time – *at least till the CBI had submitted its report and the court proceedings had begun.*

In two months, the CBI report was out. The report expectedly indicted Salim Yadav and the Bihar government on various issues. In fact, so harsh was the indictment that a court trial, though inevitable, seemed like a formality! It was expected that a fast-track court would hear the case so that a verdict could be out sooner. Justice is so easy when you are in the right place.

I had been vindicated, but I still felt hollow inside.

❖

I went to meet Sharadji after the indictment and did so with a heavy heart. It almost felt like the last step in an inevitable journey of which I'd been a part. Sticking to the promise that I'd made to Rohit, I had gone to discuss quitting my Lok Sabha membership. I would soon be back in Kishanganj, at home with my husband. I should have been happy but I felt strangely detached.

However, as always, destiny had something else planned for me.

Sharad sat in his office with two women – Sarojini Srivastava, the National Council for Women Chairperson and Urmila Deshmukh, the Minister for Women and Child Affairs. I was a little surprised.

'Come, come, Shruti. We were waiting for you.'

Waiting for what?

I had briefly met Urmila once in Parliament and had exchanged greetings with her, while Sarojini was unknown to me, except that I had seen her in debates on TV and attended some of her press conferences as a young reporter... That both were so warm towards me, was surprising.

Sharad introduced the two women to me, though of course I knew who they were, and then said, 'Sarojini, as you know, is the NCW chairperson. She completes her term next month... She and Urmila, asked me to suggest someone who could take up the position and I suggested your name.'

I was stunned by this sudden turn of events. I still had to do my part of the talking – to apprise Sharad of the reason I was there. 'But, Sharadji...' I began

'No ifs and buts, Shruti. I simply recommended your name, but Sarojini and Urmila are more than keen to have you...'

Sarojini said, 'Ideally we'd have liked to appoint someone senior, but your case is special. At this point, we can't think of anyone more gutsy and inspiring than you.'

I tried to tell Sharad what I'd come there for, but Sharad didn't leave me with an option. It had all been decided before I could open my mouth.

'Congratulations, Shruti, on your new assign-ment! May this be the first of many big assignments that come your way.'

At that point Sharad received an urgent call on his cell and excused himself to talk on the phone. I was left with the ladies who talked enthusiastically about how I was the perfect candidate for the post.

❖

That night I called Rohit and tried to explain what had happened. He heard me out in complete silence. I knew he'd be upset. But did I have an option? I didn't want to be a quitter again.

And then I got angry with myself. Why the hell was I already calling myself a quitter? When was I a quitter the first time around? Perhaps I was scared to admit to myself that in my subconscious mind I had considered my decision to agree to marry Rohit an act of quitting. Perhaps in doing so I had quit my ambitious spirit. I couldn't overlook the fact that while, if not exactly an act of quitting, my marriage in some sense had been a compromise; a cop-out.

When he finally spoke Rohit sounded unusually defeated on the phone – making the kind of choked, inarticulate sounds that tells a spouse that something is drastically amiss. Despite my persuasion, Rohit did not tell me what was bothering him.

Three weeks later when I learnt the reason behind Rohit's anguish, I was aghast.

7

When I had been away in Delhi, the CM of Bihar, Gangalal Yadav, had come on a visit to Kishanganj. The official purpose of his visit had been to 'take stock of the flood situation', which was clearly not the real reason. The floods he had come to investigate were speculative and non-existent compared to the flood situation in previous years.

The CM's strange behaviour only manifested the ulterior motive behind his visit. After disinterestedly visiting a couple of places, the CM decided to meet the press at a fishermen's village called Dumkai.

'We will do everything to help the flood-affected people. Each flood-affected home will be given Rs 1 lakh for rehabilitation,' he had declared with the sarpanch of the village, by his side.

This had obviously surprised everybody as the district was not yet 'flood-hit' in the real sense of the term. So the question of 'rehabilitation' simply did not arise. Water entering homes in the low-lying areas was after all no uncommon phenomenon, especially in Kishanganj.

One of the sharper journalists present, a spunky young woman, saw something amiss. 'Are you trying to compensate the Mondal community?' the journalist had asked the CM, pointblank.

'What are you trying to say?' he had shot back.

'Sir, it's a known fact that 5 fishermen from this village were arrested last week for smuggling musk deer skin. That, we understand, is just the tip of the iceberg. We understand that the arrested persons could reveal names of some top politicians. Is this "flood relief" money a bribe to the community to keep shut?'

This was sufficient to drive the CM wild with anger. 'Shut up, you fool,' he had lashed out, abandoning all show of diplomacy and decorum and immediately ordered his goons to seize the camera reels of all the photographers present. One TV channel's camera was forcibly turned off. Then the CM had thundered, 'Thanks to incompetent IAS officials like Rohit Verma, you journalists have got used to feeding on fiction rather than real stories!' Gangalal directed his fury at Rohit. 'When *chutiyas* like Rohit Verma become IAS officers, the country is doomed. This useless man is indulging in all these antics to hide his failures. First, he makes his wife an MP and then he victimizes the poor Mondal community. What measures has he taken to prevent flooding of the district this year?'

Everybody present there had been aghast at the CM's language and behaviour. I can understand what Rohit, who wears his self-dignity on his sleeve, would have felt at that moment.

'Sir, none of my actions are fanciful. We had evidence of some of the community members' involvement. And I had personally examined the evidence before giving the police the go-ahead,' he had retorted.

The CM then went on a virtual rampage: 'Bloody fool! People like you should be beaten up in public. What evidence are you talking about? Just because Sharad Malviya has taken a fancy to your wife, doesn't mean you and your wife start operating the country's Home Ministry by proxy. Come on, get out of here, you filthy dog.'

❖

I learnt of this incident only a month after it happened, when Rohit and I were at his parents' place in Patna. We had come to attend his younger brother's engagement. Rohit's speech faltered when he narrated the incident to me.

I felt destroyed. It ravaged me to imagine a devastated Rohit retracting his steps. He had simply got into his vehicle and driven off. I don't have a firsthand account of what the CM subsequently did to the journalists present there, but none of them reported the incident. Ironically, all the news that appeared about the CM's visit to the district carried positive reports about his magnanimity.

The CM's behaviour did not surprise me as much as it hurt that Rohit should be the victim. What really disturbed me was my guilt – I knew that Rohit had begun to pay the price for my success. That Rohit had hidden this incident from me for a month only made me feel more miserable.

'Why didn't you tell me about this the day it happened?'

'What purpose would that have served?'

'I could have spoken to Sharadji. The CM could have been given a warning.'

Rohit was quiet for a moment. Then he said, 'That's exactly what I *don't* want.'

'What?'

'People insinuating that I'm incapable of fighting my battles and taking your help. I guess at some point each one of us has to look out for themselves.'

I was shocked when I heard this. How time and situations change! Just a few months ago, Rohit had been the one who had supported me to reach where I was today. And now he believed in fighting his own battles! I suddenly felt inadequate for him. 'Listen, Rohit, we can't leave it at this. I mean, if the CM has stooped to this today, tomorrow something more bizarre can happen.'

'It won't, so relax. My transfer is due next month and I'm hoping it will be to a better district.'

'Shall I speak to Sharadji and try and get you posted out of Bihar?'

'No,' was Rohit's laconic response. 'Please don't do that.'

It was getting late and we had to leave for my brother-in-law's engagement ceremony. So I had to accept Rohit's summing up of the situation, though I wasn't convinced about it.

'Listen, Shruti,' Rohit said as we left our room, 'It's a matter of time. Just concentrate on your court case. Once you're back with me, everything will be fine. Besides, everybody knows that this government will be shunted out in the next Assembly elections.'

I was completely shaken by the incident Rohit had been made to go through. Throughout my brother-in-law's engagement ceremony, I could barely speak. Rohit's narration of his humiliation, the extent these petty politicians – first Salim and now Gangalal – went to put people like us in their place, made me seethe in fury.

I had to do something about it.

❖

A week later I confided in Sharad. I knew Rohit wouldn't have liked me doing it, but then my helplessness was killing me. Sharad heard me out calmly.

'Hmm... the one thing I know is that your quitting and going back will not make sense. You will be as powerless as you were the day when I first met you.' He paused. 'But why is your husband so adamant on not taking a transfer outside the state? I can get that done within hours.'

I had no reply.

'Do you want me to have a word with him?'

I shook my head. I knew Rohit well enough to understand what was playing on his mind. He did not like my proximity to Sharad, and Sharad getting him transferred for my sake would be a blow to his dignity.

As it was pretty late in the evening, Sharad asked me to have dinner with him. As we ate our meal, he remarked: 'Human minds are very complex, Shruti. More than his insult or your court case, I think what is bothering Rohit the most is that you are here and he is in Kishanganj.'

I was amazed at his intuitive understanding of the situation. Sharad did not mean this in a wrong way. In fact, I knew it was just an impartial observation. He'd probably read my mind. Ideally, I'd have liked not to discuss it any further but for some reason, I wanted to talk to him. I wanted to share a whole lot of things that had been weighing on my mind and which I couldn't discuss with anybody.

'Sorry… what exactly do you mean by that?' I queried.

'Well, any communication is aimed at generating a certain response. The way Rohit communicated this incident to you – not when it happened, but on the eve of your brother-in-law's engagement – don't you think that had a motive?'

I took a deep breath. 'Well, I know he wants me back ASAP,' I admitted. 'It's not been easy for him. I mean, he is not such a broad-minded guy. In fact, to be honest, I'm surprised that he's stood by me so far.'

Sharad's next query was as blunt as some of his barbs at his opponents have been. 'Do you love him?'

I struggled for an answer, even as he looked me in the eye. 'Yes... as much as a wife should love her husband.'

'Are you prepared to quit everything you have achieved and go back to him?'

I was silent.

Sharad sighed. 'Fair enough. But wait till the court gives its verdict. After that you can return to your world.'

Sharad had a knowing smile on his face as he said this, which for some reason made me feel like a loser. He changed the topic: 'You were telling me about the deer skin smuggling that Rohit has stumbled upon. Can you... okay... forget it. My department will get in touch with him because there's a separate investigation that my ministry is already looking into.'

At this point, Sharad's phone rang. From the way his expression softened on recognizing the voice, it was apparent that the caller was well known: 'Hi, darling.'

Sharad's casual tone surprised me a bit. He listened for a while and then said, 'Superb. Come over tomorrow for dinner. I'll make time for you.'

He put down the phone and turned to me. 'That was Shabnam, a senior official in the Intelligence Bureau. She wants to brief me on something important.'

I felt a little awkward and left immediately.

❖

That night I went over my conversation with Sharad. I don't know whether it was the impact of that conversation but suddenly the gap between Rohit and me seemed wider than ever before. I mean, here I was, bracing up for a new responsibility – that of the NCW chairperson, which I had to take charge of the next morning. I was so immersed in my new world that it took constant reminders from Rohit to realize that I had to 'return home'.

Did I really want to go back?

No, I thought.

Would Rohit travel the distance for me?

I wasn't sure.

Surprisingly, there was something else that occupied my thoughts too. I realized it was the casual, flirtatious manner in which Sharad had spoken to Shabnam. I wondered if he liked to plan his meetings with women over dinner. I don't know why, but for the first time I was curious about Sharad's personal life; his life beyond politics. After all he was a man of many parts; some more enigmatic than others.

❖

Soon enough, the fast-track Court started its proceedings. The CBI's indictment of Salim Yadav had made it an open and shut case. The CBI had taken custody of Salim Yadav, who was now rotting behind bars. Yet, as was the norm in my life, nothing could happen for me without some horrible twist in the plot.

Salim's lawyer, S.P. Gupta threw up a defence that sounded as clichéd as the institution of sati. He again raised the issue of my photographs with Salim and alleged that I was having an affair with him. I wouldn't have minded if he had alleged that I was insane. But to be linked with this repugnant creature, whom I hated most in the world, made me seethe with indignation.

Everybody, including Salim's lawyer and the judge himself, knew how absurd the allegations were. We knew that at best, the other party was trying to buy time as it had no other defence. But given the constraints of civil society, I had to defend the allegations legally.

When the stalemate continued, Sharad, Rohit, my lawyer Gulshan Kapoor and I had a brainstorming session.

'Even if we assume that you had an affair with Salim Yadav, that does not take away from the severity of the crime. The CBI report has corroborated the rape. The act here was so shameful that the sentence will remain unaltered. On the other hand, given Salim's track record, nobody will take these allegations seriously. So in my opinion, we must ignore the barbs of Yadav's lawyer and focus on getting the conviction,' Sharad said and Gulshan concurred.

All eyes shifted on me.

I shook my head resolutely. 'If this is the fight for truth, let the truth come out in its entirety. If I did not have an affair, I will not let anybody even vaguely insinuate that I did.'

'Hmm… that's fine but that unnecessarily prolongs the case,' opined Sharad.

'Is there no other solution?' Rohit asked the lawyer.

Gulshan Kapoor thought for a while before he spoke. 'Yes. There is one.'

He told us what he had in mind. Sharad and Rohit seemed convinced by Gulshan.

But I had my doubts.

❖

In the next court hearing, I had an unlikely witness vouching for me. Abhay Sarkar was called to the stand.

'As journalists, we sometimes manipulate situations to our advantage. And we do so at the cost of killing people's character. I have to confess that in normal circumstances we would not have gone ahead with the story without verifying the pictures. But our channel was running into losses. My boss Patankar accepted Rs 50 lakhs from Salim Yadav for airing the story,' Abhay confessed. 'Our viewership had plummeted. I had little option but to go ahead with the story. Or else, I'd have been fired.'

Abhay was to be our high-risk trump card. When his deposition ended, we thought he'd done a fairly decent job and strengthened our case. We had not expected that Yadav's lawyer would have done his homework just as well. Soon, it was Gupta's turn to grill Abhay.

'How long have you and Shruti known each other?' SP Gupta asked.

'We were together in college.'

'Were you close?'

'We were good friends.'

'This friendship is a vague term. Be specific.'

'I was quite specific.'

'Even lovers are friends. Were you only friends or lover-friends?'

'I said friends.'

Within moments, even as Gupta continued to question Abhay for no rhyme or reason, ridiculously enough, heads started turning towards me – as though I had hidden something from the court.

'Your honour, Shruti Ranjan Verma is not such an innocent creature. I can prove that she has had physical relations with other men too – one of whom is journalist Abhay, whom she has known since college. In all likelihood, Abhay's act of first questioning the authenticity of her rape claims and now coming to her defence, has more to it than meets the eye. It is likely Shruti has continued to maintain relations with Abhay even after marriage. It was a lovers' tiff between them that made Abhay expose her…' Gupta roared.

I was absolutely devastated. I felt like a prostitute who could be used by anybody. How dare Gupta concoct such crap?

'Objection my lord, my esteemed colleague is indulging in character slander…' my lawyer protested.

At that point, I just lost it. I rushed to the centre of the court and screamed furiously, 'Rape for you is a sport, isn't it? You get away with it so often. But now that you've found a woman who is bent on getting you convicted, you try to prove that that woman is a whore who sleeps with every other man. Isn't that it? Honorable Judge sir, this court is meant to deliver justice, not to discuss people's sexual history. If that is all the lower courts have left to do, then let me not allow you any further entertainment at my expense. Let this case go directly to the Supreme Court…'

In a subsequent hearing the judge quashed all of Gupta's insinuations about my character and dismissed them as a hopeless effort to mislead the court. Salim Yadav and his two accomplices were sentenced to seven years' rigorous imprisonment – the maximum term that rape convictions in this country unfortunately carry. They had the option of appealing in a higher court against the verdict. But realizing that the result would be no different, the state unit of Bihar Lok Morcha had now turned its back on Salim.

It wanted the issue to die as soon as possible.

❖

Salim Yadav's conviction meant the end of a battle that I had been fighting since the moment I had been forcibly raped. I was glad the ordeal was finally over. I wasn't sure though if the ordeal's impact on my psyche could ever be erased completely.

Rohit and I took a couple of days off to be with each other. Of all places, we spent the weekend in Bodh Gaya – mostly because Rohit was in between postings; he had been transferred to Jehanabad, which was pretty close to Gaya. Gaya was chosen for another reason too – for its historical significance as an area of peace, tranquillity and understanding, which we badly needed restored in our lives.

We went to see the Bodhi tree under which the Buddha is said to have attained enlightenment. There was something going on in Rohit's mind. 'Is it possible for someone to just sit here and attain enlightenment?' he asked me, looking disturbed.

I wasn't prepared for a query so innocuous and yet so perilously laden. The disconnect between what must have been playing on his mind and his words was apparent. 'Why didn't you tell me about Abhay before? Have you been in touch with him after marriage?'

'No, we are not in touch. I haven't mentioned his name because I didn't see the need. Other than that you knew about my past.'

'Come on, Shruti. You should have mentioned it. It's… it's so bloody complicated.'

I felt a bit frustrated myself. I realized that Rohit would need reassurances all the time, right through our married life. I mean, if he'd really understood me, he'd know that despite Abhay coming and bailing me out in court, I had not even exchanged a word with him. I could have told Rohit about Abhay the day he broke the malicious news story about me but how could I trust a husband who, I knew, wasn't entirely sure of my innocence? At least, that's what Rohit's telephonic conversation with his friend had indicated.

Rohit's behaviour under the Bodhi tree belied all hopes of him ever being rid of his misgivings.

We sat under the tree. He lay his head on my lap, and I ran my fingers through his hair.

'Shruti, I want to become a father.'

My eyes grew moist thinking of the baby I had lost. At a time when we should have been planning our first child, we were instead consumed in fighting an absurd war. Rohit's words took me back to that moment in Darjeeling when I had first expressed my desire to have a child. Yes, life had been cruel to us and now it was up to me to move speedily to bring it back to normal. A fear loomed in my mind, though. When Rohit spoke those words to me, I'd been waiting to tell him something too; something I knew he wouldn't take well.

'Rohit, I'm in a dilemma,' I said hesitantly. 'I don't think I will be able to attend your brother's marriage next month.'

'Why?'

'Unfortunately, the date clashes with the start of the International Conference for Women in Geneva where I have to lead the Indian delegation.'

He looked tense and upset.

'But I will definitely attend the mehendi and sangeet.'

Rohit struggled for a response. He was clearly very angry. Still, he had the maturity and heart to tell me, 'It's a very important conference for you. You must decide your priority.'

On my way back to Delhi I felt I was being selfish. I had virtually decided to give Geneva a miss. After all, citing 'personal reasons' could get me that exemption. But when I reached Delhi, Rohit called me from Jehanabad. He sounded annoyed. 'Listen, you don't need to come for the pre-marriage rituals either. You must concentrate on your work.'

'But, Rohit…'

'No, don't bother. In any case, you'll be quitting this circus soon…'

Rohit's insistence on my quitting had begun to irritate me. So this time, when he reiterated it, I decided to concentrate on my job.

❖

On the evening before I was to depart, the President of India hosted a dinner for all the MPs. It happened to be Gandhi Jayanti. I had been meaning to meet Sharad before my first official trip. However, the meeting had not been possible as Sharad had been away on an official trip to Kashmir. Eventually, it so turned out that my meeting with him was scheduled just an hour before the dinner at Rashtrapati Bhawan.

I carried a gift for Sharad – a small idol of lord Krishna. Sharad's tact and his intelligence reminded me so often of this god.

'I'm very happy for you, Shruti,' he told me when we met. He looked genuinely pleased.

'It wouldn't have been possible without you, Sharadji.'

'Well, we're all catalysts who make possible what God wants. I don't want you to think that I went out of my way for you. I did what I had to do.'

'I think it's your magnanimity that makes you so modest. I don't know what my life would have been like had you not brought about this change.'

'So what have you decided?' he asked.

'About what?'

'Are you quitting your Lok Sabha seat?'

I sighed deeply. 'What should I do?' I finally asked him, virtually submitting myself to his counsel.

He looked at the idol of Krishna I had given him and smiled. 'Krishna will never advise you to leave the battlefield.'

'But, Sharadji, I've won my battle.'

'You haven't won the war. And you'll realize that only when you've quit this world.'

The enigmatic smile on Sharad's face when he spoke that last line said more than his words did. I would be lying if I said I wasn't in awe of him. There were things about life and the way it ought to be lived that I really wanted to learn from him. In some obscure corner of my mind, I was worried that 'going back' would deprive me of more than I had ever lost.

❖

That evening, nearly 500 MPs gathered for an official dinner at the Rashtrapati Bhawan. What struck me most about the President's speech was what he said about 'attaining the moral high ground'.

'Gandhism, in its most simplified form is about attaining the moral high ground. At every point, it is important for us to ascertain whether we are morally correct – as individuals, as society, as a party, and as a nation. If we do that, then most of our problems will end.'

I tried to mull over what the President said. Of course a lot of what was going on in my mind had to do with concerns about my future in politics.

But the need for a 'moral high ground' existed in the conjugal relationship between a husband and wife as well. Would I lose that if I chose to continue in politics? My rumination was cut short by a comment from Sharad. He said, 'The moral high ground is fine everywhere else, except in the case of Pakistan.' He had a few of his followers support him on that.

The other important thing that I remember the evening for is that it gave me my first opportunity to interface with some leading politicians I would have to deal with if I continued in this world.

The new PM, Yashwant Modi, was a suave, soft-spoken septuagenarian with a pleasant disposition. 'You have become an inspiration for the masses. Make sure you keep inspiring other women,' he told me affectionately, with a gentle pat on my shoulder.

For as long as I could remember, I had heard stories about the PM and Sharad not getting along with each other. As such, I had been a bit sceptical of how Modi would react to me. His warmth allayed my fears. Considering the twenty-four year age gap between Modi and Sharad, I felt it was only natural for two generations not to think alike.

Harish Chandra Solanki was the leader of the Opposition. I didn't like him one bit. Nor would any sensible educated person if they overheard the snide comment he made to Sharad. 'Not bad, Sharad. You've always been a little ahead of the times. Even before the Women's Reservation Bill is passed, you've started promoting women.' The pointed reference was to me.

Sharad shrugged off the remark with an acerbic riposte: 'I feel sad for you, Solanki. When in Opposition, you have neither power, nor women. And this is how the rest of your life will be...' Sharad's words were once again as ambiguous as ever. He gave nothing away.

Ratna Pandey, the leader of our party – the Nationalist League – was in her early fifties. A fourth-time MP, she was the senior-most woman in the party. I'm not very intuitive most of the times, but in her case, I could sense negative vibes towards me. I didn't know whether that was because of her insecurity but I didn't quite like her either.

Ratnesh Prasad was the party's leader in the Rajya Sabha. In his late fifties, he was reasonably young by Indian standards. Though from the similarity in their names Ratnesh and Ratna sounded like they were siblings, they couldn't stand each other. Much of their animosity had to do with the fight for 'control' within the party. It was Ratnesh's election as the leader of the party in the Rajya Sabha that had forced Ratna to go through the torture of fighting a Lok Sabha election again – a fact she did not care for one bit.

In the gathering that evening, Ratnesh heaped lavish praises on me and my ability to develop into a 'top leader' in the future. I suspect he did this on purpose – to drive home a message to Ratna. Ratna left the gathering early. I had begun to realize how much politicking went into everything that politicians did or said. To my own surprise, it did not perturb me.

❖

The four days that I spent in Geneva weren't easy for me. The days were spent in heated debate on issues like 're-defining sexual exploitation at the work-place where women at some point were willing partners'; 'defining rape in a failed live-in relationship'; and the age-old issue of 'domestic violence'. At night I was left alone with my thoughts, and I'd keep thinking about Rohit and our marriage. I'd promised to call and speak to Rohit's family members from Geneva on the evening my brother-in-law was getting married. That night I tried the number once but nobody picked up the phone. I did not try again as I felt awkward calling and wishing them when I couldn't be there. I felt rather miserable. We were still a year or so away from when mobile phones entered our lives and calling was not easy.

❖

Even as I dealt with my loneliness in Geneva, Rohit put up with his in the presence of all his family members. In addition, Rohit had to contend with insinuations of another kind and level. I would avoid the use of the words 'smear campaign' as it involves the family. My mother-in-law was naturally upset over my absence. When a close relative tauntingly asked my mother-in-law why I had chosen to skip such a 'special occasion', my mother-in-law lost her cool: 'We'll give *you* her office number. Why don't *you* call up Shruti directly and ask her?' she apparently exploded. The she went on to say, 'We're only concerned about our son. There must have been a bad planetary alignment when we got him married to this Draupadi. Oh God, save us from misery...'

I was told of this incident by one of my relatives who had attended the marriage as she was close to both families. This was the first time that someone had referred to me as 'Draupadi'. Of all people, the person saying this was my mother-in-law.

I was always given to consider Draupadi's 'poly-androus' history with sympathy – after all, an intelli-gent, strong, good-looking and wilful woman like her had nothing but her fate to blame for the unpleasant insinuations that her reference drew. I couldn't gather if I was being called 'Draupadi' because I had been raped, or because I was not ingratiating myself to my husband and his family.

Whatever it was, the reference devastated me. What my mother-in-law probably forgot was that Draupadi's mother-in-law Kunti was no less polyandrous.

Besides, Draupadi's fate was in so many ways her mother-in-law's doing. I was told that my mother-in-law had quickly realized the folly of her public outburst and calmed down. But the damage had been done. Rohit, who had become increasingly vulnerable to other people's jibes, was determined to have his way this time round.

When I landed back in Delhi two days later much after midnight, I was surprised to find Rohit waiting in the guest house. 'Rohit, I didn't expect you'd be here,' I said, surprised.

He didn't say anything. I knew he was upset, and had reason to be. His red eyes battling sleep and tension spoke more than any words could. He held out two typewritten sheets of paper for me.

'What is this, Rohit?'

He just kept looking at me with his bloodshot eyes. I read the papers. The first was my letter of resignation as MP; the second, my letter of resignation from the NCW.

I couldn't but look at him, dazed.

'Tomorrow morning,' was his ultimatum as he opened the door and stormed out of the room.

❖

I felt a chill go down my spine. I felt as nervous as I'd done that night when Rohit and I had first discussed the idea of me contesting the elections. Time had indeed come full circle. Having completed the circle I felt the same emptiness that I'd felt on starting out on this journey. What increased my fears this time was the stark realization that my journey back would be an even more isolated one than the one I had been on so far.

By the next morning, when Rohit and I sat together silently over breakfast, I had come to terms with the situation; I had decided I would quit my temporary world to go back to where I belonged.

My remembrance of the core thought of renunciation/relinquishment as enshrined in the Gita, made me stronger. I was happy that Rohit too felt relieved by my decision. I requested him to accompany me to Sharad's residence and he agreed.

Alas! My destiny and I seemed to always be at loggerheads.

Just as Rohit and I were preparing to leave for Sharad's house I heard some commotion at the gate. My guard was negotiating at least three groups of journalists who insisted on meeting me. I was surprised. I mean, what could it be about the Women's Conference that could interest them so urgently? I walked up to the gate with Rohit following me.

'What is the matter? What is it that I can do for you?'

One of the journalists responded, surprised, 'Madam, you really haven't heard the news yet?'

'What news?' I asked, as Rohit and I looked at each other in bewilderment.

'Ma'am, a Cabinet expansion is taking place today. And we have news that you are being inducted as Deputy Minister.'

The news would have made anyone else in my position ecstatic.

I was aghast.

Rohit and I looked at each other, as speechless as we were the previous night.

❖

A few hours later, I took an oath of office for the second time that year.

'*I, Shruti Ranjan Verma, do swear in the name of God that I will faithfully execute the office of Deputy Minister of the Republic of India…*'

...As I read my oath my voice shook. My eyes searched the audience for the face from whom I feared I would have a complete disconnect now...

'....*and will to the best of my ability preserve, protect and defend the Constitution and the law, and that I will devote myself to the service and well-being of the people of the Republic of India...*'

There was no sign of Rohit.

And I was now Deputy Home Minister under Sharad Malviya.

PART TWO

PART TWO

8

Hindu mythology portrays a glorious bond between Krishna and Draupadi. On one occasion, when Krishna had cut his finger on the Sudarshan Chakra, Draupadi tied it with the torn edge of her sari and that, according to one version of the myth, became the origin of Rakshabandhan.

Draupadi's father, Drupad, wanted to marry his daughter to the most eligible man on earth. On Krishna's advice, a Swayamvar was organized for Draupadi to which the bravest men of the time were invited, including the Pandavs and Kauravs. A contest was arranged to prove the eligibility of the participants and win Draupadi's hand. The contest was inhumanly difficult; looking at its reflection in a pot of water below, the participants had to target their arrow at the eye of a fish tied high above.

Karna, who had come as one of the suitors, exuded a courage and nobility that outshone the rest. However, as he lifted his bow, Krishna gestured to Draupadi to stop him. Draupadi immediately rose and objected to Karna's participation, 'Wait, King of

Anga, you don't have a royal lineage, hence I cannot marry you.'

Karna felt insulted by the taunt about his low birth and left seething in wrath. Krishna had done this to ensure that Draupadi married Arjun. He was laying down the crucial turns of history that were to follow, ultimately culminating in the Mahabharat.

But Krishna was extremely disturbed when he learnt that Draupadi had to become the wife of all five Pandavas. He chided Kunti for her careless slip of tongue that led to the fiasco.

Much later, when Duryodhana asked Dussasana to disrobe Draupadi in an open court, a helpless Draupadi prayed to Krishna for help. Krishna immediately came to her rescue and advised her to pray to the Sun god. Unknown to any human, Krishna met the Sun god. The god instructed Chhaya (literally, 'Shadow') and Maya (literally, 'illusion') to dress Draupadi. Unseen by everyone including Draupadi, these two kept dressing her, as Dussasana kept disrobing her.

Whenever in need, Krishna, thus, stood by Draupadi like a rock and bailed her out of all difficult situations.

❖

You are probably wondering why I'm telling you this story about Krishna and Draupadi. Well, it is not without reason. Sharad had likened our relationship to the one that is said to have existed between Krishna and Draupadi. Again, he did not do it without a reason.

Soon after my swearing-in ceremony, a rather vicious story broke out in a section of the media – of a supposed affair between Sharad and me. It suggested that the 'affair' was instrumental in my meteoric rise. Well, yes, by my own unassuming standards, my rise had indeed been 'meteoric'. I didn't know what to attribute it to, though – my rape, the forces of my destiny, or Sharad. I found the reports as much a slur on my character as the rape itself.

I was deeply disturbed by the nasty rumours and the speculation in the media. So I went to meet Sharad that evening. He was absorbed in listening to the music of Hari Prasad Chaurasia. I was asked to wait in the office from where I could hear the melodious notes of the flute playing in the background. In a way, I envied Sharad his calm. How detached he was from natural emotions like anger and hurt. Or did he feel neither? Well, he certainly had built a wall around himself – one that provided him immunity from obstacles that swayed lesser mortals. One part of me wanted to be like him; the other was scared of who I'd be if I became more like him.

After a few minutes of waiting I lost my patience and virtually barged into the living room. Noticing me, he lowered the volume of the music.

'What's happened?' he asked, calmly.

'Don't you know?' I asked in shock. 'Haven't you read the stories linking us together?

He took a deep breath, turned off the music and then spoke as serenely as ever: 'I thought these things won't bother you anymore. Rumour and propaganda are a part of public life. You have experienced all this before, even when you weren't in public life.'

For once Sharad's reasoning failed to impress me. Life was not as simple as that. Was he really unaffected by our link-up? Worse, did he really want it that way? My quandary led me to finally ask him this more directly. 'Sharadji, do I really *deserve* to be a Deputy Minister?'

'Yes, you deserve all you've got,' was his laconic response. As if in afterthought, he added, 'You know what, when your past is laden with heavy emotional baggage, it makes sense to accelerate your journey into the future.'

His words carried a personal sense of ownership that only deepened my doubts about the disparity between what I really deserved and what I'd been given. I didn't think my rape entitled me to political clout. 'Sharadji, I need to understand, why are you putting so much at stake for me? How do we define our relationship?'

'It's pretty similar to the one that existed between Krishna and Draupadi,' he replied enigmatically.

I was silenced yet again. While I knew that Sharad fancied himself a modern-day Krishna, I wondered what uncanny resemblance had led to me being referred to as 'Draupadi' twice in the last few weeks.

Draupadi, apart from her instant and obvious reference as a woman with five husbands, was known for her tact and pragmatic approach. She was wilful and self assured and knew exactly what she wanted. Many would blame her for the Mahabharat. But then, if there was anyone who did exercise control over her it was Krishna. Had Krishna not hinted to her to stop Karna from participating in the Swayamvar, Draupadi would not have humiliated Karna the way she did. Had Draupadi been Karna's wife, there wouldn't have been a Mahabharat.

Did Krishna want the Mahabharat all along and did Draupadi tacitly agree to his plans?

I realized that, in much the same way that Draupadi must have been, I was turning into Sharad's protégé and puppet. My life, from the time that I met him, was moving precisely in the direction he wanted it to. And it left me wondering, yet again, if Sharad indeed had the powers to foresee the future the way Krishna did. Was he bracing, in some twisted manner, for another Mahabharat?

A Mahabharat with me at its centre, playing the role of Draupadi?

❖

As the Deputy Minister for Home, I got on with my responsibilities. One of the areas that I was to look into was Police Reform. Sharad had, understandably, kept the important responsibility of Internal Security, which included both external terrorist threats and the Naxal menace, with himself.

My efforts to drown myself in work could not erode the depression that had built around my personal life. It had been two weeks since I had taken my oath of office and last spoken to Rohit. He had left for Jehanabad that evening itself. After he left, I called him up at least half-a-dozen times, everyday but he'd disconnect the phone immediately on hearing my voice.

Sharad, whom I bumped into at least once during the day and had lengthy meetings with twice in the week, sensed my unhappiness. On one occasion, when he saw me pre-occupied during an important meeting, he looked at me with empathy before providing the solution to my problems: 'Karma, my dear, Karma... that's the biggest healer.'

With nobody else to look up to, I think I was beginning to lead my life by his principles.

9

Soon after I took over as Deputy Minister, a savage incident occurred at Alleppey in Kerala. A Syrian-Christian professor's limbs were chopped off for reportedly saying something that was construed as offensive to Islam. The brutality of the retribution shook the state as much as it did the rest of the country.

A one-off incident like this would ideally have best been dealt with by the state government itself. But a few days later, the Kerala CM made a rather uncharacteristic remark. He alleged that a fundamentalist organization, the Radical Front of India (RFI), had plans to completely alter Kerala's religious demography in twenty years. And it was using money and 'love' to achieve its aim. The very next morning, Sharad called me for an important meeting.

When I entered Sharad's chambers, he was already seated with Shabnam, the IB official whom he had so casually chatted up and asked to come home for dinner the other night. Shabnam looked every inch an assertive, informed professional. She was making an AV presentation to him, where one slide after another focused on the rather morbid situation in Kerala. It was clear from the way that Sharad was listening to her that he respected her opinion. When he saw me, Sharad quickly apprised me of the situation. 'The chopping-off of the hands of the professor in Kerala two weeks ago had led the state police to carry out raids. They've unearthed some very incriminating findings...'

Two days later, I was in Kerala, on my first official visit outside Delhi. I was accompanied by two officials from my ministry. My task was to get a first-hand account of the reported 'communalization' of the state that had been covertly going on for the last few years.

We had our first briefing from the DGP, U.K. Cherian.

'Ma'am, the situation is quite grim. Some of the documents that we seized in our follow-up raids after the professor's hands were chopped off, are unbeliev-ably shocking. We have found Lashkar-e-Hindustan training tapes, Taliban-style courts, literature on conversion, explosives and documents indicating an interest in Indian Navy installations. Based on our findings so far, we believe that the chopping off of the professor's arm was a pre-meditated act that was taken by the "top bosses" of the organization. It was aimed at sending a clear message, and creating a fear psychosis in the state.'

'What message?'

'That religious bigotry could be the future of Kerala.'

'*What?*' I blurted in anger. I mean, the senior-most police official of the state speaking in this manner was downright absurd. But the situation on the ground didn't give much room for optimism. On the same day that I was in Kerala, the local papers reported a case of 'Love War'.

It was only recently that I had heard the term 'Love War' but in Kerala it seemed like everyone knew about it. According to the newspaper report, there were unconfirmed reports that revealed the blessings of some outfits for a concerted effort at religious conversions, at least 3000 to 4000 incidences of which had taken place in a four-year period. The report found indications of 'forceful' religious conversions under the garb of 'love', suggesting that such 'deceptive acts' might require legislative intervention.

What the media was infamously calling 'Love War' was allegedly an underground movement through which young boys belonging to a certain community in Kerala and coastal Karnataka were reportedly targeting college girls belonging to other communities for conversion by feigning love. Even though investigations so far had been unable to establish 'organized activity' of the sort taking place, the sheer magnitude of the menace left me intrigued.

In the last few years, there had been hundreds of young girls from across the state who had gone missing. The consistent pattern across several districts over the years had led to investigations that exposed the state's religious underbelly. Apparently forced conversion had not only started becoming rampant but they seemed to be following a pattern. It also turned out that the hotbed of these activities were the campuses of educational institutes.

The act as it came to be understood involved boys belonging to a certain community feigning love for their female colleagues belonging to other communities. The 'obsessive' love the youth professed would have the youth crave for marriage at the earliest with the condition that the girl converted. Once married and impregnated, the girl would be abandoned while the boy supposedly moved on to his next 'prey'.

While this was just one news report, unconfirmed reports and estimates pointed to a far more alarmist situation. For instance, there had been unconfirmed stories of how many of these converted girls were later deported to the Gulf to be used for prostitution. And then there were stories of how some of them were being used for terror activities.

Just to be doubly sure, I decided to meet an 'affected' family firsthand. And so, the state government officials set up my meeting with a father and his 'rescued' daughter.

Nilleswari was a 22 year old girl who seemed to have experienced the worst of the menace. Three years ago while studying at a local college in Idukki, she was relentlessly wooed by her college mate, Aslam. Aslam told her he was crazily in love with her, twice piercing his skin to write her name in his blood. Once he almost bashed up an eve-teaser to death. (Nilleswari later realized that the eve-teaser was his friend and that the act was staged.) Within a month, he started putting pressure on her to marry him. When she objected, he threatened to commit suicide. Nilleswari's parents were dead against the match. But when Aslam one day did in fact try to kill himself, Nilleswari was left with no option but to relent. On his insistence, she eloped with him. For a while the two lived with one of Aslam's relatives on the outskirts of Mangalore. Aslam soon impregnated her, and then he just disappeared. Later, Nilleswari realized that the people she was staying with were not Aslam's relatives. They were a group of hardcore fundamentalists who were obsessed with ideas of religious bigotry. There were at least a dozen other girls who'd had similar fates in the vicinity.

Luckily, she suffered a miscarriage. A year later, she eventually managed to escape and after an arduous trial, was finally reunited with her family nearly a year and a half after she eloped. Nilleswari was lucky. Many other girls continued to be reported 'missing'. Nobody really knew their fate.

Significantly most of the major bomb blasts that have occurred in the country in recent years seemed to have a Kerala imprint. Equally significant was the fact that Kerala had been spared of these blasts, lest the security agencies' focus shift there.

An assessment on the ground this time though only corroborated some of our worst security fears.

❖

'The situation in Kerala can aptly be described as an obnoxious cocktail of religious extremism and hawala,' Sharad summed up the situation for me, sipping his white wine, even as a ghazal played on the music system.

'Your calm response suggests you've known about this for a while?'

'Come on, Shruti, who doesn't? Centuries ago, we were invaded and forced to convert. After Independence, it is this proxy war of conversion. But it's an extension of the same old battle – to convert this piece of land from the Himalayas in the north to the Indian Ocean in the south, into an Islamic state.'

I was shocked to hear him say this. Sharad was a man whose words and actions carried great conviction. Did he *really* mean what he had just said? I mean, to hear the country's Home Minister speak this way would shock anybody. But Sharad was a walking encyclopedia on Indian history and he went on to explain what he had said.

Just then, we were joined by Mohammed Salim, an MP from Kerala and someone Sharad held in high esteem. Salim was just as upset about the situation.

'In Kerala, there are two distinct reasons that have led to the situation being what it is today. And strangely both have had to do with the unabashed greed to win the minority votes.'

We heard him out as he spoke on.

'On one hand, you have the state's leading party wooing a gentleman who has spent several years in jail for his alleged involvement in a major bomb blast; on the other, Kerala's links with the Gulf countries have been strengthened by allowing fake passport agencies to flourish. Ill-equipped airports have been given the status of international airports to further boost this trend, even endangering passenger safety in the process. A lot of unaccounted for hawala money flows into Kerala from the Gulf. We can't rule out a portion of it being used for nefarious purposes.'

Kerala's links with the Gulf countries was indeed one aspect that truly fascinated me. It's strange, but almost every Malayali home there has at least one relative – close or distant – who has found employment in the Gulf. In fact, the 'Gulf man' is much sought after as a potential bridegroom.

Mohammed Salim enlightened us further: 'An interesting history precedes this Gulf boom. Huge oil reserves were discovered in the Arabian Peninsula and the Gulf in the 1930s, and commercial extraction began in the early 1950s. Soon, these countries became the major oil exporting countries of the world, and amassed huge riches within a short span of years, a feat that perhaps has no historical rival. However, these nations were handicapped by their small population and thin labour force with low level of skills. Thus, they had to procure manpower from abroad to meet the challenge. A newly independent India, grappling with its own unemployment woes grabbed the opportunity, with Kerala leading the trend.

'Today, the Gulf countries have a Keralite population of nearly 3 million, who annually send home a sum of $7 billion. That, of course, is the official, accounted figure. Kerala, we understand, is also the hotbed of unaccounted for hawala money flowing into the country. It is a scourge we have been able to do little about.

'So, yes, money from the Gulf countries does enjoy a free flow into the state. Whether this free connection has encouraged some anti-India forces sitting abroad to pump money into the country through the hawala route for ulterior motives is something that still requires intensive investigation. The little that the situation has already thrown up would make it fallacious for us to rule out the possibility.'

I reflected on what Mohammad Salim was saying. It was strange how religion often confused people instead of solving their confusion. The misplaced fervour only led to its abuse at the hands of its propagators. So while the pro-Muslim Commoners' Party had always been a force to reckon with in Kerala, the extremist groups were now accusing it of being 'ineffective' and 'weak'. They actually believed that chopping off people's hands would serve religion better.

What was worrisome was that the situation left the average peace-loving Malayali Muslim with a tough choice. It was a difficult situation really – the RFI would not be growing if newer chunks of people were not buying into its indoctrination, or perhaps, being forced to do so. I felt many of the supporters of the RFI were probably drawn from those who had supported the Commoner's Party previously. If the Commoner's Party, which had over the years diligently worked on getting a moderate image, now suddenly decided to up its ante to thwart the designs of the RFI, the situation would only grow worse. What added to the problem was that a key party of Kerala did not have any reservations about tying up with the RFI for electoral gains. It goes without saying that the politics of Kerala had heaped this fate upon its people.

Mohammed Salim left soon after, but not before sounding a caveat. 'What these extremists don't realize is that the Hindu extremists can't be lying idle for long. They've been restrained so far, but God forbid if they decide to give it back, it might just lead to one of the worst communal riots.'

After he had gone, Sharad grew ruminative. 'Shruti, you know, I have the highest regard for Bhim Rao Ambedkar,' he said.

I looked at him in surprise, wondering where the reference came from.

'Throughout his life, Ambedkar fought to get the Dalits an equal status in Hindu society, before he finally converted to Buddhism just months before his death in 1956.'

I still didn't get the connection; Sharad explained further, 'Ambedkar resisted the option of converting to Islam. Had he converted to Islam and done so twenty years before he finally did, India would have been a different story.'

The smile on Sharad's countenance, even as he took another sip, said a lot.

'It's a sad commentary on Hinduism that many sections of Dalits somehow have come closer to Islam and Christianity. They've always been soft targets. Even today, it's the Dalits who are the prime targets for conversion.'

'Can't we bridge this gap?'

'Well, that's what our reservation policy was meant for, except that it has resulted in subsequent generations being more and more conscious of caste distinctions than they used to. I would say the divide hasn't been reduced.'

It is indeed interesting that 'Dalit–Muslim' invariably becomes a hyphenated term at the time of elections. A strong Dalit leader is expected to draw Muslim support as well and vice versa.

'History repeats itself and those who do not learn from their mistakes are only condemned to repeat them,' said Sharad before ceding a piece of information that stunned me: 'Today we have several popular Dalit leaders. And some of the intelligence reports that we have suggest that at least one of them is being wooed to convert.'

'Oh God! And what implications would that have?'

'Well, many of them may follow suit,' Sharad said, adding another piece of vital information: 'It's an international conspiracy.' He took a sip of wine before adding, 'We have to defeat it. Tampering with the country's demography will ruin it.'

Sharad was mildly inebriated. But knowing him, nothing could blunt the sharpness of his thoughts.

❖

The thing about a mentor–protégé relationship is that the quest for knowledge often leads to a sense of ingratiation towards the mentor. The journey towards enlightenment is a truly enchanting one.

I would wonder how the focus of my interest had changed completely in a little over a year. From solely fighting for personal justice for my rape, to championing feminist causes to now taking care of the country's security – life had indeed come more than a full circle. And yet, I'd always have to buffet doubts – was all this for real?

I would be lying if I said I was comfortable with my new-found status. Thing is, when you get too much too early it makes you insecure. Unless you have earned them the hard way you are insecure of your attainments. And to be honest, I was very unsure of myself. Every night, when I went to sleep, I'd mull over the situation. I shuddered to think of a life of drudgery in some semi-urban, mofussil town – be it Jehanabad or Kishanganj.

Hence, quite naturally, I wasn't too inclined now to make the extra effort to reach out to and cajole Rohit. My folks were anxious to know where things stood between Rohit and me and kept bombarding me with questions. I kept avoiding them because I too had little clarity on the matter. Then one night my father asked me pointedly over the phone, 'Is it over between Rohit and you?'

After a pause, I said, 'Maybe. Maybe not.'

❖

After months of empty evenings spent alone and eating whatever was served, I decided to cook. I made some parathas and baingan ka bharta. As my loneliness refused to go away, I called up Sharad and asked if I could drop in and share my meal with him.

Sharad sounded a little mellow and lost in thought but asked me to come over, nevertheless.

When I reached Sharad's house, he was talking on the phone. I was about to retreat when he gestured that I should stay in the room. I'm not sure if I wanted to overhear his conversation.

'It's been eighteen years, Rhea, but it seems like yesterday... time just flies. Or shall I say, I'm selfish to not think about it.'

There was a long silence as he listened to the voice on the other side.

'To be honest, I'm not as strong as the world might think me to be. Had it not been for my obsession with work, I'd have collapsed long ago.'

Another long pause ensued as he listened into the line. As I watched I saw his eyes moisten, and I couldn't believe it. 'I'd like you to come back, Rhea, and help me out with my work. Sooner than later, unless something unforeseen happens, I should be the PM. There's so much to do for the country. Your presence here will make me stronger.'

The conversation ended on what seemed like a note of disagreement. Sharad put down the receiver and turned sadly to me. 'Rhea is my daughter. In fact today happens to be the birthday of my deceased wife, Mala.'

Sharad was clearly emotional; I had never known him to be this way. He opened his desk drawer and looked nostalgically at a picture of his dead wife that he had kept between the pages of a diary.

'She passed away eighteen years ago, when Rhea was just five – neither too small to forget nor big enough to get over the death. I still vividly remember Mala pleading with me on her death bed to re-marry soon, for Rhea's sake.'

A deep silence descended on the room.

I cleared my throat, 'I guess you loved your wife too much to think of marrying again.'

Sharad took his time to reply, 'I too thought so for many years,' he said looking at me, then looking away.

His words once again left me confused, my mind brimming with more questions. Yet I knew it would be premature to query him on stuff that I would have considered deeply personal. I'm not sure whether he would have volunteered to share his feelings. Somehow a part of me was scared to discuss his personal life with him. I don't think I was ready to venture there.

We had a quiet dinner together. He loved the baingan ka bharta and even promised to cook khichdi one day, with which, he said, the baingan ka bharta would go even better. He knew that I was feeling lonely and asked me about the latest between Rohit and me. Once again, I did not have an answer.

I realized I had begun to develop a comfort zone with Sharad. I mean, I felt so protected with him around. Be it about the ministry or about life, his insights opened up a new worldview for me. Yes, he was enigmatic in many ways – especially when it came to his personal life. But then I was not sure that I wanted to delve into his private affairs either. With him as Krishna, I realized that I for once didn't mind being Draupadi. I could sense a positive energy and optimism in me that I hadn't known before. There was only Sharad to whom I could attribute this change in my outlook to. Life seemed okay. Things were just fine.

It wouldn't be okay for long, though.

❖

One morning, when I entered office, I was greeted by the news of the arrest of a man called Ajmal Pathan. Ajmal was said to have been involved in at least three bomb blasts in the last two years, including one in an election rally the previous year that had killed more than fifty people. Ajmal had been nabbed when he was crossing over to Nepal from a district called Bettiah in north Bihar. The mood in the ministry was naturally upbeat as he was expected to spill the beans on local terror modules.

Sharad was locked in meetings throughout the day with the Minister of State for Home Shashi Deshmukh and other important officials of the Ministry. I was not a part of these meetings. Not that I expected to be; after all I was privy to only a tiny fraction of all the information that the Home Ministry sat on.

What threw me was a piece of news that came in late at night – news of the arrest of Maulana Ashar from Kishanganj. I learnt of this on the late night news. I was completely stunned. The news anchor claimed that the Maulana was associated with Ajmal. I knew that this was impossible. From the little that I knew of the Maulana, I knew he could never be involved with anything unethical.

I tried calling Sharad. I was told that he was still in a meeting and had asked not to be disturbed. I called back twice again in the next half an hour, still failing to get through. I found it strange; I mean I was now a Deputy Minister under Sharad. How come he had thought it prudent to keep me in the dark about this? My frustration reiterated my basic query – was I *really* here on merit? For the first time, I was angry at Sharad; something I had thought myself incapable of being till just a few hours back. I kept wondering if he had avoided me all day on purpose.

There was little that I could do at night except wait for morning. I arrived early at my office and was told that the policeman in charge of the jail in Kishanganj where the Maulana had been imprisoned had called my office twice. The Maulana he said had pleaded to speak to me. I felt extremely guilty. I knew I would call up and speak to the Maulana, irrespective of my being advised by my ministry officials against doing so. After all, I wasn't yet selfish enough to forget that the Maulana had played a pivotal role in getting me into Parliament.

But before I had a word with Maulana, I needed to know precisely what the case against him was. From the information that the officials gave me, I was even more convinced that the Maulana had been framed. Apparently it had been alleged that Ajmal had stayed in the mosque for two weeks, some two years ago and that he called up the Maulana pretty frequently — almost twice every week. Did that constitute a case of complicity against the Maulana?

I finally managed to speak with the Maulana, who gave me a completely different picture.

'Two years ago, this person whom the media calls Ajmal had indeed come to my mosque. But then I knew him by the name of Taufiq — at least that was the name he told me. He was extremely sick and needed help. Where does the Koran tell me to abandon the sick and needy? I allowed him to stay in the mosque, arranged for a doctor and took care of his treatment. He stayed here for almost three weeks, till he had recovered fully. And then he went off. He told me he was a small-time trader from Asansol and was travelling around in Bihar to explore new business opportunities. I trusted him and did not ask him anything further. While leaving, he told me he would remain indebted to me for giving him a new life. In fact, he'd call me frequently and consult me on any problem. He told me I was an angel sent by Allah. Now you tell me, does that qualify me as an "accomplice"? Next time around I will have to think a million times before being good to someone.'

I heard out the Maulana and promised to bail him out at the earliest. I apologized to him for what he was going through. He was gracious enough to say, 'It's okay. Terrorism is a curse. I know I am innocent and it will be proved so. But make sure that people like Taufiq get the severest punishment.'

By the time I finished my conversation with the Maulana, I was livid at Sharad.

For the first time since I knew him, I was prepared to confront Sharad. I stormed into his office. Seeing the anger on my face, he asked his secretary to leave the room.

'Sharadji, *you* know the Maulana is innocent...'

'My knowing doesn't make a difference. There are certain leads that point towards his involvement. He has merely been taken into custody for questioning.'

'But, Sharadji, you've seen how he had helped us.'

'The law does not operate on emotions.'

I felt helpless at his obstinacy, which for once, I thought was not backed by reason. 'Sharadji, why are you doing this? You are putting me in a very awkward situation. The Maulana just spoke to me –'

He cut me short. 'You should be responsible enough to know that as a minister, you shouldn't be speaking to people in custody.'

At this I lost my cool. 'Sharadji, you know as well as I that the Maulana is innocent. God, to make up for his absence, sometimes sends us angels. He is one such farishta. He's told me everything about his association with Ajmal. The Maulana had basically nursed him back to health when Ajmal was sick. If he hadn't, Ajmal would have been dead.'

I could see a look of determination descend on Sharad's countenance as he said: 'The Maulana will have to prove that he did not know Ajmal was a terrorist when he provided Ajmal shelter. If he can prove that, then of course, he is innocent.'

What Sharad said beyond this made me lose all patience.

'We have to send a message to some of the other madrasas that are sheltering wrongdoers. Maulana's arrest will send that message. It will act as a deterrent to others.'

I was shocked to hear this. I wondered how this Krishna could suddenly become a Chanakya as well. I hated him for what he had just said.

On his part Sharad looked a bit abashed about voicing what was on his mind. 'Don't worry. I'll see to it that the Maulana is not harmed. Everybody knows that the Maulana campaigned for us during the elections. If he had not been arrested now, the Opposition would have ripped us apart. I'll take care of the situation and perhaps bail him out after we've arrested some real culprits.'

My shock at seeing this shrewd, politically con-niving avatar of Sharad left me flustered. 'Sharadji, I'm not with you on this,' I said exasperatedly.

There was little that I could say beyond this. For his part, Sharad's countenance showed the same cocksure conviction that it always did – as if he knew exactly what he was doing and that my reaction was immaterial to him.

❖

I felt quite terrible that night. My differences with Sharad had been an eye-opener of sorts – everything was not hunky dory in my new office; there was a lot of ambiguity beneath the noble intentions that were constantly being professed. I was fine with nobility; but would I be fine with the accompanying manipulations and deceit?

It was, after all, part of Krishna's philosophy to employ incorrect means if that helped the larger cause of a noble objective. I understood that by going ahead with the Maulana's arrest Sharad had tried to kill two birds with one stone. One, he'd sent a clear and stern warning to all those madrasas that were suspected to be sheltering anti-social elements, and two, he had attained a moral high ground vis-a-vis the Opposition parties who would have accused him of inaction after taking the help of the Maulana in the elections.

I wasn't sure if I was game to this kind of manoeuvring even if it helped in attaining the desired 'larger objectives'.

My meeting with Sharad had ended on a note of confrontation. I somehow expected him to call me and reason things out with the indulgent kindness that I had got used to from him. I don't know what gave rise to this expectation. Perhaps it was my dependence upon him, which for some strange reason had me hoping to see a reciprocal dependence in him for me.

❖

As a result of the stand-off between us I did not show up in office for the next three days. Every day, I sat waiting, hoping that he'd call me. But he didn't. To give him the benefit of doubt, Parliament was in session, and perhaps he thought it more important to discharge his 'karma' rather than bother to nurse the grouse of a lesser mortal.

The reason I stuck my ground and did not apologize to him was because I believed just as much in the stand I had taken. If Sharad had been a godsend for me, so had the Maulana. Politics was only temporary in my scheme of things; but humanity was permanent.

On the fourth day I switched on the TV to watch a debate in Parliament on the issue of the recent terror arrests. One slimy member from the Opposition benches sarcastically asked where I had disappeared and if by any chance, I too was involved in the terror nexus.

Sharad got up and said that I was unwell, but I could see that his face was grim. Perhaps the tension was due to the stand-off between us and not the terror trail, which he was pretty seasoned at handling.

With every passing moment, I felt the situation become more and more absurd. I wanted to break down and cry like a child. More than ever I wanted to abandon everything and go back to Jehanabad. Then I wondered if that option was still open to me.

But that evening, an unlikely visitor bailed me out of the situation.

❖

My brother-in-law, looking tense and distraught, showed up at my doorstep. 'Bhabhi, Bhaiya is unwell. He has been suffering from jaundice for the last two weeks. Yet he refuses to rest and goes to work every day. He says being at home alone in this condition is far more hard to take.'

I couldn't believe what I heard. Ajit told me that Rohit's parents were in Florida to be with his sister and his newly born niece. On Rohit's insistence they had not been informed of his illness.

'Bhaiya's obstinacy is further destroying his health. He has become very pale and doesn't listen to anybody.'

For a change I took the news in my stride. After all, this new development was a minor twist in the many convolutions that my life had become habituated to.

10

I wiped Rohit's bare back with a wet towel. It had been raining incessantly for the last two days. Although Rohit was running a mild fever and was weak, bathing him wasn't a good idea.

It was a strange situation, really. I mean, after all the animosity that our relationship had been through, even with communications between us having completely broken down, here I was nursing him and trying to bring him relief. I'm not sure whether the physical contact in this case could be considered sensuous, but yes, it definitely felt unnatural. In the sense that while it was an intimate gesture, the intimacy was inhibited by all the baggage our relationship had accumulated in the last few weeks.

Being the Doubting Thomas that Rohit was, it seemed he wasn't entirely convinced that I had come back for him. Speculations about my fall-out with Sharad had been reported in the media. And Rohit was well aware of these reports. The interesting thing was that, this time I too wasn't entirely sure about my unselfishness towards my husband.

'So, how has your experience in the ministry been so far?' he asked me blandly.

'So far so good,' was my laconic response. In the changed equation between us, I was stingy with my words.

'It seems you've started guarding your words like politicians do.'

I did not react.

'So is it all over? Or you intend to go back?'

He was deliberately provoking me. I decided to give back as good as I got: 'Are you trying to suggest that I'm here because I had no option?'

'Well, you were never short of options,' he smiled wryly.

At this, I lost my cool. 'For God's sake, Rohit, will you shut up? I mean, I didn't come back to hear this. When your brother told me about your condition I felt so helpless…'

'You're not responsible for my condition. If guilt is what has brought you here, please return.'

I said, 'It's neither my guilt, nor my helplessness that has brought me here. It's that thing called home and that thing called marriage which brings me back.'

'Didn't you remember about your home and marriage when you took oath as minister?'

'Is my being a minister what bothers you?'

'*You* bother me… your *attitude* bothers me.'

'Fine then… I'm leaving.'

Our confrontation was acrimonious, but this was not my doing. I wasn't the one who had brought it about. That night I felt completely orphaned and lonely. I realized that I had no dwelling to call my home; nobody to consider my own.

My conversation with Rohit left me with no option but to leave him. However, as I sat by the window and looked out, I thought I heard the sound of someone crying. I turned around in shock to see Rohit weeping profusely and apologizing for his intemperance. 'Shruti, I'm really sorry, I think I am speaking to someone other than my office peons and servant after almost two weeks. And I just messed it up.' Saying this, he put his head in my lap and broke down completely. On seeing him in this state, I had to abandon my thoughts of fleeing for the moment.

So there we were, locked again, by the course of destiny, under the same roof, doing neither knew what.

Three days went by. Rohit's condition improved marginally. We sat in front of the TV set watching a debate that was live, from the Lok Sabha. News had just come in that the government had released Maulana Ashar as it could not find any evidence that to establish his involvement with Ajmal's activities.

I knew it was a tough time for Sharad. But the way he was mauled in Parliament only reiterated the ruthlessness of parliamentary democracy.

Initiating the debate, the leader of the Opposition, Harish Chandra Solanki, called him a 'whimsical' and 'vindictive' Home Minister. A lesser-evolved MP from a regional party went a step further. He wondered if the release of the Maulana was due to 'pressure from Sharad's absentee junior minister'.

Sharad for his part was as dignified as a strong and principled man can be. 'Honourable sir, I wish to inform you that at no point has my ministry acted in contravention of norms or established procedure. Given the vast number of calls that were exchanged between the Maulana and Ajmal, we felt it in the national interest to interrogate the Maulana. Since after questioning him, our doubts were allayed, we found no reason to hold him back. I assure you that the government has shown no prejudice whatsoever in dealing with the case.'

Sharad's explanation made logical sense. He displayed the sense of fairness that I expected from him. In his position, it wouldn't have been difficult for him to have the Maulana's detention extended. But he chose to let truth prevail.

The Opposition, though, was not one to buy his reasoning. One member of the Opposition asked him to clarify if the Maulana's arrest was indeed a result of the fall-out between Sharad and me, to which Sharad replied, 'Shruti is not well.'

The Opposition flared up at this and accused Sharad of hiding the real facts behind the arrest and release of the Maulana. They staged a boycott and walked out of the House. While talking to the media later, Ratna Pandey, a senior leader of my party, made a rather tongue-in-cheek remark: 'Politics and personal life should be kept away from each other. It is my firm belief that those holding responsible posts should take care not to allow themselves to be influenced by personal factors.'

The remark was so slimy that it didn't require anybody to guess whom it was aimed at. However, given that freedom of speech is an integral constituent of democracy, Sharad had no option but to take it in his stride. About the only consolation for him was that the PM, Yashwant Modi, showed faith in him.

That evening I felt guilty about Sharad's plight. He had been a man of honour in letting Maulana go. But my continued absence had become the bane of his existence. Feeling contrite, I called him that evening. 'Sharadji, I'm really sorry for what happened today…'

'When are you joining back?' he asked non-chalantly, as if he knew my mind better than I did.

I mumbled, 'Soon'.

'Come back and we'll talk,' he said and hung up.

Sharad's behaviour would often leave me wondering how a man like him could carefully contain feelings of anger, hurt and betrayal to live up to his dignified persona. I wanted my man to be like him. But then in the past, I'd wanted him to be like Abhay.

That night, Rohit attempted physical proximity but I was too weary to renew my relationship. Sensing my disinterest, Rohit let it go. The next morning, he made an extra effort to initiate conversation. 'What have you planned, Shruti?' I looked at him askance, expecting him to be more specific. So he asked, 'Are you going back to Delhi?'

I hesitated before my ambivalence gave way to a concrete nod.

Rohit's face darkened. 'Why?' he demanded.

'To compensate for my failings and to live up to the job I've been entrusted.'

'Why did you come here then?'

'To take care of you.'

'No. You wanted to run away from the mess that you found yourself in after the Maulana's arrest. And now since the matter has been resolved you want to go back; you needed refuge.'

Rohit's words hurt me. I had expected a little empathy, if not gratitude. Here, there was neither. We spent the day avoiding conversation. While I was devastated by what Rohit had said, what made my woes worse was that I knew he wasn't entirely incorrect. An emotional refugee is what I had become from the time that I was raped. I had relinquished control over my life – handing it first to my husband and, now, more prominently, to Sharad. Of late, I was experiencing something unusual; I felt caught between two men. I'd feel a more profound sense of responsibility towards one and then the same for the other.

In the same way that problems create themselves, there are times when solutions are handed out to you. My solution came via an unsavoury incident that took place in a village in Mahasamund in Chhattisgarh during the course of the night. Next morning, I learnt that in an unprecedented Naxal strike, more than 125 CRPF jawans had been killed.

I was left to choose between being an absentee minister and an absentee wife.

I instantly chose the latter.

❖

The next morning I was waiting at Raipur Airport for Sharad to arrive from Delhi. That my dependence on him was complete was a truth that had gradually begun to dawn upon me.

Sharad was clearly surprised to see me. I could see a combination of anger, surprise and relief on his face. For the first time I saw him looking perturbed – sleep-deprived and terribly exhausted. It made me wonder for a moment if he too had begun to depend on me. Not one to betray his emotions, all that Sharad told me was, 'Good to see you back....' And I nodded like an obedient muse.

Sharad, the Chhattisgarh CM Prashant Singh, and I paid our respects to the bodies of the CRPF jawans. It was the most numbing experience I've ever had. Each one of the 125 dead soldier's faces seemed to chide us for our inability to protect them. It made me wonder once again if it was we who'd made our country a 'soft state'.

Sharad was understandably furious. In a press conference convened soon after, he advocated air strikes against the Naxals. Then we flew in a helicopter to the village where the incident had taken place. The idea was to get a first-hand account of why things had gone so irrevocably wrong.

The strange thing is, when talking to a villager in these parts, you don't know whether you're actually talking to a Naxal, which in turn makes the whole debate over who Naxalites really are all the more contentious. Sharad, for one, was convinced that they were all 'terrorists', funded in some parts of the country by the Chinese and in other parts by Pakistani war groups. Sharad's claim was substantiated by the weapons that the Naxals had used to kill the CRPF jawans. In all likelihood, a high-intensity, remote-controlled detonator had been used. And those CRPF jawans who hadn't died instantly had been taken down with machine-guns. Sharad made a valid point in questioning how illiterate tribals who weren't even aware of modern techniques of agriculture, were equipped to handle modern ammunition that couldn't be used without effective training.

However, our interaction with a respected social worker, Shivcharan Sahu, provided us a different picture. 'The Naxal movement is a myth. It has no ideology, nor is it an organized revolution,' he said.

'Then what is it?'

'It's a reaction. When you suppress, or abuse someone for decades, there comes a time when the sufferers join hands and start reacting. That's all that this tribal uprising is about.'

Sahu elaborated by giving an example. He said that many tribal men went to the cities in search of a livelihood. In their absence, the security forces patrolling the areas preyed on their women. In many cases, even the women would give in readily, in exchange for money or because of their bodily needs. This illicit sexual activity would anger the men and make them want to take down the armed forces. So what was termed a 'Naxal strike' was really an act of revenge. 'These tribals are simpletons, now when they see a man in uniform they see a rapist.'

I doubted if the matter could be reasoned out so simplistically. Was Sahu a Naxal in disguise? Even a fool would not be so naive as to believe that these so-called Naxals did not have educated and well-equipped sympathizers backing them. The matter was definitely far more complex than either of the extremes that Sharad or Sahu spoke about.

After a gruelling day, we finally boarded the copter back to Delhi. Sitting next to him, I finally had the opportunity to offer my apologies. 'Sharadji, I'm sorry. These are tough times for the country. I don't think I should have gone away like that,' I said, attempting to restore normal conversation.

Sharad was visibly weary and sighed deeply in response. 'Is everything okay back home?' is all he asked.

I tried to nod, but couldn't. I ended up looking out of the window of the ascending aircraft as the settlements below grew increasingly smaller, till a patch of cloud obscured them altogether. I could see this as symbolic. My political ascent implied that my personal issues would need to become invisible, just like the settlements below. They were too small to impede me in the tasks that were assigned to me. I had to choose between two disparate worlds.

Accommodating both didn't seem possible.

❖

Back in Delhi, it did not take much time before political mud-slinging on the massacre began.

Ratna Pandey, who for some strange reason, had perfected the habit of rubbing Sharad the wrong way, was at it again. In an article in a leading daily, she wrote:

'The Home Minister is hopelessly out of sync with the government position on the Naxal problem. It is purely a political problem that demands a political solution. The least that is expected of the Minister is to stop making absurd and irresponsible statements like wanting to carry out air strikes on the Naxals. One wonders if such statements are influenced by the minister's inexperienced deputy.'

Sharad was understandably livid at these remarks. Now politics is such a strange game that it's not just inter-party; most of it is intra-party. He knew that Ratna would not have made such remarks and got away with them had it not been for support from the biggest name in the party. Had the PM actually lost faith in him, first due to the Maulana fiasco and now this unprecedented Naxal strike?

What made my position equally miserable was my guilt at the thought that Sharad was paying the price for backing me over some party seniors. But why did he need to do that?

The PM had called a meeting of the Cabinet in the afternoon. A couple of hours before, Sharad and I met at his office. He looked betrayed and hurt. 'Shruti, I'm planning to offer my resignation at the Cabinet meeting today,' Sharad told me in strict confidence.

'But why? It's not your doing...'

'I know. Leaders and champions have an image to live up to and when that gets sullied you lose your charisma. The last two weeks have been tough. Nothing has gone in my favour. People now talk of me like I can't do anything right. The resignation will help me keep my image intact.'

I tried to persuade him to hold back his resignation as that wouldn't serve any purpose. I'm not sure whether my reasoning made any sense; I doubted it did because Sharad was his own man. But an hour later at the Cabinet meeting, thankfully no offer of resignation was put forth by Sharad. Instead he was at his vehement best, ripping apart critics with authenticated fact files. 'Here, this file contains a whole list of cases of women who have been sexually abused and forced by Naxals to operate for them. It also lists the brutality that has been carried out on men to support them.'

Sharad furiously pulled out another file: 'This file carries a report of how some Naxals went to Dubai to meet the absconding gangster Ali Aslam, who reportedly offered them Rs 100 crore that would be routed through hawala. Also present at the meeting was a senior Pakistani official. The money reportedly belongs to the Pakistan government.'

The entire Cabinet heard out Sharad in silence. He wasn't done yet. 'And this file carries details of a few of our ex-armymen who went for an advanced level training to China. According to intelligence reports, three of them have been training Naxals in three different parts of the country and preparing them for bigger strikes.'

Sharad's offensive had put his opponents on the defensive. Even as the PM flipped through one of the files, Sharad took his fight straight to the enemy camp. 'Now will Mrs. Ratna Pandey explain her fondness for the Naxals? Will she explain how the menace is a political problem and not a law and order one?'

Ratna was taken off-guard. Fumbling for words, she retorted, 'I was only miffed about your comment on carrying out air-strikes on the Naxals. That is not a practical solution.'

'Have you ever seen 125 young soldiers lying dead in front of you? If you did, you'd not bother about sounding practical! Prime Minister, sir, I stand by my views on Naxals. They are pests and rodents and the worst form of terrorists and should be eliminated from any civil society.'

Having made his stand clear, Sharad walked out of the Cabinet meeting, With his uncompromising and no-holds-barred attack he had clearly set the agenda. In the twenty minutes or so that the Cabinet meeting lasted after his exit, the PM merely asserted that the Naxal problem was a 'serious' problem and that it demanded stern measures. In other words, the PM reposed faith in Sharad and allowed him to deal with the situation in the way he deemed right.

❖

Sharad and I had dinner together that night.

'I must say you know how to get your way all the time,' I said, in admiration.

He smiled nostalgically. 'I think the last person to have said that was my wife. There's something similar between you and her.'

I found it strange that an innocent remark of mine had me sound similar to his deceased wife. I found it much more comfortable to veer the conversation away from the personal. 'So now that you have got your way, are we going all out in our crusade against the Naxals?' I queried.

He smiled and then his smile grew wider. 'Politics is a game of glorious uncertainties. Wait and see what happens.'

A month later, much to everybody's surprise, Sharad was at a tribal village in Orissa's Keonjhar district, barely a few hundred kilometres away from where the massacre had taken place. He was there to address a massive tribal rally. Sharing the dais with him was a gentleman called Bulbul Mahato, who had spent a good number of years in jail for being a 'Naxal'. The purpose of the rally was to protest the government's sanction for setting up a chemical plant that would result in the taking over and subsequent erosion of 500 square kilometres of forest land. The tribals were naturally furious at the government's decision. What made Sharad's presence all the more significant was that the final nod for the project had come from his bête noire, Ratna Pandey, in her capacity as the Minister for Industry.

'Not an iota of injustice will be allowed. Anybody who dares take away your rights and your belongings will be cut to size. I am your warrior in Delhi and will ensure that your voice is heard by the PM!' Sharad roared at the rally, winning him an incredible show of support. The tribals cheered for him as though he were their new messiah.

When I saw the footage of Sharad's address to that rally I was mesmerized. His dexterity in transforming from a die-hard crusader against the Naxals to a pro-tribal leader made it all seem so effortless.

❖

That night, the PM and Sharad met over dinner and drinks. 'Great job, Sharad,' the grand old man conceded. 'The biggest challenge for a political party in India is to be a party of the poor by day and one of the rich by night. With your move, we're definitely going to be there soon.'

'Yes, that's the key to be in power forever,' said Sharad holding up his glass.

The next morning, when Sharad told me about his meeting with the PM, I thought their celebration was premature, until news came in that in an unprecedented strike carried out by our security forces in the jungles of Mahamasund in the wee hours of the morning, a record 37 Naxals had been killed and another 50 had been captured.

Sharad's smile was as wide as on the night when I'd failed to crack its enigma. Now his genius lay unveiled in front of me.

Yes, he'd truly become the leader of the poor by day and of the rich by the night – the perfect combination to rule in a democracy like ours!

My awe of him grew deeper and deeper.

11

Gandhi and Nehru: two of the most influential men in the history of Indian subcontinent. Yet it is difficult to ignore their differences not just on political matters, but even their personal outlook, especially when it came to women.

Gandhi, with a view to re-integrate our virtuous past into the present and future used the symbol of Sita to motivate Indian women during our freedom struggle. Sita stood for chastity, sacrifice and her selflessness towards her husband Rama. As a firm believer in a woman's homemaking abilities, Gandhi encouraged their participation in politics within certain parameters. By inference, thus, Gandhi expected a strong woman to support her husband and provide him the strength to rise up and perform greater deeds for the country.

By contrast, Nehru's idea of a woman was inspired by Tagore's Chitrangada, the intrepid Manipuri princess who fought convention and epitomized equality. Talking about his deceased wife Kamala, Nehru wrote in his book, *Discovery of*

India, 'Like Chitra in Tagore's plays, she (Kamala) seemed to say to me: I am Chitra. No goddess to be worshipped, nor yet the object of common pity to be brushed aside. If you design to keep me by your side in the path of danger and daring, if you allow me to share the great duties of your life, then you will know my self…'

It can be thus inferred that while Gandhi was still largely conservative in the role he envisaged for Indian women, Nehru, in a truer sense, saw them as equal companions.

This fundamental difference in outlook between Gandhi and Nehru extended to the way each carried out their lives. While Gandhi preached 'abstinence' and control over one's sexual desires, Nehru was liberal. While the way Gandhi conducted his life bordered on the ascetic, Nehru was a romantic at heart. While Gandhi advocated some unnatural experiments in his ashram which even his staunch supporters found unacceptable, Nehru pursued some interesting relationships, which many believe provided the right intellectual stimulation to the genius that he was.

❖

Sharad and I lay on our backs with the upper half of our bodies arched upward and our faces turned to the sky. It was a yogic posture that I'd somehow found very sensuous every time I had seen it being performed on TV. And here we were, Sharad and I, doing it together.

I had been having a mild backache the whole of last week and Sharad had attributed it to my long hours of sitting in the office. Sharad himself was quite a fitness freak – performing anywhere between 50 to 75 surya namaskars a day. This time round, he wanted me to try the namaskars to keep fit.

I had had some amount of hesitation in accepting his offer to join him for yoga, but realizing that there wasn't much logic for me *not* taking it up, I chose to join him. It is strange but most of our lives, we do things that are expected of us rather than doing what we want to. A few weeks ago, given the fact that the media and general public hadn't been too kind about our 'association', I think I'd have refrained from giving an impression of such 'proximity' between us. Not anymore. And some of the reason was that I felt terribly let down by my husband. Who knows, perhaps he felt the same way about me.

I managed about 15 surya namaskars before I bowed out. Sharad performed more than thrice that number. 'This is what gives me the energy to slog for 16 hours a day,' he beamed.

I felt in awe of him again. This time my admiration was fuelled by his superior physical prowess. I could sense a change in the way I was responding to the situation, and to him.

❖

The situation in Kashmir suddenly worsened with mobs in different places starting to throw stones at the police and armed forces right in the heart of Srinagar. What triggered this was the 'killing' of a youth by an army-man a week back, whom the locals claimed was 'innocent'.

In any another place in India, it would have been easy to combat these motley groups of stone-throwers; not so in Kashmir. For the death of any of these protestors in police firing would provide adequate reason for the entire valley to go up in flames. That it happened to be the holy month of Ramzan did not make things simpler.

In the week since the stone pelting menace started, some 20 people had been killed. What was particularly painful was the Jammu and Kashmir CM's cavalier approach in dealing with the problem. Instead of coming down hard on the protestors, he seemed to relish the opportunity of reiterating the state's eternal demand for autonomy.

The situation troubled me. The fact that the problem came under the jurisdiction of the Home Ministry and yet the ministry could do little about it, made the situation harder to handle. I have to confess that at that point I was pretty ignorant of the history of the Kashmir problem so I read up extensively on the facts.

The Kashmir problem I learnt was exactly the same age as our nation – it was born with the

Partition. Several characters had a bearing on the situation back then, prominent among whom were Maharaja Hari Singh, then the king of Kashmir; Sheikh Abdullah, the most popular leader in Kashmir at that time; Jawaharlal Nehru; Sardar Patel and Lord Mountbatten.

Maharaja Hari Singh, who refused to throw in his lot with India at the time of Independence, did so just months after that when an intrusion from Pakistani tribals left him with no option. Thus Kashmir's accession to India was effected in rather unnatural circumstances. Nehru's then friend, Sheikh Abdullah, who was at the forefront of Kashmir politics, took centrestage by raising his own army of young men who patrolled the streets of Kashmir before the Indian forces could arrive. The critical role that Sheikh played in the situation increased his stakes.

Even though Sheikh Abdullah was subsequently made the PM of Kashmir, as time went by he was never content with Kashmir being a part of India.

Now, in hindsight, several actions of the time are questionable – the most notable among them being Nehru's decision to refer Kashmir to the UN Security Council in late 1948 when Indian troops were perfectly capable of flushing out the intruders from the region of Kashmir. Nehru, the genius, came with his share of problems – the most detrimental of which was his obduracy and his distrust of sage counsel. So, in handling Kashmir, he seemed to have toed Mountbatten's line more than Patel's.

Yes, Nehru did play a pivotal part in Kashmir becoming a part of India. And yes, Nehru in many ways can't escape censure for the problem that Kashmir is today.

By 1953, Sheikh Abdullah had had a falling-out with Nehru and was incarcerated for several years on charges of 'anti-national' activities. Much later, just before Nehru's sudden death, Sheikh and Nehru did become friends again. But it would be foolish to expect anyone in the Sheikh's position to remain unprejudiced towards India. To the credit of the Abdullahs, they never once advocated joining Pakistan. Yes, they were unhappy with India and autonomy had been their perpetual demand.

Nowadays it is ironical that some of the most extremist reactionary groups are offshoots of more moderate movements. So while Kashmiri leadership has stuck to its demand for autonomy or self rule, several sections of people in the Valley had gone far beyond that. And it was the elements of a dual trust deficit – one between New Delhi and Srinagar and other between the people of Kashmir and Kashmir's leadership – that had made the situation intractable.

❖

Sharad and I visited the streets of Kashmir on the day before Eid. The very streets that ought to have worn a festive look for the Valley's biggest festival, were largely deserted. As all separatist groups had anyway decided to boycott Sharad's visit to the city, black flags could be seen by the dozen. In the sparse movement of people on the streets, the tension was palpable.

On arrival at the Srinagar airport, we had a brief meeting with the CM, Anees Baig and the state finance minister, Haroon Rashid who, of late, had not been getting along with the CM. But given that at 35, he exercised a considerable influence on the youth of Kashmir, the CM did not want to risk his alienation. Interestingly, Rashid belonged to the Jammu region and much to the surprise of the Kashmir leadership, enjoyed Hindu support as well. Rashid had alleged sometime back that the CM's lifestyle had made him aloof and that there was a disconnect between the CM and the state.

❖

Sharad and I were quickly briefed about the situation, which was grim. However, given Sharad's penchant for catching the bull by the horns, he suddenly decided to attempt something that everybody, including all our intelligence agencies, had advised him against.

Instead of the original plan of meeting a select group of citizens at the Town Hall, Sharad threw caution to the wind and decided to address the people of Srinagar right in the heart of the city, at the famous Lal Chowk. Our entire team had a deep foreboding of doom. But then Sharad, once he made up his mind, was not one to budge.

Sharad asked our cavalcade to stop at Lal Chowk. While his security had been beefed up for the visit, it was hopelessly inadequate for the madness that he was determined to enact. He asked his security personnel to arrange for a mike, which they quickly managed to hire from a tent shop nearby.

Anees, Haroon and I stood witness to a rare act of mad courage by India's Home Minister as Sharad addressed the people scattered all around who stood as dazed as us.

'My beloved brothers and sisters of this paradise on earth, I have not come here to offer you jobs and economic incentives – I know they can't assuage the anger and resentment that you have been living with. Nor am I a fool to expect that that will buy me your loyalty. I won't threaten you with dire consequences; not because the Indian state is scared, but because she respects and loves you like she does every citizen of this country. You may have been sceptical of our intentions, but that hasn't diminished our affection or our concern for you...'

Raising his voice, he roared, '...but this violence has to end. If the separatist leaders on Pakistan's payroll feel that they can intimidate us with might, let me tell them that they are demented. Guns cannot replace education, violence cannot replace employment. Your constant grouse has been the deployment of an overwhelming number of army personnel. I challenge the separatist leaders to come on a public platform together and swear on the Koran: one, that they will not incite violence and two, that should violence still break out, they shall come on the street and risk their lives as I have done today, to quell that violence. The moment, these separatist leaders do that, I promise the presence of army will be reduced to a quarter of what it is in the state right now...

'The Separatist leaders are the biggest cowards that I have seen on earth. With Pakistan's funds they can provide you ammunition. But that ammunition will never let your future generations live in peace... India has always wanted the best for Kashmir. We have always wanted to set up an IIT and an IIM here. In fact, my government wanted to make this dream a reality. But I have advised the government to put the plans on hold till I'm convinced that such prestigious institutes won't be hijacked by the enemies of India to pursue baseless anti-India propaganda.'

Raising his pitch once again, he roared:

'I challenge the so-called separatist leaders – the agents of Pakistan in disguise – to a debate right here. You accuse us of using the army to kill you for no reason. I challenge you to bring such instances directly to my office in Delhi. I will provide you a helpline number. And my ministry will ensure that the Army and the National Human Rights Commission (NHRC) get to the bottom of each case ASAP. But please don't cultivate propaganda as a tool. If you shout a lie a 100 times on the streets of Srinagar and expect Delhi to treat it as the truth, then you're mistaken. This is not the previous government in Delhi which liked being taken for a ride. My government still believes in what India has always believed in – humanity. But when the enemies of India treat that as our weakness, then my government will not hesitate to vanquish such enemies…'

And finally an earnest appeal.

'For Allah's sake, you can't afford to give the control of your life to those brokers of Pakistan who've disguised themselves as political leaders out here. Come with us. Today I won't promise you anything except respect and that all your grievances will be patiently heard. Can't you once trust this friend of yours and see the difference…? That's all that I have to tell you. May Allah bless you this Eid with lots of happiness.'

After Sharad was done talking, the crowd was quiet. It was as if the people were numbed by the guts of this Indian minister coming from nowhere and holding their attention; something only the separatist leaders did. The calm finally broke with the applause of a fifty-something, burqa-clad woman coming from within the commoners.

She looked frailer than her age – possibly because of some personal tragedy that she'd have gone through. She spoke in chaste Urdu.

'Saheb… I am impressed. If an Indian leader had done what you've done today in the late eighties, Kashmir would have been a different story.'

Waheeda Begum's young teenaged son had left home in 1989. In 1993, he had been killed by the army in the Baramullah sector. A huge amount of explosives were found in his possession. Besides, the literature found from his hideout corroborated his training in Pakistan-occupied Kashmir.

Sharad put his palm on her head in blessing and said, 'Give me your trust – that's all I'm asking for, Ammi. I want happier Eids in Kashmir.'

The lady hugged him even as she couldn't prevent herself from breaking down. The crowd, which had now swelled to nearly thrice its size, looked on in sheer amazement.

❖

Sharad had pulled a coup of sorts with his deft performance. Lal Chowk, which was hitherto synonymous with protests by Kashmiri extremists, for a change played host to the Indian Home Minister – one no less a genius than Nehru but just as different in his approach from India's first premier.

❖

The day wasn't done yet. After lunch, Sharad and I had a closed door meeting with Haroon Rashid. I was given to understand that we would discuss a special economic package for Kashmir, especially as Rashid was the state's Finance Minister. It didn't take me much time to realize that an economic package of another kind was on the agenda. 'Rs 100 crore,' said Sharad, as Haroon looked surprised and I, confused.

'That's the amount we can give you if you break away from the present government, float your own party, and contest all Assembly seats in the next elections.'

'What else does the deal entail?' Haroon asked.

'Nothing, except unflinching loyalty towards India. In fact you have to leverage your clout among the youth to make them realize the futility of this anti-India nonsense.'

'And may I know what gives you the confidence that I'm worth this amount?' he asked.

'Politics is like a racehorse. We throw in our lot with the horse that is most likely to win. Anees has lost the trust of people. You are more popular than him. Besides, you have your roots in Jammu which makes us think you won't have the same fixated mindset as many of the Kashmiri leaders.'

'And what if I fail?'

'The horse gets replaced.'

❖

It was late evening by the time we took the flight back to Delhi. We were definitely relieved by the way things had gone. Given the turbulence in Kashmir anything was possible – even us not returning home alive.

Sharad, as always, remained guarded in his joy. 'It's a part of life. Some days, you win. On others you lose. The idea is to start thinking about the next day.'

Sharad informed me that his histrionics at the Lal Chowk were entirely impromptu and unplanned. 'I decided to go for it after hearing about the CM's helplessness at the airport.'

'And it didn't take you much to risk your life?'

'Death does not scare me,' he smiled.

Even as I mulled over the nonchalance with which he said that, he looked straight into my eyes. 'Are *you* scared of death?'

I realized I wasn't sure about the answer. I guess death is scary when you have someone to live for. Did I have anybody?

My inability to give an answer made me change the topic and question him about what had surprised me the most – the deal with Haroon Rashid. Sharad's response was as nonchalant. 'Let's see how it pans out. It's like a game of chess where you've got to anticipate not one but three future moves of your rival. The bottomline remains the same – to protect and retain this vast land from the Himalayas till the Indian Ocean.'

Half way through the plane journey, I began feeling unwell. It started with a feeling of nausea and led to an acute piercing pain in the lower abdominal region. In no time, I realized that something was terribly amiss – the pain was constant; so much so that I was immobilized by it. I finally informed Sharad. Soon enough, I was virtually shrieking in pain.

I was rushed to the hospital as soon as we landed in Delhi. I was given analgesic injections while an emergency sonography and other tests were performed late in the night.

It must have been the wee hours of the morning when Sharad walked into my hospital room. I was desperately waiting for an update on the tests.

'The doctors have discovered an unusual growth in your uterus that needs to be operated upon immediately. They were debating an emergency operation and required the consent of a family member of yours.'

I listened to him in complete daze.

'I have given them the permission saying you've authorized me to take all decisions for you.'

Sharad looked tense, which only added to my fears. What did the next couple of hours hold for me? Were they by any chance going to be my last? Sharad's quietness indicated that there was something more he had to communicate. I looked at him enquiringly. He knew he could say what was on his mind.

'Shruti, the doctors want you to know that this operation might permanently impair your chances of becoming a mother.'

I was simply clueless on how I was supposed to react to this. Sharad held my palm firmly and reassured me, 'Don't worry – everything will be fine.' Saying this, he bent and kissed me on the forehead.

As I was being readied to be put under the doctor's knife, I realized I had the answer to what Sharad had asked me on the plane: I was indeed scared of death.

12

Eight days had gone by since that night of madness when I was operated upon. The tumour which had turned out to be benign had been successfully removed, but it altered my life in a way that I didn't like. I was now living in Sharad's house – a room had been provided to me with all the amenities. It was so comfortable that I felt I was in my own home. And it had happened in a rather unsuspecting manner.

Three days after my operation, when I was still extremely weak, though ready to be discharged, Sharad took charge of my transportation back home. That's when I realized he had brought me to his house. I protested. But then knowing just how stubborn Sharad was, I knew my protests were futile.

'Listen, don't get into this business of what the world will say. Think about your health. You need utmost care right now and I can't leave you alone,' Sharad said in a no-nonsense voice.

There were two things that confounded me – one the absence of my parents throughout this fiasco. Apart from my mother calling up Sharad's residence till she managed to speak to him, there was little to suggest that my parents still cared for me. Thinking about their indifference, Sharad's extra care did not hurt me much. Rohit too hadn't enquired about me. Frankly, I didn't expect him to.

The other, was the role of the media. On the day after my operation itself, one vernacular paper quoted my parents-in-law casting doubts about my fidelity. The news report speculated that I was carrying Sharad's baby and it was a complicated miscarriage that very nearly took my life.

Sharad was understandably outraged. He kept the paper away from me, lest after reading it, I decided not to stay at his place anymore. Following this newspaper report, even the prestigious newspapers and TV channels were now openly talking about our 'affair'. And yet I was surprised that Sharad stuck to his stand that I should stay in his house a couple of weeks more, till I had recovered fully.

'Rumours are a part of public life, Shruti, You need to decide whether you want to live your life or let rumours dictate how you should lead it,' he said.

'What about your public image? You are a potential PM after all.'

'The public wants change. They're sick of stereo-typical images. I don't think they'd mind a gallant, manly leader who is unabashed about taking care of a woman colleague of his. If they think beyond this, it is their imagination that is at fault.'

I found myself in an awfully strange position. The fact that I'd virtually been cut off from the rest of the world and marooned in someone else's house brought with it a whole gamut of strange emotions. I mean, apart from the media, once Sharad would leave for office at around 10 in the morning, I was left all alone in his house. Being on bed-rest, my movements were restricted. What overwhelmed me was that every couple of hours, Sharad would call and ask if I'd had my juice and medicines. His staff had been instructed to provide me two glasses of watermelon juice and a glass of apple juice spread over the day. I spent the day watching TV or reading the papers.

This was the third time I had been sharing a roof with a man, not related to me by blood. First, it was Abhay. For two years, we had lived as man and wife sharing every bit of each other including our most intense sexual engagements. And then it had all ended abruptly, like a snatch of music suddenly cut off.

Later, I had shared a roof with Rohit for a little over a year, a man who was my husband but with whom I always felt like a stranger, unable to open up completely and share my true feelings with.

And here for the last eight days, I had been sharing a roof with a man who seemed like God's messenger for me, yet with whom I found it extremely difficult to define my relationship.

It makes me wonder if all our bonds and relationships in this life are extensions of those that we have lived in a previous life. Today, Abhay was history to me, as was Rohit, whom I struggled to accommodate in my life. Was this strange phase of my life – when I was being provided a sense of familial belonging by someone who I thought was sworn to the country – also as ephemeral?

Lying in bed, I wondered why Sharad was doing so much for me, Did he still see a Krishna–Draupadi kind of bond between us? For I can tell you, his sense of extreme protectiveness towards me allayed all the fears that I'd experienced with other men. He'd been good to me at a time when the world had ganged up against me.

That evening Sharad returned home slightly early. He sat beside me and played a raga for me – it soothed me more than all the medicines that I'd been having.

A little while later, Sharad sipped his wine, as we sat listening to classical music. Strangely, I found Sharad in a somewhat melancholic frame of mind. That I'd only once seen him reveal his emotional side to me, made me curious. A few sips more and he sounded ready to share with me matters he'd never broached till then. 'Your staying here reminds me of something… someone…'

I waited for him to go on.

'Of my wife and the last few days that we spent together…' And he went on to tell me the story of his married years.

❖

Sharad and his wife, Mala studied in the same college in Delhi: Kirori Mal College. Both were students of History. While Sharad wanted to compete for the civil services exams, Mala was more interested in pursuing a teaching career. Sharad was a bit of a flirt. Even though Mala didn't like this much, she knew Sharad was committed to her. Sharad knew it too.

However, the 1970s was not an easy time for personal relationships to flourish, especially if the people involved in the relationship were affected by the political turbulence in the country. Sharad was an active member of a student group that strongly opposed the Congress government of the time. He even went on to become the organization's vice president in 1974.

Having failed to make in to the civil services, Sharad took up the job of a journalist in *The Indian Express*, the most famed anti-establishment paper of independent India. Mala, in the meantime, pursued her Master's degree and subsequently took up the post of junior lecturer in Daulat Ram College.

Sharad's and Mala's romance thus was a classic case of college companionship and sharing, it must have been akin to the life I had shared with Abhay. For in due course, in their relationship too, the differences came to the fore.

Mala and her parents were sceptical of Sharad's rebel instincts. The fact that he had been showing interest in pursuing a political career worried them because the politics of those days was still bereft of the affluence that it subsequently gifted itself.

Under some pressure from Mala, Sharad and Mala tied the knot on 24th June, 1975. Even as the long-drawn-out north Indian marriage rituals went on till the wee hours of the morning, news of an unprecedented development poured in. A state of national emergency had been clamped upon the nation.

No sooner were the rituals over that Sharad went away for a meeting with other members of the youth wing of the political organization that he was associated with. He returned only the next night. The consummation of his marriage became all the more intense due to Sharad's feelings of political outrage. What followed were some very fiery articles for the newspaper, as a result of which Sharad was awarded a solitary honeymoon in jail.

Fifteen months later, when Sharad was finally released, Mala was a different person. There was a sense of detachment about her. In all their conversations, he got the impression that she was not really involved in the marriage anymore. What made matters worse was a male friend of Mala's, a fellow lecturer in the college, Arvind Singhal.

Mala got along very well with Arvind and there were occasions when they'd have long discussions on the phone, ostensibly about some college stuff.

Sharad felt an unusual anxiety about this, which he found strange. Had his spell in jail changed him? He'd never felt insecure about any of his girlfriends before. But now things were different. It was as if the situation had reversed completely. In their courtship days it was Sharad's behaviour that would make Mala feel insecure; now it was the other way around. Besides, the spell in jail had given him some sort of a complex.

He had spent fifteen months of his life behind bars but what had he achieved? Even without him making that sacrifice, the fate of the country would not have been any different. On the other hand, both his personal and professional life would have been less screwed up. After battling his demons for weeks, Sharad confronted his wife over her friendship with Arvind.

'Sharad, I had never liked you getting so actively involved into politics, but I let it be because I believed both of us ought to have the freedom to pursue our dreams. But to what end? Do you realize the state of mind of a woman whose husband disappears straight from the marriage pandal for fifteen months? And does so to glorify an activism that I find banal?'

'Mala, wasn't it about your choice, as well? I mean, you could have been a part of my struggle?'

'Sharad, frankly I did not find anything wrong with the Emergency. This country had brought it upon itself...'

Sharad was stunned when he heard this. Had she always thought this way? If so, why didn't she let him know before? If not, was this new thinking the result of her newer associations?

'Arvind is a colleague I relate well to. Being a senior he has helped me a lot. Besides, we think alike on some important issues...'

'Like your views on the Emergency?'

'Maybe...'

'What else do you think alike on?'

Sharad felt utterly defeated. The only thing a crusader expects from a spouse is empathy towards the cause he espouses. Here there was none. Sharad had two options at this stage – either to restrict himself to being a journalist and a good family man, or to go all out and pursue what he believed in.

He chose the latter.

A year later, Sharad and Mala had their first baby – a girl whom they named Rhea. However, the new entrant to the family could do little to reverse the increasing alienation between the husband and wife.

Six years went by with Sharad and Mala coexisting with all their differences. And yet there must have been something that kept them together apart from Rhea.

'I think it was Mala's strength of character. Every time she contradicted me, I felt offended. Yet a couple of days later, I'd warm to her point of view and try to correct my stance. I think her alter-ego approach towards me somehow made me a more rounded personality. Despite our differences, we shared a bond that always pulled me back to her. And I guess she felt the same.'

As Sharad said this, his expression changed. His eyes grew moist as he prepared himself to make a confession: 'Disillusioned with our growing differences, I was briefly involved with a woman journalist working in my organization. I hated myself for doing what I was doing and yet at that point, my senses had gone for a toss. Sandwiched between a discontented family life and an equally frustrating political career that wasn't taking off, I took refuge in an illicit affair.'

I noticed a tear trickle down Sharad's cheeks as he spoke: 'Mala knew about it. But her greatness comes in the fact that she divulged this to me only on her death bed. She told me that since she'd not been the wife that I'd expected her to be, she did not feel like making an issue of my indiscretion. If that compensated for the tough time that she'd given me, it was okay by her. She said this to me just hours before leaving me forever. Her words have haunted me ever since.'

Strange indeed are the ways of destiny. Through the early eighties, even as Sharad, disgruntled with the mortal existence of a mere journalist, tried in vain to pursue a political career, the distance between his wife and him grew wider. Their interactions became sparse for fear of their thoughts not meeting the right understanding or empathy in each other. Most of their conversations thus centred around their daughter Rhea.

In the latter half of 1984, Mala fell ill. A splitting headache like she had never experienced before is what started it off. Sooner, she was experiencing all sorts of problems – constant nausea, listlessness and weight loss. A comprehensive set of tests revealed that she was suffering from an advanced stage of brain tumour. It was a spooky coincidence that the information of the brain tumour arrived on the same day that Sharad got a ticket to fight his first Lok Sabha elections.

Sharad was shattered by the turn of events. He had decided to give up the ticket when he was surprised that his wife persuaded him against it.

'I never opposed you directly but I'm sure you could sense my disapproval. And being an attached husband somewhere I'm sure my reactions have hindered your growth. This is God's way of preparing you for a new beginning. The doctors are pretty clear that I can't be cured. So don't waste your efforts on me. For my sake, win this election so that I can go in peace.'

Sharad was stunned by Mala's unselfishness. Was she always like this and was it his self-obsessions that had him not acknowledge this side of hers? He had no answer.

'You have to win this one for our daughter. Come on, don't waste your time here. Get on with your job,' Mala had exhorted him.

For twenty days thereafter, Sharad was on the streets all day campaigning for the elections. People in those days didn't have cellphones. Many a times Sharad had no contact with his wife or know about her condition all day. It was an excruciating time for Sharad – more painful than the years of incarceration.

Worse, in his heart of hearts, Sharad knew that he was fighting a losing battle on both fronts. After Indira Gandhi's assassination there was a huge sympathy wave in favour of the Congress who had managed to glorify Mrs Gandhi's martyrdom. So what would have been an even contest had Mrs Gandhi been alive, became a no-contest as the day of polling drew closer.

Every night that Sharad came back to his wife looking despondent, she'd encourage him like he had never seen her do. She'd boost his confidence by re-minding him of his convictions and beliefs through all his college years. *This is the opportunity to make all that come true*, she told him.

Sharad hated the way his life was playing out. After marriage, he had been gifted exile from his wife; now when he had the first real chance to make his dreams come true it too had come at the cost of parting from his wife forever.

Finally, setting his negative thoughts aside, Sharad did his wife's bidding. He packed in the most in the last few days of campaigning. His efforts bore fruit: in an election that saw the Congress win over 400 seats and some of the veteran non-Congressmen bite the dust, Sharad was among the lucky few to scrape through.

From the counting booth, Sharad rushed back to the hospital to give the good news to Mala. To his shock, Mala's condition had suddenly deteriorated and she had been rushed to the ICU. The doctor came out to inform him that due to an unexpected progression of the tumour in the last couple of days, Maya's condition was now critical; that she probably had just a few hours left.

It was on her death bed that Sharad had informed her of his victory. Her happiness knew no bounds. It was the same conversation, where driven by his guilt, Sharad had broken down and made that confession to her, only to be stunned by her reaction. Sharad and Mala spoke for an hour, like they did back in their college days, Sharad easily deciphering all her mumblings. Finally Mala was exhausted. She lay back; and then she went still. A shattered Sharad held her close and cried profusely. He then drew the curtain apart. Dawn was breaking. Mala's mumbling just before she departed, telling Sharad that a new dawn was waiting for him, ricocheted in his ears.

'It's strange that like Nehru I discovered the virtues of Chitrangada in my dying wife. It's strange that when we were together and struggling through our marriage, I tried to search the qualities of other women in my wife. And when she was gone, I tried to look for her in every woman that I met.'

Sharad was trembling at the force of his memories. He was weeping unashamedly now, the tears freely flowing down his cheeks. Seeing him in this vulnerable mode was akin to watching a monument collapse. I felt awful looking at Sharad in this state.

And then he said something which completely shook me. 'How I wish I could have given my ailing wife the care that I gave you.'

He broke down and I ended up comforting him with a hug. I was left a bit befuddled by the situation. A little while later, Sharad apologized for not having restraint over his emotions.

❖

That evening, Sharad received a call from Rhea. From what I could gather from Sharad's conversation, Rhea was going to be back in India soon. However, I knew there was something coming between the father and daughter. Whenever Sharad had to deal with that, he excused himself and took the cordless phone away to another room.

Sharad returned after five minutes. I asked him if there was a problem. He looked stressed but changed the topic.

I had never anticipated that Sharad would open up to me in this manner. And since he had, it had only whetted my interest in sorting out the many questions that still remained unanswered.

Was Sharad's taking care of me an attempt to redeem himself of the guilt of ignoring his wife?

What about the stories of his 'romanticism' – he had been linked twice before? And for all I knew must have philandered more often.

'About me being a romantic, I don't know. Let me say I'm interested, interested in all beautiful things in life. So yes, two years after my wife passed away, I fell in love with a girl called Gargi. Gargi Chauhan. Gargi, as you know, was a national-level badminton player when I was secretary of the Badminton Association of India. She was very similar to the way Mala was before marriage – calm, happy and full of beans. We were together for three years when things fell apart.'

He refilled his glass of wine.

'And then there was Shabnam, the IB official. I guess we were both extremely lonely when we met. Shabnam was in a troubled long-distance relationship with her IFS husband. We were together for a very brief while till we realized the futility of it.'

I waited to hear what he'd say about us.

When he didn't I asked him. 'Doesn't what the media say about us perturb you?'

He took a pause and thought before answering, 'Isn't ours an unusual relationship, after all?'

'Yes. But what does the future hold? I mean where are we heading?'

'How do I know? When I first met you and offered you the ticket, I had no idea we'd be sitting together and talking like this.'

Well, I too didn't have an idea then. What scared me though was I didn't have an idea even *now*. The transient patterns in my life worried me. Nothing – no relationship, city, person or work seemed to find a permanent place in my life. The really scary part was that they tended to get suddenly uprooted for no fault of mine. The pattern of my life had thus made me a reluctant but perpetual immigrant.

A myriad thoughts invaded me and kept me awake, tossing and turning, the entire night.

❖

The next morning we had a surprise visitor. Abhay dropped in to meet Sharad over breakfast. I was asked to join them.

'Abhay and I have a love-hate relationship,' Sharad had recently told me. 'At one point of time, I used to give most of my interviews to him. But then it seemed he had befriended my rivals. So I too began doing most of my interviews with his rival, Pranav. But, lately, after our Kashmir visit, Abhay has been pressing for an interview.' Now Sharad had called him over for a breakfast meeting.

I was put in an extremely awkward position. Why did Sharad have to call Abhay here? After all, he knew about our past. And why was Abhay so keen to come? To find out whether there was truth in all the stories linking Sharad and me?

'Yes, Shruti and I are having a torrid affair,' laughed Sharad, the moment I walked into the room. 'It's a partnership that will change the shape of the Home Ministry. The Home Ministry will no longer react to situations after things have gone haywire. Instead it will envision problem situations that could arise twenty years hence and wipe them out from the roots. How is that for a steamy "Home" affair?' he laughed.

For a moment, I wondered if Sharad was trying to gauge if I still had feelings for Abhay. After all, what was really on his mind could never be accurately understood by lesser mortals.

At that point Sharad received a call from the PMO. Apparently, Yashwant Modi wanted to speak to him about something important. Sharad abruptly excused himself, leaving Abhay and me struggling to make conversation. It was Abhay who made a start:

'You don't need to feel awkward, Shruti. You know I've never been judgmental. So it doesn't matter to me at all if I see you here and in this situation.'

'Does it give some kind of impression about me?'

Abhay smiled before he said, 'Only that you're as much a victim or beneficiary of nature's law of averages as anybody else.'

I felt somewhat relieved to hear this. There was a point of time in my life when Abhay's indifference had destroyed me. Today, his indifference was a relief.

I could sense, though, that Abhay was not happy. He wasn't his normal cavalier self. He had lost weight, he looked tired, and his voice sounded gruff and heavy. I asked him if all was well. Surprisingly, it seemed like he was waiting for me to ask the question.

'Does all *look* well?' he asked.

I didn't think so, but shrugged my shoulders because I really was not interested in knowing more.

Abhay, for some strange reason, did not want me to remain ignorant. 'Antara and I have filed for divorce,' he confessed.

I remained cool even as I asked him why.

'She had been cheating on me. What was most ironical was that I discovered it first-hand, much the way you had.'

'And why do you want me to know this?'

'Well, it should make you happy. You have no idea what I've gone through.'

I paused before replying, 'If sympathy is what you had expected from me, I somehow don't quite feel that yet.'

I would be lying if I said I did not feel bad for Abhay. The thing about a sensitive woman is that you can't really wish ill for a person you've once loved, no matter what that creature has made you go through. At best, you like to believe that the person does not exist for you. Like Rohit and Sharad, Abhay too had a part in me being who I was and where I was today.

At that point, a peon entered the room to inform me what I'd have least expected to hear. 'Ma'am your husband, Rohit, has come. He was insisting at the gate that he wanted to meet you. So we called him to the reception, lest some news channel makes a story of it.'

I was too frail to move, and frankly beyond caring. I asked the staff to send Rohit in. Abhay offered to leave. But deriving some sort of sadistic pleasure from the peculiarity of the situation I asked him to stay.

Rohit walked in looking all hassled and disturbed – perhaps more so on seeing Abhay there. He asked me if we could talk alone. To which I said a firm no.

'How are you, Shruti? I've been really worried about you,' he blabbered.

'What do you want now?' I asked him bluntly.

'I'm really sorry for the mess created by my parents. I have come to apologize.'

'That's it?'

He nodded.

'Fair enough. Please leave now,' I said.

He was shocked to hear this. As shocked as I was at actually being able to say it.

'For God's sake Shruti, don't talk like this. I've come all the way from Jehanabad to see you.'

I lost my cool. 'Rohit, I have nothing to do with you. Your parents have accused me of having no character. They wouldn't have dared to do this had my husband not been an extremely weak character. So, please, leave me alone. I don't need you or your concern.'

At this point, Sharad re-entered the room. For some strange reason, I did not mind exposing the charade of my marriage in front of the two other men who were, or had been, a part of my life. Perhaps I wanted Rohit to know that he was the weakest among them. The sheer awkwardness of the situation forced Rohit to make a hasty exit – a fact I did not feel in the least hassled about.

'Abhay, I'll have to rush to the PMO. Can we continue this interview in the evening at my office?'

Abhay left, leaving Sharad and me alone.

Sharad could sense my agitation and felt apologetic about it. 'I was a bit pre-occupied when Abhay called last evening and I called him over for breakfast.

I am really sorry, but your past with him just escaped my memory at that point,' he explained.

'It's okay,' I tried sounding brave even as I found it difficult to prevent myself from breaking down.

Sharad hugged me. He stroked my head and comforted me till I was okay.

❖

Sharad left for the PMO soon after and I was left alone with my thoughts. I wondered about the bizarre ploy of destiny of bringing the men of my life together in front of me. Was this one of life's metaphors?

Just as men try to see the avatar of a Sita or a Chitrangada in their women, is a woman within her rights and senses if she decides to see a Ram or Krishna or Shiva in her man? If so, who was Ram, who Krishna and who Shiva from among the three men who had been a part of my life?

I mulled the question even as the answer eluded me.

13

It was Independence Day – the national holiday that most of urban India celebrates by sleeping till late, even as the tricolour is unfurled from the Red Fort. In rural India, the indifference manifests itself in other ways.

On this day, the PM addresses the nation from the Red Fort, telling the people about the major initiatives of the government, as well as acquainting them with its position on the present and potential challenges facing the nation.

In his Independence Day address, Prime Minister Yashwant Modi showered lavish praise on Sharad Malviya. He said that Malviya had shown us the way the Kashmir problem could be resolved – not by finding solutions sitting in air-conditioned offices but by talking to the protestors and separatists, and looking them in the eye. He reiterated that while India had always favoured finding solutions through dialogue, the country will not be a mute spectator to the violence in the Valley. The PM said something similar about the Naxal menace – come for talks, but should you resort to violence, we shall give you a fitting reply.

The PM then went on to unveil a new employment scheme for villagers in three of the densest tribal belts of Chhattisgarh, Orissa and Jharkhand. Also promised was a path-breaking change in the food-grain storage mechanism. The speech that lasted for about half an hour ended with the singing of the National Anthem.

❖

Sharad looked a bit pensive as we had tea together, after the ceremony. I asked him the reason.

'You know, Shruti, the way we celebrate our Independence Day just encourages the younger generation to be more and more ignorant of so many facts about our country, which they ought to know,' he complained.

My interest in what he was saying goaded him on.

'For instance, this unveiling of the flag, followed by the PM's lecture – it's so mechanical. And it's gone on for decades, making the younger generation disinterested enough to give it a miss.'

He took a sip of his tea and continued, 'The idea should be to spread knowledge and awareness, which does not happen. For instance, how many school and college-goers know how the name India was derived? How many know what the colours of the Indian flag stand for? The way history is taught in our schools is so boring that very few youngsters want to pursue it in college. That's a weakness of our education system. We must realize that we cannot dream of a bright future if we ignore our history.'

Had someone else been talking like this, I'm not sure it would have elicited interest in me. I guess it's not so much the content itself as the trust factor that makes the content believable. I trusted Sharad's intentions for the country. Almost everything that he told me seemed like an eye-opener. Was I this ignorant or did Sharad belong to that rare breed of people who had arrogated a humungous sense of purpose to their living, which mere mortals like me could never really decipher. What Sharad went on to say set me off to discover a whole new ocean of thoughts.

'The India that you see today is essentially the result of four gargantuan efforts in history to unify this vast piece of land and its people in the last 1200 years. In early 9th century, Adi Shankaracharya, a philosopher from Kerala, travelled across the country espousing his doctrine of Advaita Vedanta. Adi Shankara founded four mathas to guide the Hindu religion. These are at Sringeri in Karnataka in the south, Dwaraka in Gujarat in the west, Puri in Orissa in the east, and Jyotirmath (Joshimath) in Uttarakhand in the north. Even today the Shankaracharya of these mathas trace their lineage to the south, thus asserting that the idea of this vast piece of land being one country existed far before the Mughal and British invasions.

'Then in the early sixteenth century, Chaitanya Mahaprabhu, a saint and reformer in eastern India, believed by his followers to be a re-incarnation of Lord Krishna himself, travelled across the country unifying people via his Bhakti philosophy. He re-discovered Vrindavan and Mathura. He is a man who single-handedly brought about a cultural renaissance in Bengal. After him, the Bhakti Movement drew followers from other parts of the country as well.

'In the nineteenth century, it was the turn of Rama Krishna and his disciple Vivekananda to do their bit for the cultural revival of the country. Their efforts in unifying this land via culture and humanism remain of the highest standards ever.

'And finally, starting around 1920, it was the turn of Gandhi to launch an all-out peace offensive that eventually got us freedom and gave us self-rule, which had been usurped many centuries ago.'

I listened to Sharad attentively.

'Unfortunately, our Nehruvian historians, who were as conceited as Nehru himself, glorified all the humiliations that were heaped upon this country. An invader, no matter how heroic he must have been, can't be the hero. What has happened is that subsequent generations that have grown up studying a concocted version of history have revelled in their aloofness.'

I could sense that Sharad felt very passionately about this subject. I was thus, naturally inclined to deduce that he advocated cultural nationalism as a pillar on which the foundation for the country's future ought to have been laid. There was a fundamental point though, on which I tended to disagree with Sharad: Sharad's idea of cultural nationalism underlined and reiterated the distinction between the original inhabitants of the land and the invaders, a distinction which to my understanding holds little relevance in present-day democracy.

Sharad had more ideas to share. 'If I had my way, I'd have Independence Day brought in with firecrackers at midnight and then celebrate it with the colours of Holi during the day. A huge national temple that houses the prayer halls of all independent faiths should have been built as a national monument – basically something like a temple of Bharat Mata, as Swami Vivekananda would have envisaged.'

He added with some amount of remorse, 'We revel in our chaos – the fact that we are perhaps democratic in its truest sense, unlike China or many countries of the Arab world. But let me tell you that even chaos needs to be controlled. It ought to be controlled by someone who understands and appreciates the ancient culture of this land. Or else, this chaos will at some point singe this land from within.'

Sharad's musings that evening and my rapt absorption in the same were much akin to a mentor enlightening his disciple. Of course the fact that I had come to him with little ideological baggage helped in me becoming an easy student. But did Sharad's thinking carry a bias? His point was simple actually: Who should be our real heroes – those who ruled us by force or the silent majority who withstood force to still help the original virtues of the land survive?

Well, the question will remain a contentious one.

History is depressing; its ignorance and unlearnt lessons, dangerous.

❖

Next morning, when I sat with Sharad over breakfast, I had a question. 'Sharadji, I kept thinking about what you told me yesterday. I agree with all that you said except for one fundamental difference of opinion.'

He looked on, a bit surprised. I was just as surprised with the gumption that my speech had:

'Much before these movements that you mentioned occurred, India was ruled by Ashoka whose conquests extended till central Asia as well as South East Asia. And it was he who spread Buddhism in those countries. In fact some of those countries, Sri Lanka included, have the most devout Buddhist following even today.'

'What are you trying to say?'

'Two things. One, a conqueror must have loved a piece of land to own it. Two, it was but natural for the conqueror to promote his religion. I think in the present age, one has to bury the debate of original inhabitant versus invader. It takes us back in time and spirit.'

A deep-breathed 'hmm' was all that Sharad responded with. I was his protégé but a protégé need not subscribe to her mentor's views on every issue.

❖

As we were talking, Sharad received a call, following which he switched on the TV. A leading Hindi news channel that specialized in 'sting operations', had broken a scandalous story about us. The story asserted that pregnancy and not a uterine tumour is what had led to that covert emergency operation being performed on me. It said that I was pregnant and that an urgent abortion had to be performed to hide it from the world. Snide references were made to the 'alleged' rape case in my past. What was worse was that the article created a whole mystery about the father of the child. Without naming Sharad, it kept harping upon Sharad's unusual interest in me, leaving little to public imagination.

I felt an unprecedented indignation as I watched the story unfold. What on earth had I done to deserve this trial by fire once again? Didn't such a report after all amount to a rape of my character?

Sharad was just as livid, furiously pacing the room. He received a host of calls that morning – some from well-wishers and others from rivals who wanted to shed crocodile tears. He ignored most of them.

An extremely awkward silence prevailed between us. In some sense I'd seen it coming all along. It just wasn't done for the country's top politician to have his deputy stay in his official house, irrespective of the reasons attached to the situation. Why then had Sharad been so complacent? And why had I not been stronger about putting my foot down? I blamed myself for not pre-empting this situation.

What added fuel to the fire was an interview that Sharad's bête-noire gave to a TV channel and which beamed out live right in front of us.

'Ministers need to follow a certain protocol. If Sharad does not realize this, he needs to be told that he has set a wrong example for the people of the country and disgraced the position that he holds...'

Minutes after the interview aired, Sharad received a call from the PMO. He left immediately.

❖

I did not wait for Sharad to return. I told his staff to help me shift back to my residence. I also insisted that Sharad not be informed about my departure. He had far more pressing problems to deal with. In the stage of recovery that I was in, this kind of physical and mental pressure was extremely detrimental. I was least bothered.

That day, the PM, gave a piece of his mind to Sharad for the first time. Sharad was apparently told that his indiscretions had greatly harmed the image of the government; a fact that could prove costly considering that the government enjoyed a very slender majority. Besides, it was time he realized that for all our projections of modernity, India remained deeply conservative at heart. A large chunk of the population still seemed to want a father-figure in in their leaders.

And finally, the PM doled out a piece of advice for Sharad. 'Let Shruti shift to another ministry. We can even give her an independent charge as Minister of State in say the Environment Ministry. But the Home Ministry can't afford to be seen as a family enterprise.'

Sharad warded off the pressure saying that I was privy to some important strategic plans that we were working on together and that my shifting out at this stage could kill those initiatives. For his part, he promised to maintain protocol in the future.

❖

That evening I sat alone, back in my own house. I could sense a change in me. For once, I did not harbour the remotest thoughts of escaping from the world I was in. But what if this world chose to banish me? I think for the first time, I was prepared to believe I could fight it out. It is true I had been brought here by Sharad, but with all my limitations, I had done nothing that would amount to a betrayal of anybody's expectations. I was inclined to believe that the PM was right; it would be good if I could take up an assignment independently, away from Sharad's tutelage, and prove my mettle.

That whole day I did not take any calls or meet anyone. Sharad dropped into my house later that night, and I immediately pinned him down with my question: 'Why Sharadji? Why are you destroying your career for me?'

He avoided a direct answer, harping on the usual stuff – my competence, his implicit trust in me, et al, all of which sounded absolutely unconvincing.

My refusal to budge had him blurt out something else: 'I don't know. I don't have an answer. But yes, I feel a dependence on you that I haven't felt for anybody.'

I heard him out in disbelief. So far I'd thought I was depending on him.

'I don't know when it happened but somewhere along the way, I think... well... I developed feelings for you.'

I was stunned. I almost hoped that I'd heard wrong. But alas, he had said what he did and I had heard it just the way it had been said. I could also sense that after telling me what was on his mind he felt as confounded by the declaration as I was. The two of us just stood there for the next ten minutes, trying to say something at various points and then cutting it short.

Exasperated, Sharad finally walked abruptly away. I'm not sure what hurt him more – the fact that he'd actually messed up a platonic relationship that I wanted to believe was still as pure, at least on my part; or the fact that he had to state what I should have known.

I was left wondering whether Sharad was as much a victim of circumstances as I was. He certainly had never had a happy personal life – destiny cutting short his fulfilment each time. Or was he the sort who lived in perpetual quest of all that was elusive?

I stayed awake that whole night mulling over this and by next morning my decision was made. I would personally meet Sharad and request him to get me transferred to another ministry. Shouldn't a parent let go of his child after a certain age and let it battle the rigours of the ruthless world independently?

I wanted to serve as deputy to Ratna Pandey. I wanted to prove that even as deputy in her own ministry I could outshine her achievements. I was also conscious of the fact that these thoughts were the first manifestation of the rebel in me. I was no longer willing to take things lying down. From being a reluctant politician, I was ready to be a more pro-active one.

For the first time in my political career I was determined to survive in this world without Sharad.

It was strange, but that obnoxious TV report had led to what I felt was my coming of age in Delhi. I was no longer the lost child that I had been so far.

Predictably, the unsavoury chain of events led to some amount of distancing between Sharad and me. Three weeks later, when I rejoined work earlier than I had been advised to by my doctors, I withdrew myself from the long interactions that Sharad and I used to share in office and out of it. Now, I'd stick to my work and go back home. Our meetings were formal and did not broach subjects outside work. This despite the fact that days after Sharad had blurted out his feelings, he had come to my cabin to apologize to me. 'I'm sorry, Shruti. I shouldn't have said what I did.'

I had struggled to answer.

'I promise that I won't let that conversation ever come between us,' he had assured me.

❖

As the days went by, we got reports that the situation in Kerala was worsening. Much of it had to do with the arrest of a popular hardliner Abdul Latif in connection with a bomb blast that had taken place in the neighbouring state of Karnataka a year ago. Intelligence inputs warned us of simultaneous terror strikes being planned in three or four places in Kerala during that year's festive season.

Buoyed by the improved situation in Kashmir and the Naxal belt, Sharad decided to shift his focus to Kerala. He decided to initiate a series of combative measures that would prevent Kerala from becoming the future trouble zone for the country. With that end objective, Sharad decided to pay a two-day visit to the state. On the first day he was scheduled to meet peoples' delegations in Alleppey and Trivandrum to get a first-hand account of the situation. On the second he was supposed to address a rally in Kochi.

Ideally, I ought to have accompanied him on the tour since I was handling Kerala initially. But then given the way things stood between us, I decided to give it a miss. Instead I met Sharad for an hour on the evening before he was to depart and discussed my understanding of the problem once again. Given the maverick that Sharad was and the fact that he had been lying quiet for some time, especially in the aftermath of the pesky media stories, I had an intuition that Sharad was gearing up for another stellar performance – of the kind that he'd demonstrated first in tribal Orissa and then in the heart of Srinagar.

One part of me missed not accompanying him. I kept wondering what unexpected move Sharad would come up with on this tour. My sense of involvement with him had me wonder if my sentiments were similar to the ones that Sharad had ended up expressing that rainy night. A clear answer eluded me. I didn't want to think about us and so I chose to immerse myself in the stack of files lying in my office.

Addressing a huge rally in Kochi, Sharad held out a clear warning for the fundamentalist groups: 'For a long time in this country, fundamentalist groups have been indulged for the sake of votes. Now that trend is going to change. Those who deserve to be behind bars will be sent there and not to the State Legislatures and the Parliament. The hawala funding that is freely flowing into the state and being misused will become history very soon. This is your chance to own up to your country...'

Sharad got an unprecedented response from the crowd. People of all religions lauded him for directly taking on an issue that previous governments had been deliberately ignoring for a very long time.

After the rally Sharad proceeded to the state headquarters of our party, the Nationalist League. In fact, the state unit of the party was so buoyed by the positive impact of Sharad's visit that for the first time the party was contemplating fighting all seats for the Kerala Assembly elections scheduled next year.

On his way to the party office, Sharad spoke to me on the phone and informed me about the developments. I felt he was being extremely gracious in so including me.

'Our present distance notwithstanding, you've been an important member of my team. Besides, you were the one who'd prepared the groundwork in Kerala for this visit of mine. So you ought to know the results,' he told me.

My eyes were moist with emotion. I felt good at the prospect of an India not at war with itself. I was pleased for Sharad. I was happy that our country still had someone like him to pull it out of the mess that some of our previous governments had landed us in.

My ecstasy was short-lived. I received a phone call exactly an hour after Sharad's call – a call after which everything changed for me.

A few hours later, after midnight, I stood outside the ICU ward of Christian Medical College Hospital, Kochi, praying for Sharad to survive even as an emergency operation was being performed on him to remove the two bullets lodged inside his body. A first-hand account of what had transpired was told to me by a party worker.

Apparently, barely minutes after completing his conversation with me, Sharad reached the party office. Here, right at the main entry, there was a huge commotion. A blind couple had created a huge furore over the 'humiliation' that had been heaped upon them. Even as the security guards tried to push them back, they relentlessly demanded an appointment with Sharad. Sharad found it a bit strange and decided to personally interact with the couple. This wasn't the first time he had contravened protocol to reach someone in need.

The only difference was that his interface with this apparently blind couple had him staring at death. No sooner had he asked his security guards to move aside, the man had pulled out a revolver from under his shirt and shot at Sharad from close range. Sharad immediately ducked for cover. But so close was the firing range that it couldn't escape Sharad. He sustained three bullet injuries – two in his ribs and one on his left arm. Immediately after shooting him, the man shot himself dead; the woman tried the same but was nabbed before she could succeed.

What had seemed till a few moments ago like another feather in Sharad's cap had now turned into a nightmare. There was panic and gloom all around with his condition stated to be critical.

I flew down to Kochi immediately and joined the others waiting outside the operation theatre. It had been eight hours since Sharad had been shot. One bullet still remained inside, lodged right over the spleen. The bleeding which had continued since had made Sharad's condition worse. This operation that was being performed on him had started an hour and half ago. Yet there was no indication of how things stood.

I was an emotional wreck. I felt devastated and completely distraught. I cried and cried not caring what the people thought, with no one to give me shoulder except the memories of the wonderful moments that I had shared with Sharad. Also present now outside the OT were at least three Cabinet Ministers, each hoping against hope that Sharad would be pulled out of this one.

And then there was buzz that Sharad's daughter who had just flown in from London on a chartered flight had reached the hospital. In no time, in walked a pretty young girl. She was beautiful and looked confident enough to control her emotions. Absurdly I felt a rush of concern towards her as I saw her walk in from a distance.

Rhea was accompanied by Sharad's secretary. She quickly enquired about her father's health from the other ministers. I felt she was deliberately ignoring me and in the same moment hated myself for thinking like that. I walked up to her and introduced myself. 'Rhea, hello... I'm Shruti. Shruti Ranjan.'

There was no warmth on Shruti's face. Instead there was some amount of disdain. 'I see...' was all she said before adding, 'You're the one who has been causing my dad problems in the ministry.'

I wasn't in the least prepared for this.

She gave me a baleful stare and then turned her attention to the medical team who had arrived to brief her about the situation.

I felt angry and humiliated. As I moved away, her words ricocheted in my mind with increased intensity.

14

Sharad came out trumps from the jaws of Yamraj – the god of death. After being on the ventilator for ten days he showed the first signs of improvement when he regained consciousness. I haven't said this to anyone before but I was on a fast until he regained consciousness – having only fruits and liquids to sustain myself.

Why did I do that?

Sharad, by virtue of his contribution to my life, had already assumed a position where giving up my life for him seemed like no big deal. When he was in coma I dreaded what life would be if he were gone, so addicted had I become to his protection in the last two years. Of course I knew that his recovery had more to do with his steely will-power than my prayers.

My days in hospital were not easy. Whenever I'd come in front of Rhea, she'd give me a stare that would somehow make me feel very guilty. But her dislike and disapproval was not going to keep me away. While Sharad was in the hospital in Kochi I just parked myself in one of the hospital corridors and prayed all day, waiting for updates and talking on the phone all day long with bureaucrats in the ministry. I did return to Delhi once to attend a meeting with the PM, wherein the law and order situation in the country was reviewed in the light of what had happened.

On the fifth day, Sharad had been flown to Delhi in a comatose state, which in fact made it easier for me to go back to office to finish urgent work and then return to take up my vigil at the Apollo Hospital.

And then on the tenth day, hope won.

When Sharad had regained consciousness and was able to communicate at least by signs and gestures, I was told he had enquired about me. I then visited him in his room.

Trapped with all sorts of tubes and bandages Sharad looked like a grievously wounded tiger. So while the spirit to fight back was intact, he was handicapped by his physical state.

Even in that state, he enquired about the work of his ministry.

'Don't worry. Everything is under control. One of the assailants had shot himself dead. The other is in police custody and has provided us vital clues that have helped us arrest 22 people from different parts of the country. It was a massive conspiracy and the role of an international terror group can't be ruled out.'

Sharad heaved a sigh of relief.

❖

Things changed drastically post the incident. One, I felt increasingly awkward going to meet Sharad. Rhea, by virtue of being Sharad's daughter, clearly enjoyed a greater ownership over the man and she chose to look through me all the time and made me feel wretched. Two, on the professional front, I had a new boss. Shyamachand Gupta, a septuagenarian who was the Defence Minister was handed additional responsibility of the Home Ministry till Sharad recovered and was ready to join office again. A moderate estimate of the time that Sharad would take for recovery suggested six months.

Gupta was the antithesis of Sharad – a pacifist who was extra cautious not to rub people the wrong way. So instead of adopting a pro-active approach to combat trouble, which was demanded of a Home Minister, he let things be as they were. This approach was fallacious to say the least. What added to my woes was the ignorance that was meted out to me. To begin with, my powers were clipped immensely. So I was merely left handling 'Police Reforms'. A new Deputy Minister was appointed who was now handling the areas that were previously with me.

Now there are certain ministries where continuity or at least a cautious transfer of power hold pivotal importance. This is because the people manning these ministries are privy to some extremely sensitive information and strategies which can get nullified if the successor doesn't make use of them. That caution was purposely thrown to the winds in this case caused immense heartburn to Sharad and me.

'Don't worry, it's a matter of a few months. I have a hunch that the PM too wanted to clip my powers, lest I become powerful enough to unseat him,' said Sharad.

What he had said was completely true. It is indeed sad that instead of rewarding merit, our country invariably rewards mediocrity. So what followed were two serial blasts on two consecutive days in Ahmedabad and Bangalore. The only consolation for us was that casualty figures in these blasts were low.

'It's a matter of time before I take charge again,' Sharad said to pep me up even as my patience began to wear thin.

❖

Sharad was discharged from hospital a month after he had been attacked. In the days that followed I realized that all was not well between Sharad and Rhea. At the core of the problem was the generation gap. But somewhere I felt there was an unusual bitterness in Rhea – maybe one that had resulted from not having got enough time or attention from her father in her formative years. Rhea's anger was understandable. As a girl who had lost her mother at the age of five, she had needed her father more than ever. That the father was absorbed with bigger issues of the country had probably led to a feeling of neglect in her. Gradually this neglect had manifested itself in her becoming a rebel of sorts.

I was sitting quietly in a corner of his room when Rhea had walked in. As usual she pointedly ignored me. She was speaking to her father about mundane things when she abruptly informed him about her American boyfriend, Derek.

'Come on, Rhea. You should focus on your career at this stage,' was Sharad's first reaction.

I am pretty sure that Sharad was not so much perturbed by her daughter having a boyfriend as he was by the antecedents of the guy whom she'd chosen.

When Rhea rubbished his concerns about her career, Sharad's next query was, 'How serious are you about this relationship?'

Rhea was her father's daughter. 'As serious as you are about your political career,' she said.

Sharad knew how much of a hara-kiri his daughter, who after all was his political heir, would be committing if she chose to go ahead and marry an American. Derek was of mixed blood, with a British father and Mexican mother, and had been brought up in Florida in the US. After all, Sharad's party at one point had run a massive campaign against the foreign antecedents of their opponent.

The issue had become a bone of contention between father and daughter, adding to his stress during his recovery.

Did Sharad need me during this difficult period – as friend and confidante?

I would think he did.

I was also inclined to think that at least part of Rhea's problems with Sharad was because of the preconceived notions she'd formed about the women in Sharad's life.

Sharad had mentioned to me once, in passing, that till a few years ago, Rhea had been keen that he get married again. 'In those days, I scoffed at the thought of it,' Sharad had said. 'Now she realizes that I'm married to power and that I'll be harming the woman's life I get married to. She probably thinks that women who get close to me do so for selfish gains. It's complicated.'

It was complicated indeed but the thought that Rhea's antipathy towards me wasn't personal, consoled me a bit.

❖

Not surprisingly, once again the way out of the mess that I found myself in came via extraneous developments that took place many hundred miles away.

By now, I had realized that democracy in India is a mockery of numbers. This time the mockery was enacted in my own state, Bihar.

Some six months were left for the Assembly elections in the state, when one-third of the MLAs of the ruling Bihar Lok Morcha, headed by Chintu Yadav, the brother-in-law of the CM, decided to break away from the party. Chintu was increasingly being sidelined by the party, who had closed down his illegal money minting businesses. Chintu in turn had revolted, alleging that he was merely the front-man for others who were the real kingpins. Without explicitly saying so, he had assumed the role of what in legal parlance is considered an 'approver' and looked determined to make the CM bite the dust.

This break-away faction was willing to support us – the Nationalist League – to form the government in the state. Now we were in a dilemma. Given that we liked to project ourselves as a 'principled party' it was clearly unethical to form the government in this manner. However, the other line of thought was that elections under Gangalal Yadav would anyway be rigged. (The Election Commission in those days wasn't half as effective in curbing the menace of rigging.) Therefore it made sense to form the government, launch some fresh populist initiatives and then go into the elections a few months hence, with full control over the state administration.

However, there was another problem that confronted us. While we did have three or four reasonably popular leaders in the state, there was none who could match the stature of Gangalal Yadav. It was in this situation that I got a call from Sharad, who wanted to meet me ASAP.

I went over to his place.

I was happy to see that he seemed much better. He still couldn't walk without help and had been advised to strictly avoid any physical movements that could cause exhaustion.

'Would you take over as Bihar CM?' he asked, sitting up in his bed, shocking me.

It took me a minute or two to realize the gravity of the offer that I'd been made and I stared at him in bewilderment.

'Think about it. I've already discussed this with the PM. No state-level leader in Bihar right now suits the profile we need. Besides, in Delhi, things aren't moving for you. It's a matter of six months. You'll have to lead the party in the Assembly elections. After the elections, we can take a call again. By then, I should also be back at the helm of the Home Ministry.'

On another occasion, I'd have dithered. Not this time. I wanted to get away from Sharad and Rhea. Sharad wanted the best for me. I wanted to escape from the snares that I'd invite in Sharad's absence. I needed an identity of my own. I realized that here was the opportunity which would help me prove my mettle; prove to the world that I was no pushover.

I accepted the gargantuan challenge.

❖

Two days later, I was sworn in as CM of Bihar. Among those present at the ceremony were the outgoing CM, Gangalal Yadav and a host of other politicians. What really surprised me was the presence of my folks – both my parents were there along with some relatives who had been close to us.

A whole gamut of memories – some pleasant, some not so pleasant and others outright horrible, swamped my mind. Indeed, a few hundred kilometres, north-east of Patna is where my story had begun; it had travelled to Patna where Rohit and I had pleaded helplessly for justice with this man who had now been shunted out of the office of CM.

And indeed these were the same parents who had virtually abandoned me when my mother-in-law made some sordid remarks about my character. Sharad would have been there had he been fit to travel. Instead there were two ministers from the Central government who graced my swearing-in.

This was my third oath-taking exercise in just a little over two years – the first as an MP, the second as a Deputy Minister and now as CM. I'm not sure if the frequency and the range of posts qualified me to be a record-holder of sorts.

Was I missing someone who'd complete the picture? Well, yes and no. I couldn't possibly forget the character who had stood by me through my worst and who disappeared when things got better. Did

Rohit drive me out of his life or was it the other way round? I doubted whether the query had an answer at all.

It would have taken me few days to get the official CM's bungalow. But since I was not willing to stay with my parents, I had insisted on being provided government accommodation immediately. And so I was temporarily allotted the bungalow of the Speaker of the Legislative Council, since he had moved into his private house and was not availing the facility.

❖

My first night in my new Anne Marg residence was intensely lonely – the sort of night that leaves one battling for sleep. I desperately needed to talk to someone. I felt burdened by the onerous position that circumstances had suddenly made me occupy. The next morning I was given a first-hand briefing of the problems confronting the state by the Chief Secretary attached to the Chief Minister's Office.

At least one-third of the districts had been reeling under drought. Some others were experiencing incessant killings – at times by the Naxals and at other times by the private armies formed by landowners. There were intelligence reports of a massive impending strike by one of the private armies called the Ranvir Sena. Besides, unemployment and crime were perennial problems.

With less than six months left for the elections, I knew I had to get down to the job with utmost urgency.

My first challenge was to constitute my ministry. And in so much as I disapproved of it I ended up employing what the situation demanded. I was expected to base my selection upon caste and not merit.

As I normally did in unfavorable situations, I turned to Sharad for counsel.

As usual he had a pragmatic answer.

'Make sure the ministry has a visible "backward" skew,' he told me. I immediately understood what he was getting at. His reasoning made mathematical sense. The upper castes were anyway with us and fragmented. But with the level of patronage that the backward castes enjoyed under Yadav, if we suddenly ignored them now, they would never stop voting for the Bihar Lok Morcha.

And so I did what the situation demanded; I appointed a deputy CM from the OBC.

This 'backward-bend' of Bihar was an interesting subject in itself. I had read about it intensively.

Two of Bihar's greatest leaders, Dr Rajendra Prasad and Jai Prakash Narain, never espoused caste-consciousness or the politics associated with it. The seeds of this shift were sown by Karpoori Thakur – a socialist leader who became CM of Bihar twice in the seventies. Interestingly, both Laloo Yadav and Nitish Kumar consider him their guru. A champion of Dalits and backward castes, Thakur's espousal of caste politics is what probably set the precedent for its more vicious variants to surface in the succeeding decades.

Since the politics of Bihar and U.P. are often intertwined, the socialism of the seventies led to the emergence of a host of powerful Yadav and Dalit leaders in the eighties and nineties in both states. What is disappointing is that these leaders had little to offer by way of principles and instead made socialism their first casualty.

But my last two years in politics had taught me to embrace the existing system before daring to change it. So I wasn't complaining.

A week into my chief ministership, my parents called me over to have a meal with them. It felt strange to go back home for a meal. Relations between us had been strained for a long while. It angered me that even my educated, doctor-parents did not have the social courage to openly acknowledge me; that they were ashamed of my being raped rather than being outraged about it. But my loneliness made me eager to grab the opportunity.

As we sat down to a dinner of my old favourites, I turned to my dad. 'Are you happy, Papa, with what I've achieved?'

This simple query from me had made him think. 'Yes Beta, we're happy,' he said, then paused before adding, 'We'll be even happier if you can be in a happy marriage.'

'Is a woman incomplete without marriage?' I asked, completely frustrated by their blinkered outlook.

'Both a man and a woman are incomplete. The responsibilities of raising a family are just as important as "karma".'

I had nothing to say to this or to them. I finished my meal in silence and returned home shortly thereafter.

❖

A couple of days later when I returned to my official residence late in the evening after a gruelling day of tours I found an unexpected visitor waiting at the gate. It was Rohit.

'I... I... well I just felt like talking to you,' he mumbled, seeing the shock on my face.

Half an hour later, we sat together sipping coffee. The conversation was still as sparse. 'Why are you here, Rohit?' I finally said, tired of the charade.

'Shruti, I want you back. Why can't we make a fresh start?'

I didn't find the statement as strange as the sheer absence of motive behind it. Did he miss me or did he hate being the CM's husband?

'Life has been incomplete without you,' he said unconvincingly.

Had he put this option to me earlier in my career, I would have succumbed to it. But the vagaries of destiny had made me my own woman. I needed a concrete and satisfactory rationale to precede my decisions. Here, I didn't seem to find any. And so I chose to do the next best thing I could – to try and avoid hurting him.

'Rohit, I don't think getting back is a wise idea. But I'll think about it.'

The complex being that Rohit was, he misconstrued my harmless words.

'Of course, it won't be a wise idea for a CM-wife to go back to her IAS-husband. It will be against, what you call it "protocol". We're glorified servants, anyway,' he said, his words dripping sarcasm.

'Is that the real reason why you want me back?' I snapped looking him directly into the eye.

'Don't forget that you are not here on your merit. First it was your rape and then your–'

'– Affair? That's what you want to say...'

'I'm glad that I didn't need to say it.'

'And you still want a "whore" back as your wife? Don't you have any standards?'

The vitriolic exchange was good in a way. The animosity between us only vindicated my unwillingness to give the relationship another chance. Rohit, quite naturally, didn't have an answer. I could see a strange obsession in him. It was as if being the estranged husband of the CM was some sort of a curse that he wanted to get rid of by showing to the world that he still possessed me. How could I make him realize that he had *never* possessed me?

His behaviour was to manifest itself in a bizarre, violent form. On an impulse, he suddenly forced himself on me, giving me no time to react at all. He pushed me onto the sofa, intending to forcibly have sex with me.

I was overpowered. I had the option of screaming, in which case, my security would have saved me. But I was found wanting in my resolve to ward off my second rape – this time at the hands of my own husband. Maybe, a part of me was curious to know the extent to which Rohit could go. Maybe a part of me didn't mind re-experiencing that which had become history for me.

As he lay on top of me, still holding me hard, Rohit realized the futility of his act. He broke down and confessed that he had lost it completely.

Ironically, even as he retreated and sought for-giveness, he had no shoulder but mine for support. I was left perplexed by the sheer absurdity of it all. I deserved a more sorted personal life. Actually, we both deserved a more sorted personal life.

15

Good and evil keep happening in this world. It just takes a little longer for us to take the bad in our stride. And just when we think we've come to terms with the bad, we're shocked to be haunted by that one query whose answer is ever as elusive – why on earth did it have to happen to me?

I strode into Patna's Beur jail. My face wore a look of extreme anger as two police officials led me to the cell I wanted to be taken to. Upon reaching my destination, I asked them to leave.

I was left facing Salim Yadav. A thick, overgrown beard was the only difference to his demonic countenance. He was stunned to see me there.

'Why?' I demanded and then screamed. 'Why the hell did it have to be me? Why did you rape me?'

Salim was stunned.

How often does it happen in any part of the world that a rape victim, by virtue of having lived that cruelty, goes on to assume a disproportionately powerful office and then comes back to the rapist to demand an explanation for what he had done.

Well I wanted an answer, an explanation. What if he couldn't come up with a satisfactory answer? Could I then avenge the heinous crime by inflicting the same upon him?

I could have him raped by one of the slightly deviant jail employees. I could let him loose upon this devil of a man! A rapist after all ought to feel what he makes his victim go through.

My blood was boiling. In a fit of sheer fury, I pulled him by the collar of his shirt, banged his head against the wall, unleashed a knife and stabbed him repeatedly in the groin while he howled in pain.

I woke up screaming in a cold sweat, my heart pounding. God help me. Would I ever erase that indelible scar from my mind? Even today, with Salim in jail, and after winning the case, my mind was still obsessed with it. Would a more retributive justice have given me closure? Can rapists be castrated for the evil they have done? Did my new empowerment mean that I could actually initiate a law like this?

I know my meteoric rise had little to do with personal accomplishment. When you get things you know you don't deserve, it affects you in either of the two ways. Either it makes you complacent; you start abusing the power you've got as you don't know its worth. The other possibility is that it humbles you and makes you extra modest about what you've achieved.

In my case, it was decidedly the latter; I went about my job as CM with extra caution, suppressing the anger in my heart.

❖

I felt completely lost and inadequate for the first couple of days in my new office. So vast was my area of work that I didn't know where to begin. Where do I start from? What do I prioritize? The sense of indirection reminded me of my initial days in Parliament and of the day when I'd first gone to meet Sharad at his South Block office. For some uncanny reason, it reminded me of the inscription in Sharad's office: *'Liberty will not descend to a people: a people must raise themselves to liberty. It is a blessing which must be earned before it can be enjoyed.'*

I quickly had that inscription installed in my office. Soon my days started to sort themselves out.

My day started at about 6:30 a.m. when I would try doing some surya namaskars – my way of living up to Sharad's idea of a stress-free and healthy life. By 8:30, I was interacting with the people who came to my residence for a 'darshan'. Cases of unpaid pensions, unjustified rustication, unemployment, grievances against a government department, pleas for medical aid, the police not reporting a rape case, etc. would be some of the issues that would stare me in the face the first thing every morning. I'd hear each one out before deputing my secretary to take the issue forward.

Personally speaking, I didn't approve much of the idea of people landing up at my residence with a bagful of complaints every morning. But that's because I would get deeply disturbed by the stories I heard. When an old man would tell me of his teenage son having been beaten up by policemen on frivolous charges, the story would linger in my mind the whole day, distracting me. I personally preferred to depute a full-time secretary in the CM's office who could handle just these grievances.

'Relax, Shruti, in public life, all these are a means of mass contact. Just desensitize yourself a bit and adopt a more clinical approach. Then such things won't hurt you.' That was how simplistically Sharad had summed up the situation when I'd spoken to him on the phone a couple of days ago.

However, on a short trip to Delh, when I met him a few mornings later, he sounded uncharacteristically depressed. I was worried about his health. Had there been a setback in his convalescence? When I asked him what the matter was he said, 'I'm fine. It's Rhea who is giving me a tough time. Her boyfriend Derek is in town and they are seen together all the time at the city's nightspots. At one point, we'd campaigned against the foreign antecedents of one of our rivals.

Now, the Opposition is going to use her behaviour to embarrass me. I wish she would realize this is not the life that I've slogged so hard for. It just hurts.'

I heard Sharad out. There was really nothing that I could suggest to him as a solution except to try and let go. Sharad had lived his life on his terms. Rhea being his daughter was entitled to live it on hers.

❖

Two months into my job, I was getting a hang of the rigmarole. Thanks to the massive overhauling of the administration, the crime rate had dipped. But that I was told would not suffice in undoing the regressive social engineering that Gangalal Yadav had manufactured over a decade. What were needed therefore were some populist schemes like making rice available at Re 1 per kilo in villages or promising free TV sets in the election manifesto. Personally I disliked gimmicks that drain the public exchequer. But if that is what wins you elections, does it leave you with any choice?

No politician is in politics to lose elections.

❖

While I was busy planning election strategy, I heard that Rohit's parents had gone over to meet my parents one day. This time around his mother was not hysterical.

'What has happened has happened. Now with Shruti as CM, she's at totally another level. We need to think of ways to end this relationship at the earliest,' is what she told my parents.

There was an obvious intent in my mother-in-law stating that I was at 'another level'. It was meant to reinstate Rohit as the sufferer between us. Had I been convinced either about me contributing to the deterioration of my marriage or about Rohit's strength as a husband, I'd have happily quit my role in politics and gone back to family life.

When Sharad discussed his daughter's problems with me, in a strange way it would remind me that I might never have a child or a normal family life, and the thought greatly saddened me.

What then held me back?

I think I was beginning to get the answer: I was finally unequivocally convinced that I could not spend the rest of my life with Rohit. Given his insecurities, if I tried getting back with him I'd be twice the unhappier. Besides, I did not want my personal life to be the butt of jokes. I think I had given our marriage a fair chance. Not everybody, after all, is destined for such pleasures. Ours was a dead marriage and acknowledging it as such made a lot of sense.

I called up Rohit. 'Rohit, I think we should go for a divorce.'

A silence preceded his response. 'Are you sure?'

I somehow felt Rohit still thought we could work it out. But I'd run out of patience and energy. 'Yes.'

'Okay,' was all he said before he hung up.

The only person I could talk to about these latest developments in my life was Sharad, who despite being several hundred kilometres away, felt closer to me than anyone else I knew.

'Well, I'm glad you think that way. What doesn't come naturally can't be stretched for too long,' he reasoned rationally, before adding something that augmented my woes. 'But just hang on for some time. The Indian public still likens its women to Sita – the epitome of sacrifice. If they get to know of your divorce prior to the elections, it will mar our chances.'

Two days later, on the insistence of Rohit's parents, the two families met, along with Rohit and me. It reminded me of the day when they'd first come to discuss our marriage. The irony in my case was that our divorce needed to be planned more meticulously than our marriage.

'I'm glad Shruti has agreed to a quick divorce,' said Rohit's father. 'We wish her luck in the future. Our son too needs to move on quickly.' Rohit's parents were enormously cautious. A quick divorce was in their interest.

'Rohit, can I have a word with you in private?' I said, surprising everybody.

We stepped out into our garden.

'What is it, Shruti?'

'Rohit, can we wait for a few more months before the divorce?'

Rohit was surprised. 'Wasn't it you who wanted it?'

'Yes. But… but… let's see for a few more months.'

'Till the elections get over?' he asked snidely.

I ran out of words, as guilt or maybe my helplessness got the better of me.

'I've suffered enough. I'll be filing for divorce right away. Come what may,' Rohit sounded uncharacteristically assertive as he walked away.

I felt like crying but I quickly abandoned the thought. Strong women, especially those in politics, should after all, be able to contain their emotions.

Next morning Rohit went and filed for divorce in the family court. In fact, the court issued summons to me for a hearing, which I conveniently skipped. I appreciated Rohit doing things discreetly. After all, if the media had known about this latest development, it would have found a new stick to beat me with.

❖

Two weeks later, after recuperating for four months as against the six he had been advised, Sharad rejoined office as the Home Minister. His voice was frail, even as his determination seemed stronger.

'I have an unfinished agenda,' was the only sound bite that the media got from him when he was quizzed about his priorities after rejoining office.

As elections in Bihar were drawing closer, I had to discuss the state's requirement for additional security forces during the elections with the Home Minister. The task had me land at Sharad's office and I sat with my mentor over another long, intense conversation.

'What's the latest on the investigations into your shooting?' I asked him.

'Ah… well… the investigations have managed to gather concrete evidence against eight Indians, four of whom are behind bars. The major breakthrough is of course nabbing Ismail Pasha, who we all believe heads the Lashkar-e-Hindustan. But there's something to worry about: this attack has a definite imprint of both the fugitive Indian don, Danny Khan and Pakistan's ISI.'

'Hmm… the usual suspects,' I said, before turning somewhat philosophical, 'Life can really be so predictable in its unpredictablity. There's often just a single moment that separates life from death, isn't it?'

'That's right. But the key is to minimize the possibility of that moment ever surfacing,' Sharad said pensively. By now I knew him well enough to know that a larger idea was perhaps brewing in his mind. And so it was.

'I want to end this menace of mercy petitions,' asserted Sharad. 'Why should we even consider mercy for the enemies of the country? Did the culprit feel mercy for me before attacking me? Was I allowed to file a mercy petition before anyone?'

Mercy petitions in India are indeed a joke. I would think that even death sentence in the Indian legal context is a joke, albeit a sick one; at least the data available with me seems to suggest so. There were over 300 convicts in India who had been sentenced to death by various courts and whose execution remained uncertain, in many cases because of the convict having challenged the verdict in a higher court. Worse, only 56 convicts had actually been hanged to death since Independence. Some 29 mercy petitions were pending before the President. Of these, seven pertained to terror cases.

Well, either the law of the country keeps the provision of death penalty or does away with it. To have a provision in the law which is liable to be entrapped in mercy petitions, which take as much time to be decided upon as the legal case itself, does not make sense. In my opinion, the death penalty is about as fair as the fate of the victim. If a society preserves its enemies, it makes itself liable to be attacked again and again. The provision for a mercy petition only worsens the problem. Indian Presidents apparently like to take an unusually long time to decide upon the petition. As a result, while the convict rests in jail, the country remains susceptible to potential attacks to free these convicts.

I was glad Sharad had made up his mind to fix the problem.

'It's been ages since we did something that shook up the world. It's high time the world stops seeing us as a meek nation,' Sharad asserted.

I looked on in anticipation as he spelt out his plan.

'I'm going to get all of these seven odd mercy petitions involving terror cases and pending before the President cleared in the next one month. In some cases, it's the concerned state government's home ministry that is to blame as they've been slow in providing additional information sought by the President's Office. It will be a humongous task but I have to do it.'

Truth be told, I was as surprised by Sharad's plan as I would've been had I been told that India had decided to wrest back Pakistan-occupied Kashmir by waging war.

'But what about its political fallout?' I queried.

'If I were to think about that, I'd be the same as any other Indian politician. India needs to send a message to the world: We are capable of rising above petty politics and take on the enemies of the land,' he looked into my eyes and added, 'I have to make this happen, Shruti.'

I knew Sharad better than most of the world; if anyone could bring about this change it was him. Besides, Sharad's anger could be rationalized.

Investigations into the attack carried out on him had corroborated the involvement of at least three banned outfits spread over six states across the country right from Kozhikode in Kerala to Jorhat in Assam. Moreover, these outfits were taking instructions from an agency in Islamabad.

His eyes shone with excitement as he spoke:

'Imagine seven terrorists being hanged to death one after the other. It would shake the world! More importantly that would be our manifestation of being a true superpower: one that can shun vote-bank politics and assure potential investors across the world that the Indian government is indeed capable of protecting the country!'

I was happy to see the old drive alive in Sharad. About the one difference that I could notice in him now was that he wasn't as unaffected by personal emotions. Having known Sharad so well, I knew what was bothering him.

'Rhea's behaviour saddens me. I want her to inherit my legacy one day. But she seems disinterested,' he said.

'Once they grow up children can't be controlled,' I tried to reason.

'It's not about controlling children. It's just... I don't know... I guess I'd be fine even if she tells me candidly that she's not interested in politics. But I want to see a sense of purpose in her. She's my daughter. She can't be wasting her life pub-hopping and holidaying, especially with that firang.'

For the first time I noticed that Sharad had a problem. Without meaning to, he tended to expect people to be like him: the closer the person, the higher his expectations. I'm still not sure what made us click. Maybe he saw in me what he was not, but would have wanted to be like had he not been so hard on himself. I saw in him what I was not but would have wanted to be to stop being such a loser in life. I'm not sure whether Sharad or I had influenced changes in each other's behaviour, but we did bask in the comfort of mutual disagreements.

'Shruti, can I ask you for a favour?' Sharad asked me suddenly in a mellow voice.

I nodded.

'I'd like you to sit and chat with Rhea. She knows I'm close to you. Somehow I haven't managed to be friends with my daughter. You're younger, maybe you'll be able to put across my point better.'

'But, Sharadji… it seems so odd.'

'It doesn't, Shruti. I can't ask anyone else to do this because in more than a decade now, I've not shared my personal life with anyone.'

I couldn't refuse Sharad. For his part, he explained exactly what he wanted me to do.

❖

That evening, Sharad, Rhea and I sat over dinner at his place. Derek, Rhea's boyfriend had gone to Agra with another American friend. Fifteen minutes into our conversation, Sharad excused himself on the pretext of an important con-call. I knew he wouldn't be back for half an hour.

'Gosh! Dad and his Thursdays! What has a day of the week got to do with your choice of food?' Rhea complained, looking at Sharad's plate that was devoid of all things non-vegetarian.

'Are you fond of chicken?'

'As much as I am of all the good things in life,' she replied.

For the next couple of minutes, both of us struggled to make conversation. I felt nervous sitting with Rhea. She was the same brat who'd given me the cold shoulder at the hospital. And now her father had entrusted me with the task of reasoning with her.

As I sat, preparing myself for the conversation, I was surprised by the strong maternal instinct I felt for her. Even though I was only a decade older than Rhea she brought back memories of my unborn child. She reminded me of the time when I was pregnant. What if I had a daughter who behaved just like Rhea? How would I have handled her?

'You aren't eating...' Rhea pointed out sensing my absent-mindedness.

'Rhea, would you like to go on a drive after dinner?' I said, surprising myself.

And then Rhea surprised me more by agreeing to my suggestion.

An hour later, we sat on the terrace restaurant of a five-star hotel over steaming mugs of coffee. A gentle, soothing breeze blew across, easing our tense dispositions. 'So, dear, tell me. How does it feel to be living in India after so long?' I asked.

'Well, the country has certainly moved forward but the people haven't. And by the way, I'm not living here yet. India is not my home.'

'You may be right.'

'I'm not wrong.' Rhea exuded a brash confidence that can so easily be construed as conceit. But at least, she was willing to chat.

'But don't you miss your dad when you're away?'

'Ah… well, when I'm abroad, I feel more at ease. I'd stopped expecting attention from Dad even when I was a kid. So now when I get that extra attention, the first natural reaction tends to be defiance.'

She got more emotional as the conversation got deeper. 'I love my dad, you know. I'd have loved it if he had given me more time when I was a kid. But that's okay. He had other priorities, which were equally important. But then at this stage, it gets difficult for me to live a life that he wants me to lead.'

'How serious are you about Derek? I mean, are you convinced that he is the guy you want to marry?'

'Yes. We've been together for five years. Of course, I couldn't tell this to Dad because I knew he'd always expected me to complete my studies and then get back to join him. But my life can't be that conditioned or planned. I love Derek and just can't think of ditching him…'

I heard her out. I was in a dilemma. I was meeting Rhea with a specific agenda. But I saw more reason in what she was doing. And since I had been feeling maternal towards her, I couldn't possibly have persuaded her to do something I did not think was in her best interests. Would I then go back to Sharad and convince him to not impose his decisions upon her? Even as I ruminated on this it was Rhea's turn to cross-examine me. 'How well do you know my dad?'

'Quite well, I should think. But of course not as well as you know him.'

Rhea then said something that left me stunned. 'You know what… I sometimes feel the two of you should get married.'

'What?'

'Both Dad and you have incomplete personal lives, which complement each other. Of course, the choice is yours – whether you decide on your own, like I did, or whether you let societal considerations prevail upon you,' Rhea said, sounding far more mature than her years.

I couldn't believe that it was Rhea saying this – the same girl who apparently detested me. I had found it unusual to feel motherly towards her. I found it more unusual now to see her prepared to accept me as her mother. The evening ended with a hug and yet another realization that my life wasn't done with its share of surprises.

That night, I kept thinking about my conversation with Rhea. From being complete strangers we had parted like kindred souls. Not the first time I had seen such a thing happen in my life. Obviously, there was just one thing that Rhea had said that lingered in my mind.

It kept me awake till the wee hours.

❖

The next morning, Abhay came down to see me before I boarded my flight to Patna. Somehow I had softened towards him after knowing what he was going through with Antara. He had made an effort to be in touch with me and I had tried to reciprocate that. Maybe I didn't want him to go through all that I had to undergo, because of him. I didn't know why.

As I was still preoccupied with my interaction with Rhea, I ended up telling him what Rhea felt about Sharad and me.

'Well, that's how the entire country feels,' Abhay smiled.

'Really?'

'Shruti, if you look at it closely, marriage is just a bourgeois necessity. You may not be married to someone and yet be more than husband and wife.'

My confused expression at what he said, made Abhay elaborate: 'It's always people around us who are more bothered about our marriage than we are. If you ask me, what is more important in your case, is to have that steamy partnership, as Sharad calls it, that would change the politics of this country, besides leaving a legacy behind.'

My surprise at having this conversation with Abhay notwithstanding, I thought his words made sense. The ease of our conversation had me enquire about the latest in his life. He told me of the emotional mess that his four-year-old daughter was going through.

'Abhay, can I suggest something to you? I think Antara and you should give it one more try, at least for the kid. From what I know you really love her. Try and forget that incident, and think about her.'

Abhay looked even more defeated when he heard me.

'I *have* forgiven her. After all, I've been in her position before. But getting back is impossible as she doesn't regret it. She said something about our relationship being "a confused and overstretched affair". When Abhay mentioned those words, I couldn't help laughing, a little sadistically, I'm afraid. Abhay too laughed with me for want of an option.

Strangely enough we were sharing a laugh after ages. The laughter though was shortlived, as Mishra, my secretary, walked in with a piece of terrible news:

In an early morning massacre at a village called Logai some twenty kilometres south of Jehanabad, a private army of the upper castes called the Ravinder Sena had gunned down sixty Dalits, half of whom were women and children.

This was the last thing I'd have wanted before the state went to the polls.

16

Have you ever wondered why so many families in Bihar have done away with their surnames and opted instead for names like Kumar, Ranjan, Suman, etc.? Well, surnames represent caste and in a society divided and polarized on caste lines, it makes sense to do away with something that has the potential to become a cause of friction in society.

Caste consciousness in Bihar is surprisingly an inherent phenomenon. I remember being a student of Class 4 at the Notre Dame Academy in Patna. Even in those days the upper-caste girls would poke fun at two girls in my class who went by the names Preeti Yadav and Rita Paswan. Where does a ten-year-old learn about caste discrimination, unless she hears her parents talk about it at home? Often parents don't do so deliberately. In discussing social or political developments, they end up letting out information that impressionable minds are liable to interpret in their own way. The years when I was growing up saw a huge socialist revolution in Bihar, which ironically only worsened the caste divide in the decades that followed.

So, in 1992, when Gangalal Yadav became the CM, he virtually created a separate electorate, based on caste equations. Social engineering became so over riding in his politics that development was systematically shunned and crime encouraged, by turning a blind eye to it. Upper-middle-class and rich residents of Patna still recall horror stories of extortions, kidnappings, threats and murders during Yadav's regime.

My rape, obviously was the culmination of this 'Jungle Raj'. It is worth noting that the migration of Bihari professionals to other states touched unprecedented figures during these years. So much for the lofty ideals of socialism that our leaders never ceased to glorify!

Interestingly, the resurgent socialist movement of the seventies had coincided with an extremist offshoot of the Marxists in Bengal starting the Naxal movement. Landless, suppressed peasants from backward castes were mobilized to attack upper-caste landlords. The movement was bound to spread to neighbouring Bihar, which along with Bengal led the Naxal movement.

Now every action has an equal and opposite reaction. Upper-caste landlords in Bihar, particularly Bhumihars, formed their own private army called the Ravinder Sena, to return the favour of Naxals. This group would select small Dalit majority villages in central Bihar – particularly those in Gaya, Nalanda, Biharsharif, Jehanabad – and bleed them at will. Bihar, thus, suffered twice over – from Naxalite strikes and then from retaliatory upper-caste strikes. As the years went by, on many occasions, the Ravinder Sena would strike first, following which the Naxals would retaliate.

❖

I reached Logai, a small village that housed some 500 Dalits at 2 in the afternoon. 12 per cent of the village's population lay in front of me in the form of corpses. This was the second most morbid experience for me after the massacre at Dantewada. Had Sharad not been with me at Dantewada, I'd have possibly fainted. Strangely, giving me company this time round was Rohit Verma, my estranged husband, who happened to be the Deputy Commissioner of the district. Also present were Home Minister of Bihar Suryakant Pathak, Director General of Police B. C. Sen and the local MP Sukhjivan Ram.

How I wish I could have avoided the sight of sixty corpses burning together. I couldn't. Seeing my distress, Rohit came forward and held my hand – a gesture I was thankful to him for. I was weak and anguished and was about to hug him when the sight of TV cameras focused on me held me back. I did not want Rohit to suffer, once again, the consequences of TV footage that showed him that close to the CM.

After the mass funeral, things were bound to go out of control. Incensed family members of the dead converged around me, wailing and shouting out their grievances. Apparently, the Ravinder Sena had warned the village of a 'calamity' nearly a month back, after one of the villagers, Bhiku, working in a landlord's house, had fled with cash and jewellery on the eve of a marriage in the family. Bhiku had since not been traced. The villagers, on the other hand, denied the allegations and instead alleged that Bhiku had been murdered by the landlord. Whatever the truth, it did not justify the massacre of innocents. I shuddered to think that some parts of our country still witnessed such medieval barbarism.

Even as public anger was hard to contain, the local MP, Sukhjivan Ram, who belonged to the Opposition Bihar Lok Morcha alleged that he had met Rohit personally a week ago to request for additional police cover to the village especially in the wake of the Ravinder Sena threat. If Rohit had heeded his advice, he said, the massacre could have been averted. The state DGP at this stage only seconded the MP.

'In fact I had passed on intelligence reports warning of a possible attack on this village to both the DC and the SP. I wonder why no action had been taken.'

In no time, the onus had entirely shifted upon Rohit, putting me in an even more embarrassing situation.

'We will order a high-level inquiry into the lapses,' I said, attempting to defuse the situation. 'I promise the finding of the enquiry will be made public within a month.'

Just as I thought the situation was under control, a young female TV reporter virtually pounced on me: 'Ma'am, how can you treat the matter so casually? Should your husband not be answerable, right here and now, if he is responsible for not taking the threat seriously?'

Before, I could answer, the MP joined in: 'Of course! This useless DC can't get away just because he is lucky enough to be the CM's husband.'

In no time, the villagers were up in arms against Rohit and the SP, demanding an answer. I hated my fate for putting me in yet another difficult situation. I felt terrible for Rohit. I was even more worried about the situation turning violent at any point of time.

'Yes, I had been informed of the threat. But the extra policemen who were supposed to join us from the Raxaul district took time to arrive here. And just when they were supposed to reach here, I got a request from my counterpart in Gaya asking me for extra forces for the rally of Sharad Malviya this weekend.' Rohit's reply only worsened the situation for me.

'Did you ask me before letting the police team go to Gaya?' the DGP asked him sternly.

'No, I did not because I was told by my Gaya counterpart that the instructions had come from the state Home Minister, Suryakant Pathak.'

Pathak defended himself by saying that Rohit could have simply asked for another police team for the village, given its threat perception.

'Come on, sir. You know that with elections round the corner there is heavy demand in every district. I have already put in two requisitions in the last two weeks but there has been no response,' Rohit tried to reason with his accusers.

By this time, the villagers were running out of patience. Sensing their mood, the opportunist MP, Sukhjivan Ram, went for the jugular: 'The fact is Rohit is an incompetent officer who does not even attend office regularly. So now he is making up all sorts of silly excuses.'

The police formed a barricade to keep the angry villagers at a distance. They were now generously hurling invectives at me and Rohit. In the crazy situation that prevailed, I ended up publicly berating Rohit: 'Rohit, you are an experienced administrator. You can't be making excuses. If you were facing such a grave crisis, you could have just called me.'

Rohit was stunned to hear me speak to him like this. 'Why don't you ask your Home Minister under whose instructions it happened?' he retaliated.

'Come on, don't blame me. You know the requirements of your districts the best,' Pathak cleverly put the onus on Rohit.

At this point, Rohit went berserk with anger and started shouting at me: 'Fair enough, Shruti. I am responsible. As your husband, I am responsible for the death of sixty people. Is everyone happy to hear that? Why don't you ask Sharad Malviya to have me hanged along with the terrorists?' Saying this, he stomped off.

I was left in a pathetic situation.

I turned to the crowd and pleaded with them to give me three days, promising to personally investigate the lapses and take action against the guilty.

'Madam, can we expect you to sack Rohit Verma for abdicating his responsibility?' the MP asked cheekily.

❖

On my way to Patna in the helicopter, I kept thinking about the unnatural turn of events that took place at the village. The death of villagers was devastating; what was more unnerving for me personally was the death of the Rohit I had known in the early months of our marriage. I recalled the persuasive, never-say-die crusader that Rohit had once been. To see him reduced to a pale shadow of his former self, hurt me to no end. What if Rohit had not been able to concentrate on work due to his personal problems?

In that case, since the personal problem involved me, could I shirk my part of the blame? I knew I couldn't escape my guilt.

That night I stayed awake, pacing the empty rooms of my house all night. I knew that for Rohit's sake, I had to get out of his life at the earliest. At the same time, doing so right away would mean committing political hara-kiri. That night, for the second time in my life, I seriously felt like ending my life. This time too, I went for the sleeping pills.

However, just as I was about to pop them, something held me back. It was the revulsion I felt for everything around me. I would have to set certain things right before I left or my guilt would not let me die in peace. Instead I popped a solitary pill that helped me fall into a deep, dreamless sleep.

❖

A month went by. Election dates had now been announced. In order to ensure maximum security on each polling day, the elections were to take place in four phases spread over a month. The first polling day was just ten days away and since Jehanabad was to go to the polls in the first phase, campaigning for the elections had me visit the district yet again. At the eleventh hour, Sharad Malviya decided to join me. His point was that a senior national leader visiting a place that has recently been struck by tragedy, leaves a bigger impact.

The thought of addressing the people of Jehanabad made me feel awkward. One, because I still hadn't come to terms with making a political issue out of personal tragedy. Two, I'd have another brush with Rohit, what with him overseeing all security arrangements during our visit. I hadn't spoken to Rohit since our last encounter at Logai village, despite getting another court summons in the divorce case filed by Rohit. The fact that an investigation was still on into possible administrative lapses leading to the Jehanabad massacre had left very little room for conversation between Rohit and me. I was in fact, waiting for the elections to get over quickly so that I could free Rohit from the bondage of our failed marriage.

I drove down to Jehanabad from Patna, while Sharad arrived directly in his helicopter, which landed in a small field, adjoining the municipal grounds, where the rally was being held. In a rally attended by nearly 15,000 people, we promised to eradicate caste violence from the state. We pledged to make 'development' the only guiding agenda of our politics in future. Most importantly we assured peace and safety for women. As I addressed the gathering, I was surprised to find the people paying close attention – more so during my speech than during Sharad's. I felt good about it. If I did win these elections, it would mark my coming-of-age in politics. I was also relieved I had not encountered Rohit so far.

It remained a bit cloudy that day and just as we were coming to the end of the rally, it started to rain. In no time, wind and thundershowers had taken over. The rains had us wind up a bit early. After a brief spell of thundershowers, the drizzle continued. It was getting dark and since we were scheduled to hold a press conference in Patna late evening, Sharad and I decided to fly down to Patna without waiting further. In any case, the drizzle seemed pretty innocuous.

Just as the door of the helicopter was shut and we were all set to take off, the pilot reported that there was someone outside who was gesturing at the helicopter to stop. I looked out of the window. It was Rohit, drenched to the skin, walking towards the helicopter. He was waving his arms, signalling to us to stop. I knew Rohit was in great distress. There were five other people in the helicopter who I did not want to be privy to our conversation. Instead, I asked the flight attendant to open the door. Before Sharad could say anything, I stepped out of the helicopter, and walked towards him least concerned about the rain.

'What happened, Rohit? Is everything okay?' I asked him, worried.

His face was contorted with stress. It took him a while to speak and when he did, it left me distraught.

'Shruti, please, let me go. Give me the divorce.'

'Rohit…'

'All you need to do is be present in the court and sign a set of papers. I'll ensure you won't need to appear more than once. But for God's sake, I can't afford to be seen as your husband anymore. Trust me, it's become a curse for me.'

Rohit's words were uttered in a choked voice – an indication of the mental chaos that he was battling.

Seeing him in this state, I lost my composure. 'I will, Rohit. I'll do it at the earliest.' Even as I said this, I couldn't help succumbing to my emotions. 'Rohit, I am truly sorry for what you're going through. Please forgive me... forgive me if you can for things are beyond my control now.'

By the time I said this, I was in tears. It had begun to rain heavily, and my tears merged with the rain trickling down my face. I hadn't realized how weird it may have seemed for people to see us interact like this until Sharad called from the aircraft's door.

'Shruti, is everything okay?'

I didn't have an answer.

'Can we leave? The press has already arrived for the Patna meet.'

It took me a while to gather myself before I walked back into the aircraft. As we took off I could see Rohit standing there, in the downpour.

The grief that he was battling inside made the downpour seem small in comparison.

❖

Sharad, true to his style and words, made the impossible happen. In just two months, he managed to get all the seven mercy petitions of the convicts facing death sentence in terror cases cleared. These petitions carried little merit and hence had to be rejected; that they had taken so long to be addressed corroborated another instance of stone-walling in our political system. I wondered at times whether Indian politics would ever rise above beating around the bush. Would I too lose my zest as I spent more years in politics?

Strangely, these executions were scheduled just two days prior to the first phase of polling in Bihar. Sharad knew that they would enhance the perception of a ruthless, no-nonsense administration that our party was committed to. Now it was obvious that these executions were timed anticipating their political gains; yet the Election Commission could do little about it, as technically there was no way they could be linked to the Bihar government administration.

Thus history was created when nine terror convicts, convicted of waging war against the nation were hanged to death one after the other.

A leading US daily wrote: *'India, known to glorify its weaknesses with virtues of self-restraint and patience, today stunned the world by doing something extraordinarily radical… These executions will go down as one of the most defining moments for Indian politics, post Independence. It might effectively dispel the increasing notion of India being a soft, vulnerable and helpless state…'*

The article went on to say, *'These executions have restored confidence in India's ability to fight terror on its own. Post this, India will perhaps refrain from acting as cry baby the next time a terrorist attack is sponsored by Pakistan; neither would it need to complain to Big Daddy US and coax it to impose sanctions against Pakistan. In its own way, these executions might be the first manifestation of the fact that India henceforth is prepared to act like a superpower, undeterred and unbothered by internal and external constraints.'*

I called up Sharad that day and congratulated him for the audacious step.

'Well, it had to happen. Even our PM who normally tends to disagree with me, was in agreement.' He laughed before adding, 'Of course the only people who're unhappy are the human rights groups. But that's okay. You can't keep everybody happy. And personally speaking, I don't think I'm even inclined to make the futile effort.'

Soon after the terrorists were executed, the state went to the polls. One after the other, five rounds of polling took place. And after each phase, I felt stronger. When you're a serious, seasoned politician, strong public support or the lack of it is something that you can sense. It's like waking up one day and feeling energetic or waking up another day to feel weary without reason. I could sense that we had been successful in driving home our promise of a better administration. A shoe-hurling episode at Gangalal Yadav at one of his rallies, only corroborated the public anger that had been building up against him.

When polling ended on the last day, I heaved a sigh of relief. The counting of votes was to start two days later. The exit polls however, had predicted a victory for us. For weeks during the election cam- paign, I had avoided thinking about Rohit, despite my behaviour making me feel very petty.

I had a task at hand and, as Sharad would've done in my situation, I chose to concentrate on my 'karma'. However, once the polling was through, I had to face the inevitable. I was plagued by the two most recent images of Rohit in my mind – one, when I berated him in public at the Logai village and two, that of Rohit begging me for a divorce before my helicopter took off from Jehanabad. Even if I won the elections handsomely, I knew I'd feel like a loser for what I had put Rohit through.

I wanted to apologize to Rohit and extend my full cooperation in ensuring that the divorce came through at the earliest. Unable to buy peace with my conscience, I decided to visit him immediately. I took the three hour journey to Jehanabad incognito, hoping to reduce my guilt, if not get rid of it completely.

I must have arrived at the Collector's bungalow at around 10:30 p.m., which if I knew Rohit well, wasn't late at all. Besides, all I was looking for was maybe a half-hour conversation that could make us both feel better about the hopeless situation that we were in. As I waited outside after informing Rohit's driver of my presence, a woman came out. She was in her mid-twenties, fair and with sharp features. She looked at me questioningly.

'I want to meet Rohit,' I said.

'He doesn't want to meet you,' she responded rather sternly.

'Sorry, I don't recognize you,' I said.

'You don't have to. I'm Shyamlee. It will suffice for you to know that I am Rohit's friend.'

I found it strange. I mean, Rohit was not the sort to have intimate female friends. But then did I still have the authority to question this woman? I debated for a while and then I decided against it. 'Listen, I want to help both of us get a quick divorce. That's what I'm here for.'

'He doesn't need your sympathies. If you really care for him, make sure that you are present in the court on the next appointed date,' Shyamlee said scathingly.

I felt like the official divorce notwithstanding, I had already been replaced. I retreated without uttering a word. On my journey back to Patna, I felt an even greater urgency to complete the formalities of divorce.

And so it was. Two days later, when the counting of votes began, I wasn't at the counting centre or at the party office or in the CM's office. Instead Rohit and I were at the Family Court signing our divorce papers. Shyamlee was with him. By my side stood Sharad. I wished Rohit all the best for his life ahead, even apologizing for the pain he may have gone through because of me.

Rohit, on his part, was bitter: 'I don't feel like wishing you the best. Such formalities are contrived. However, I do hope you don't have to go through the anguish that I've gone through these last few weeks.'

❖

Around the same time that I was signing my divorce papers, the election results started pouring in. We were in for a big triumph, leading in almost 60 per cent of the constituencies. The results had exceeded our own expectations. It was the biggest political triumph of my career – all the other victories had been flukes. However, Rohit's parting words kept ringing in my ears with such intensity that the congratulatory cheers seemed to pale in comparison.

Next morning, the front page of a leading daily read: *A Victory and a Defeat for Shruti Ranjan.* I was not sure my divorce was a defeat. It was a victory of hope and of life. Rohit had something better in store for him. And me? I wasn't sure. All I knew was that

I was now in a better position to plan a future on my own terms.

Life, after all, is about second chances; sometimes maybe even a third.

❖

The election results were a watershed in Bihar politics. After fifteen years, we had managed to rid the state of the trap of caste politics. Hence, expectations from the new government were quite naturally very high.

As the Nationalist League had fought the elections with me as CM, it could be implied that the mandate was for me to continue as CM. But for reasons that weren't clear in my head, I felt very uncomfortable staying back in Patna.

Even as party legislators insisted that I continue, I tried to stave them off saying I was keener to contribute my bit at the national level. Sharad knew the reason I didn't want to stay on in Bihar but felt that Bihar was where I could truly prove my mettle.

So three days after the election results were out, a massive swearing-in ceremony of the new CM and her council of ministers took place at Patna's Gandhi Maidan. I took oath a second time as the chief minister of Bihar. Several national-level leaders of our party, including Sharad Malviya, were present at the ceremony. As the swearing-in was coming to an end, Sharad's PA virtually barged onto the dais where Sharad was seated.

I knew something was terribly amiss.

And so it was.

A group of militants had taken Rhea and her boyfriend hostage near Kargil, while they were on their way to Leh from Srinagar on a holiday.

A pall of gloom descended upon the stadium.

17

The town of Kargil is located 205 kilometres east of Srinagar, almost mid-way, if one is travelling from Srinagar to Leh. The place, with its difficult terrain and equally hostile weather conditions, is a hotbed of infiltration from across the border. These factors, obviously, had proved inadequate in dissuading the rebel in Rhea from making a rather adventurous road trip from Srinagar to Leh, along with her beau, Derek, and two other friends.

The consequences, as we were to discover, were disastrous, preparing the nation for another tryst with Kargil.

Just 22 kms before Kargil, on a desolate spot near the village Karbu, three militants had attacked the jeep in which Rhea and her boyfriend were travelling and had taken them hostage. The hostages were holed up in a nearby mosque.

Before night, the terrorists had laid out their demands: Release Ismail Pasha, along with four other militants arrested in connection with the attack on Sharad Malviya and provide them safe passage, or else all the hostages will be shot dead.

The incident shook the entire country. Most of all, it devastated Sharad. For obvious emotional reasons, his daughter's abduction was a humongous blow to him. More significantly, it presented the ultimate test of his political career.

Sharad was furious and frightened. He screamed out his frustration, at times on the terrorists – 'Bloody cowards! Is this how they intend to liberate Kashmir? By attacking our women?' And at other times upon his daughter – 'Why did she have to do this? She could have at least informed me about this road trip.'

Never does a man feel as defeated as when he is let down by the people he loves the most. Even the most ambitious of men have a tender side. And Sharad's weakness lay exposed by this crisis. Even though the Indian army had encircled the mosque in question, everybody, Sharad included, was clueless about how this crisis would pan out.

A day went by.

This was the second occasion in our country when the daughter of a leading politician had been abducted and the third when a mosque was used as a battleground. In December 1989, barely days after Mufti Mohammad Sayeed became the country's Home Minister in the VP Singh-led government, his daughter Rubaiya was kidnapped in Srinagar. The abductors demanded the release of five militants and the government was only too willing to acquiesce. This meek surrender by the government is said to have been the turning point for militancy in the valley. Bolstered, the militants intensified violence to peak levels in the early nineties. On another occasion, when some dreaded militants took refuge in a mosque, instead of killing or apprehending them there, our government gave them safe passage.

With Sharad at the helm, it was unlikely that the government would bow under pressure. But what option did Sharad have? At the end of the second day, the terrorists had set a clear deadline: another 48 hours. Sharad refused to commit and instead shut himself off completely from the media, giving little hint of what his plan of action would be.

About the only development to take place so far was the appointment of a two-member team headed by the Home Secretary, D.K. Menon, which had left for Karbu to negotiate with the militants. There was a bit of confusion at this stage as rumours trickled in about there being more hostages inside the mosque, apart from Rhea and Derek.

I had virtually abandoned my responsibilities in Patna to be by Sharad's side through the crisis. I spent the night sitting in Sharad's office room at his residence. There were two other Cabinet Ministers along with me. All we could do was dole out empty assurances to Sharad that all would be well. Sharad remained grimly impassive even as he was regularly fed the latest information and updates from the ground. No headway seemed in sight. And then at around two in the morning, he got a call from the Army Chief of the J&K region.

'Sir, the terrorists want to speak to you.'

Sharad nodded his consent right away. A cordless phone was sent to the terrorists inside the mosque, and a man called Lateef came on the line.

'Janab, *kaise mizaaj hai?'* he said with a laugh.

'Tell me what you have to,' Sharad said tersely,

'Your daughter is very beautiful, looks more so when she is vulnerable, like now. Unfortunately, she could be living her last few moments.'

'Don't challenge the might of this country.'

Lateef chuckled and gave the phone to Rhea. Her voice was incoherent and choked, indicative perhaps of torture, mental and physical, or maybe both. 'Dad, save us, Dad. I'm sorry for landing you in this position. I'm really sorry, but...'

Before she could complete her sentence, the phone was grabbed from her.

I could feel Sharad's anguish and his anger. And yet, he kept his composure. At one point he suddenly turned to us and asked, 'Do you really think they'll harm my daughter? I mean they would lose their goodwill among the Kashmiri people, if they did that, won't they?'

'They may not harm your daughter. But remember, there are three foreigners as well, apart from your daughter,' remarked the HRD Minister, S.K. Mishra.

Sharad sipped his eighth cup of nimbu chai post dinner and looked on. If public opinion is what bothers politicians the most, then in this case, Sharad did not have much to worry about. People, by and large, seemed to be on his side. Even the Leader of the Opposition was being supportive if one were to take his comments at face value: 'Nobody doubts Sharad's integrity or his commitment to fight terrorism. Therefore, we'd support the government in whatever it decides to do in this grim situation.'

Sharad was experienced enough to take his comments with a pinch of salt. 'People are large-hearted towards me because somewhere they believe I'll not surrender to the militants. They may react differently if I actually do.'

At Karbu, after a series of negotiations via microphones, which went on for two full days, Home Secretary Menon was successful in whittling down the militants' demand to the release of just three militants, which obviously included Ismail Pasha. The country heaved a minor sigh of relief, anticipating the end of the hostage crisis.

There was a cause of worry, though. The militants now released photos of two other women, unrelated to Rhea's group, whom they claimed had also been taken hostage by them. The deal was that these two women, who looked like locals, would be released only a day after the government had released the militants from the Indian jail and after all the terrorists had got safe passage. This one day period would allow the terrorists to escape without being brutalized by the army. The identity of these other women remained a mystery. However, the militants holed up inside would not entertain any other discussion beyond their demand for the release of their colleagues.

The next morning, Prime Minister Yashwant Modi convened a meeting of the Cabinet to discuss the crisis. Three ministers spoke on the issue, the External Affairs Minister O.P. Krishna, HRD Minister S. K. Mishra and Sharad's bête noire, Ratna Pandey. With the exception of Ratna, the others were inclined to vest full authority with the PM and Sharad on this matter. Ratna, as usual, played the role of the Opposition within the Cabinet to perfection.

'The point is, would the government have considered releasing the militants had Rhea not been the daughter of the Home Minister? Besides, what face will it leave us with? Won't we be seen as hypocrites?'

Mishra retorted in a rather confrontationist manner to this: 'If you just concentrate on your ministry, the Food and Civil Supplies Ministry, which is by far the most corrupt in this Cabinet, things would be a lot better for this government.'

This sharp exchange led to ugly and inopportune sparks flying between the two ministers. The meeting ended by passing a resolution vesting full authority in the PM and the Home Minister to take a decision on the matter. After this, the PM and Sharad met separately at the former's office.

'We're reaching a bit of a dead end,' said the PM. 'There are only two options. One, to attack the militants, in which case we might win public support, but you might lose a lot. The other option is to release the terrorists. With your capabilities, I'm confident we can nab them back soon. What do you say?'

Sharad had never been in such a difficult situation. He took a while before he spoke. 'Sir, I don't favour releasing militants.'

'What if you lose your daughter? Are you prepared for that?'

Sharad didn't have an answer. His eyes grew moist, even as he battled to keep his emotions in check. 'I can't say I won't mind losing my daughter.'

The meeting ended with the PM deciding that the militants would indeed be released. About the only contention now was to ask the negotiator Menon to try and bargain further and bring down the militants' demand to the release of just two terrorists. That eventually did not happen. It was decided therefore that next morning Sharad would leave with the three militants for Srinagar in a special aircraft, from where they would take a helicopter to Karbu.

❖

That night I stayed with Sharad. I could not leave him alone on this dreadful night. He was a broken man: 'Why did I have to land in this miserable situation, Shruti? What will my credibility be after I escort three dreaded militants and let them go? To think, all this should happen to me because of my daughter's carelessness...'

The sad thing about these questions, which Sharad was perhaps yet to realize, was that they didn't have answers. I had lost my husband in the call of duty. But Sharad losing his daughter, for whom he'd been building up his legacy, was next to unthinkable. And hence Sharad chose to accept the situation the way it was.

'It will be the biggest defeat of my life, but the fact is I can't afford to lose my daughter,' he said, even as tears trickled down his cheeks.

We spent the rest of the night seated together on his sofa in dimmed light. I held his hand reassuringly to let him know that I still found him brave and that I was with him every bit of the way in this, his darkest hour.

The next morning, according to plan, Ismail Pasha and two other militants were released from Tihar jail. Sharad flew with them to Srinagar and then to Karbu. By two in the afternoon, Sharad, along with the three militants, stood outside the mosque where the high drama was unfolding. More than 200 army men guarded the mosque from all four sides.

Lateef took over the microphone.

'Welcome, Home Minister sahab. We're glad you've got our brothers with you.'

'Release the children. Only after we're convinced that they are safe will we hand over the militants to you,' Sharad responded.

'You think we're crazy? Once we release the kids, what guarantee do we have that you'll not attack us?'

It was then decided to release the terrorists and hostages in two lots. Sharad was adamant that all four women ought to be released in the first lot, while Lateef insisted on Ismail Pasha being released first. After a bit of a deadlock, a compromise was worked out. The Indian contingent would release two militants other than Ismail Pasha first. Simultaneously, the militants would release two women – Rhea and one of her friends. And so it was. The two terrorists started walking towards the mosque, while the hostages started walking towards Sharad and the army personnel. Soon enough, Sharad's daughter was back with him. The father, who seldom wore his emotions on his sleeves, this time made an exception. He hugged his daughter hard, like he'd grabbed her back from the jaws of death.

'Home Minister sahab... now can we have Ismail Pasha?' shouted Lateef.

'Yes. We'll release him. But you must simultaneously release all the hostages.'

'Don't crack jokes, Minister sahab. We'd made it clear that the two women will be released only one day after we've got safe passage.'

In the second lot, Ismail Pasha was to be exchanged with Derek and Peter. As movement started from both ends, the high voltage tension was palpable.

And then, right at that point, Sharad it seemed had a change of heart. He signalled to the NSG commando who stood by him and the commando responded by shooting Ismail from behind. And so it was. The fact that the NSG commando had shot with a soundless sten-gun led to some confusion about what had really happened. All this happened at a critical moment, when Derek had covered only one-third of his journey to safety.

'Fire,' Sharad shouted to the State Army Chief. 'I said attack the enemy,' he reiterated.

The army swung into action in no time. One group of soldiers rushed towards Derek in order to pull him to safety. Another set of soldiers formed a cordon around Sharad and Rhea. A third took charge of the wounded Ismail Pasha. Taken by surprise, the militants inside the mosque took a while to retaliate. Within minutes, both sides opened fire. About the only one who was not lucky enough to escape unhurt was Derek, who sustained a bullet wound to his shoulder, even as the army was pulling him to safety.

Bullets were exchanged generously from both sides for almost an hour thereafter. At least five armymen were killed. What confused the Indian side was that bullets were being fired by more than five people (assuming that the two militants just released were also firing), which in effect meant that they could not be sure about the exact strength of militants holed up inside. Nonetheless, the gun battle raged until the armymen stormed the mosque. In the end, there were seven attackers who were shot dead. Shockingly two among them were women – the same women who had been projected as kidnapped locals by the militants and whose pictures were circulated to trick and deceive the Indian establishment.

The wounded Ismail Pasha was retaken captive by the Indian Army. Rhea was safe. However, the same could not be said about Derek. Derek was bleeding profusely. Sharad had him flown to Srinagar immediately. However, time had run out for Derek, who was pronounced dead on arrival at the hospital. What thus could have been another victory for Sharad turned into a personal loss with the death of his daughter's boyfriend.

When quizzed by the media, Sharad later confessed that his instructions to the NSG commando and the Army Chief had been spontaneous and not thought-out.

'As we released the militant Ismail Pasha and he started walking towards the mosque, something happened to me. I can't exactly describe it, but I knew we'd lost another battle against terrorism. The same militant would then have regrouped and struck us bigger blows and killed far more people. At that moment, my personal loss seemed inconsequential.'

'Can it be implied that you were willing to sacrifice Derek, but not your daughter?' asked a journalist.

Sharad controlled his anger to say, 'I will not dignify the question by answering it.'

❖

Having been with Sharad through the crisis, I knew how burdened he was with guilt. The reaction to the Karbu episode was mixed. Some in the press questioned his actions. While most praised Sharad for eventually not compromising his hard stand against terror even if that meant risking his daughter's life, others were not so kind. It pained me to see the effect all this was having on Sharad's confidence. At times, he seemed as shaken as I had been after my rape.

There is no dearth of conspiracy theories in politics. And one such theory, wicked as it was, insinuated that Sharad had killed two birds with one stone by eliminating Derek. At a time when Sharad was trying his level best to build bridges with his daughter, such stories were the last thing he wanted.

One night I was witness to him virtually breaking down in front of Rhea.

'I'm sorry, Rhea. I'm really, sorry. I swear I did not want Derek killed. I was confident he would be pulled to safety. I just couldn't let Pasha escape like that.'

The daughter pulled her weeping father's head onto her lap and caressed and comforted him like a mother. He was grateful that Rhea understood and forgave him.

After Rhea went to bed, I went up to Sharad and wrapped my arms around him. He rested his head on my shoulder as his body wracked with sobs. For once he was defeated. For once he had no words to offer.

In a strange way, the incident bridged the distance between Sharad and his daughter. Sharad supported her through her personal loss while Rhea began to show more empathy and understanding towards her father. I was finally able to go back and concentrate on my responsibilities in Patna, where people and the media had become increasingly critical of their 'missing CM'.

❖

A Cabinet re-shuffle was on the cards. Two days before that, at around midnight, I was woken by a telephone call. It was Sharad. My instant reaction was of fear: was he all right? Was everything fine? What emergency would have him call at that hour?

'Shruti, I need you with me in Delhi,' Sharad said gruffly. Though he had been firm as a rock during Rhea's kidnapping, he was now falling apart. He sounded like a man who was short on confidence. And for me, who owed my confidence to him, nothing could have been a bigger shock. His voice sounded lacklustre and abject, shorn of its usual energy, 'Join me in Delhi as the Minister of State for Home. As you know, I still have an unfinished agenda.'

The next day I surprised everyone, including myself, by resigning as Bihar CM. Strangely, I didn't in the least feel insecure giving up the post I had defended so rigorously in the elections just two months ago. I had long come to terms with the fact that my political career was essentially what my mentor wanted it to be and I was just fine with that.

There was, of course, the danger of me getting dubbed as Malviya's stooge. So what?

A day after quitting as Bihar CM, I was inducted as the Union Minister of State for Home. Once again I was Sharad's deputy, helping him attain his 'unfinished agenda'. Once again, events had come full circle for me. In a strange way, I'd begun to feel such equanimity around Sharad that it almost felt as if his unfinished agenda was mine.

One day, Sharad asked me to meet him in his office for a discussion on some extremely 'sensitive matters'. Little did I know at this stage what the meeting would be about. But it wasn't a regular meeting.

Two days after this meeting, as per plan, five of the most dreaded terrorists, Ismail Pasha included, were transferred from Delhi's Tihar Jail to Nasik Jail in Maharashtra. It was reasoned that Delhi's Tihar Jail was overcrowded and that these dreaded terrorists needed to be kept separately. The terrorists were brought in a special chartered flight to Mumbai, from where they were supposed to be driven in two vans to Nasik. Interestingly, it would be past midnight when they started this journey from Mumbai to Nasik.

Igatpuri is a small town, some 45 km before Nasik. It has some of the highest peaks in the Western Ghats. However, when it featured in the news the next morning it was not for its geography. Just three kilometres away from Igatpuri, a most bizarre accident had been reported. The van carrying Ismail Pasha and his accomplice had plunged down the hills into a valley some 3000 metres deep. The three other terrorists lay shot dead on the edge of the cliff.

The police had an interesting version of the facts: according to them, on this crucial leg of their journey, Ismail Pasha had insisted on stopping the van as he wanted to pee. On getting down, he overpowered the policeman with him, shooting him in the arm. Ismail's accomplice too sprang into action and the two wrested possession of the van. Holding four policemen captive, they waited for the other van carrying three other terrorists to reach them. Threatening to shoot the policemen, Ismail made the policemen manning the other van release the three terrorists. But before these three terrorists could join Ismail and his accomplice, one unrelenting policeman began to shoot at them. Taken aback, Ismail and his accomplice just pushed away the policemen they'd held captive and abruptly took off in the van.

Left stranded between the two vans, the other terrorists tried to escape but were shot dead. Meanwhile, Ismail Pasha and his accomplice continued to drive. In their hurry to escape, the vehicle swerved off the edge of the mountain.

Amazingly, only two of the ten policemen suffered minor injuries.

❖

Of course the story had massive loopholes. And we were only too well aware of it.

'The Intelligence Bureau has definite information that terrorists from across the border are planning massive strikes to try and free their counterparts here,' Sharad had told me at the meeting a few days earlier.

'Hmm... so?' I had asked him.

'We'll have to increase our surveillance and security,' Sharad had said.

I was surprised by Sharad's words; he had sounded so timid. The old Sharad would have been breathing fire and exploring fresh solutions. That day however he spoke like any other politician. He had mellowed. His confidence had taken a severe beating. That's when I tried to re-instil his old confidence.

'Sharadji, I think now is the time to accomplish your unfinished agenda.'

He had looked at me wanting to hear more.

'If you can eliminate those terrorists, why protect them?' I had said, leaving him surprised at my suggestion.

I then spelt out the plan I was formulating in my mind. To my surprise, it was Sharad who seemed unusually defensive now. 'But doesn't that leave us vulnerable should another government come to power in the future and initiate an investigation?'

Life sometimes brings forth such unexpected role reversals. Did Krishna needed to be shown the way by Draupadi? It certainly seemed that way…

'Well, Sharadji, it was you who once said one needs to observe etiquette and norms with those who respect them. By not eliminating these terrorists, we are endangering the lives of scores of innocent citizens. By facilitating their death we're only trying to live our *rajdharma*.'

Sharad could not believe that his disciple was saying exactly what her mentor would have said, had he not been a bit out of sorts. He looked at me gratefully and then hugged me.

And with what later transpired at Igatpuri, I feel we had indeed accomplished our *rajdharma*.

❖

Hence, as it turned out I was not only privy to all the 'impropriety' that the Home Ministry undertook but the chief architect of it as well.

And I did not in the least mind being so.

In India, however, some things never change. The suspicious death of these five terrorists led to politics being played around it. 'They were accused, not yet convicted. And three of them were Indians. The government must order a CBI enquiry,' demanded the Indian Democratic Party.

The Marxists were just as unsparing: 'It's the darkest day for Indian democracy when punishments are handed out by the Home Ministry instead of the courts. The day is not far when India will become a Banana Republic.'

Ratna Pandey also had her say: 'The Home Minister must resign immediately on moral grounds. If he doesn't the PM must sack him.'

Sharad, however, stood his ground firm as ever, even refusing all demands for a CBI enquiry. It seemed that he'd taken a gamble that he was prepared to play right down to the wire. More importantly, these 'killings' were an emotive issue that were bound to divide public opinion.

Sharad had anticipated that the majority would stand by him. But that didn't happen.

In the weeks that followed, one of our key constituents, the Indian Republicans, withdrew support from our government, accusing the Home Minister of running his ministry like a mafia. With some 31 MPs gone, we were left a few seats short of a majority. The PM subsequently called a meeting of the Cabinet, where Sharad once again stuck his neck out.

'Coalition politics anyway compromises our governance agenda. I think it's the best time for us to go to the people and seek a fresh mandate. We must go in for mid-term polls,' he asserted, even assuring the Cabinet that his hard stance on national security would help the party win more than 300 seats of its own.

Sharad, obviously, had his eyes set on another larger agenda, of which I was well aware.

PM Yashwant Modi wasn't in the best of health, besides he was increasingly being seen as a weak administrator. If Sharad led the Nationalist Party's campaign in the elections and the party did indeed come to power, nothing could deny Sharad the post of PM.

'Of course I want to be the PM. Anyone who is in electoral politics in India would be lying if he said he does not want to be the PM,' Sharad had confided to me once.

It goes without saying that I personally was all for him being the PM, even though some amount of guilt did confront me, usually in the middle of the night, when I woke up thinking of the cold-blooded murder of the five terrorists that I had instigated.

Could they not have been tried in, let's say, a fast-track court?

Interestingly, as I'd already seen in other cases, an enemy's enemy tends to be your friend. So while fellow party men did not quite like Sharad's autocratic ways, they knew that if Yashwant Modi were to lead them into the next elections, the party could lose. Hence to secure their own future, they did not mind an aggressive Sharad leading them on. And the PM, faced with the prospect of proving his majority on the floor of the house, instead recommended dissolving the House.

Mid-term elections, thus, became inevitable.

❖

Sharad knew that in the next couple of weeks he'd get very busy with the campaign. It was important therefore to try and attend to Rhea before that. After Derek's death Rhea had become increasingly withdrawn. When he asked her to join us for a meal she declined, but then later, when I called, she agreed to accompany us.

Sharad, Rhea and I went out for dinner. It was an early February evening. Delhi's intense winter had finally made way for a kinder, milder weather. It was one of those rare times when the season in Delhi brings a glow to one's face. While the glow lingered, it was not strong enough to dispel the loneliness that I could sense each one of us individually battling.

'Rhea, you must start dating some hot eligible young men now or else you'll have to suffer more of these quiet dinners with oldies,' I said, trying to engage Rhea.

'And what about the oldies? How long are you prepared to suffer me?' she asked with a sad smile, leaving Sharad and me wondering how to react.

Thankfully, she was more articulate:

'At my age, I have more options than you. At your age, the options are slightly limited. Why then bother about me or the world? Don't you deserve your private life too? What are you both waiting for?'

Rhea's words filled me up with a sense of relief, which I'm sure Sharad felt too. It is indeed so strange and so much fun to see a 'daughter' match-make. Sharad did not verbally respond to what his daughter said. Instead he quietly clasped my hand into his – a clasp more reassuring than words could be. And then, as usual he had the final word, 'We promise to find you a boyfriend very soon... one you should get married to.' I squeezed Sharad's hand and smiled to indicate that I completely endorsed his wish.

❖

The country was all set to go to the polls once again in two months' time; I was re-contesting the same seat – Kishanganj. As I went about my campaign, I was flooded with memories of my first election –

when I was fighting a desperate battle for survival. I had managed to survive after all; but at a price.

Nonetheless, life had been hugely eventful for me, even making me wonder whether anyone else would have experienced as many twists and turns as I had in a short span of three years. Every time nostalgia seemed to sway me, I'd think of my 'dharma' and 'karma', words inscribed in me by my mentor.

For Sharad, this was the biggest battle of his life. He had thrust mid-term elections upon the government and the people, relying entirely upon his personal charisma. Could he pull it off? The media, by and large, had begun to refer to him as the next PM, of course always with a question mark. Sharad's efforts, this time round, were exceptional. Every day, he'd hop across the country to address at least eight to ten rallies. His first rally would start as early as seven in the morning while the last one often went on past midnight, exceeding the 10 p.m. deadline wherever possible.

'Can I travel with you for the next few days?' I asked him, surprising myself.

Sharad was just as pleasantly surprised.

'What about your election campaign? Kishanganj too is scheduled to vote in the first phase.'

'Yes, but things are fully under control there. Besides, our party unit is pretty strong in Bihar.'

To be honest, I had begun to fear for Sharad – a feeling I'd experienced only for my parents.

Sharad was virtually living life on the edge. He was overworked, always sleep-deprived, which in turn had taken its toll on his health. He had lately been diagnosed a diabetic but did nothing to control his blood sugar. Besides, in his zest to leave a greater impact upon the electorate, he'd often disregard security regulations to mingle with the janta.

'I can't shun them. They've made me reach where I am.' The media of course was more likely to buy his reasoning than me.

I knew it was the added force that a long-distance runner conjures up in the last lap of the race to ensure he doesn't come second. That Sharad had been pushing himself so hard had made me a bit fearful, though I couldn't precisely put a finger on what was bothering me. For six days Sharad and I travelled together night and day. Sample this to get an idea of what a campaign day of ours would be like: Delhi–Gorakhpur (U.P.)–Gondia (M.P.)–Bellary (Karnataka)–Cuttack (Orrisa)–Karimganj (Assam). In between flights, we'd try and catch up with each other's lives and share information about our long lost personal space.

'Rhea has been a different person after the kidnapping – lost in herself and pensive all the time. I do hope she meets someone who helps her move on in life,' Sharad said once and then asked, 'Can you think of someone who might be a good match for Rhea?'

In return I told him about the invitation I'd got from Rohit to attend his wedding. Yes, Rohit was getting married to Shyamlee.

'Does it hurt?' Sharad asked me.

'Not so much, because I've experienced something like this before.'

Sharad looked on in anticipation.

'My exes, it seems, derive some kind of joy by sending wedding invitations to me.'

In answer Sharad caressed the top of my head like one would a child's.

I feel it is very important not to let your personal life be dictated by political considerations. By travelling together, Sharad and I were taking a big risk. We knew that the media would be playing out our 'increased proximity', which in turn could become a major distraction from the issues that we were raising at different rallies. But then we wanted to set a precedent: Politicians should stop living in the fear of media. Aren't we entitled to our personal choices, in much the same way that the entire country is? Sharad trusted the masses way too much. He was confident that he'd done enough to win the people's trust. The unprecedented turn-out at our rallies further reassured us that Sharad's tryst with history was imminent.

As expected, the media made a big issue about us moving and staying together. In the six days that

Sharad and I travelled together, we grew extremely at ease with each other. After spending the whole day in front of huge crowds, we felt lonely staying in separate rooms at night. Hence, from the third night onward, we stayed together in the same room – Sharad on the bed and I on the floor. One night when I was completely exhausted Sharad slept on the floor. Another time, Sharad had a terrible body-ache. I wiped his bare back with a wet cloth and gave him a massage, much like I'd done to Rohit when he was ill. The next day, when I had a headache, Sharad rubbed some balm onto my forehead. I would iron his outfits before we set out: I wanted our future PM to look smart in front of the masses. On two occasions when it was possible I personally cooked his favourite parathas for our day long travel. Often after Sharad fell asleep, I'd stay awake just looking at him and praying that his aspirations for the country would be fulfilled.

❖

Our last rally together was at Rajnandgaon in Chattisgarh. After this rally, I had planned to go back to Patna to resume my election campaign while Sharad had planned to fly to Mumbai. The rally was supposed to a have a predominantly female tribal crowd and hence my presence was seen to serve an even bigger advantage.

'There is huge support for you; I can feel it in all my rallies,' I said as I was about to leave. 'There's little that can stop you from being the PM this time.'

In hindsight, I regret voicing that last sentence. Sharad had smiled, even as he had looked a little lost.

'I just happened to remember what you'd once said – "*Life is so predictably unpredictable. There's often just a single moment that separates life from death.*"'

I wondered what was making Sharad say that when everything looked so optimistic. Was it intuition?

Realizing the oddity of what he'd said, he quickly checked himself. 'By life and death I mean victory and defeat. There's very little that separates them, isn't there?'

His clarification did not dilute the impact of what he had originally said.

And, two hours later, I was to realize Sharad had foreseen his fate.

❖

On his way from Chattisgarh to Mumbai, some 50 kms before Nagpur, the helicopter Sharad was travelling in was caught in a terrible thunderstorm. The aircraft lost touch with the Air Traffic Controller. The moment when I was first informed of this is etched deep in my mind. I had just landed at the Patna airport and was walking with my entourage towards the exit. I immediately cancelled the two rallies that I was supposed to hold that evening, rushed to the state guest-house where I was staying, and locked myself in my room. Once there I desperately flipped news channels with one hand, while with the other I kept count of my chants of Om Namah Shivay. An hour later the news channels started flashing footage of a crashed aircraft with the charred bodies of Sharad, his personal secretary, a young journalist and three crew members, found in a village in Vidarbha.

I had experienced death in lesser forms before – when I saw Abhay and Ananya on my bed; when I was raped; when the baby in me died; when I went through the signing of my divorce papers with Rohit. But nothing had prepared me for the real thing. It was as if everything I had done or strived for, every wish, aim and ambition, was rendered meaningless. Without Sharad beside me, I had no reason to live.

Life often throws two questions at you: '*Why?*' and then '*Why me?*' Sharad's death made me question my very existence. It made me lose faith in God and everything around me. Memories of the brief period we had shared together enlarged themselves to fill all my waking hours, playing out again and again.

On a larger note, I wondered if God hated ambitious people. It was my experience that once you make your ambitions known, the world and the gods conspired to keep you from achieving them.

In 1979, a similar fate had befallen Sanjay Gandhi whom everyone had assumed would be our next PM. Now it was Sharad's turn to bite the dust. Small wonder then that of late the most timid non-leaders are going on to become successful prime ministers in our country.

❖

Life did another complete turnabout.

With Sharad no longer around to show us the way, we lost the elections and the Opposition coalition formed the government at the Centre. Though I won the Kishanganj seat again, there was little personal motivation left for me to be in politics. But if I quit, I'd be abandoning my 'karma' and 'dharma' – words on which Sharad had lived an entire life. Besides, I had another mission to accomplish – to prepare Rhea to inherit the political legacy of her father. I adopted this mission rather reluctantly, prodded by the knowledge that Sharad, wherever he was, would have expected it of me.

Life however was not so kind anymore. Once they were back in power the new Indian Democratic Party government acted out of sheer vengeance, particularly towards Sharad's improprieties as Home Minister. Every investigative agency was told to go all out and nail Sharad. It was quickly established that the Igatpuri deaths of the terrorists was a well-orchestrated fake encounter. In hindsight, I think it had been a last-ditch effort on my part to pump some confidence back into Sharad. Besides, we were just so weary of fighting the scourge of terrorism that we no longer cared for the consequences.

Had Sharad been alive he'd have been made a co-accused and perhaps the fact that he was my senior would have lessened the blame on me. Death perhaps saved him the ignominy to which being alive would have subjected him.

Based on the statement of a retired secretary from the Home Ministry – who had always felt threatened by Sharad and me and whom we largely ignored – the new government arrested me on charges of complicity in the murder of five terrorists. Thanks to the treachery that marks our politics, in a few months' time, three of those five dreaded terrorists were now being projected as 'innocents', as they had not yet been convicted.

EPILOGUE, OCTOBER 2003

I have spent the last year in jail trying not be undone by the pending enquiry and the court case against me.

To keep my sanity I immersed myself in penning a life less ordinary.

I have made umpteen appearances in court. Every time, in one way or the other, the story of my rape is dredged up and snide references are insinuated. I do not have faith in the court. And every time I wish my fate could be left to be decided by the people of my country. What wrong did Sharad and I do? We refused to treat the animals who wreaked havoc in our country like state guests. We dumped them where they deserved to be. Did Sharad and I not trust our legal system? Well, we couldn't afford to wait for the court verdict and then for the verdict in a higher court.

To us, every Indian life mattered.

As I sit back in prison, I'm aware that the Delhi High Court will be pronouncing its judgment on the case tomorrow.

I think I want to be pronounced guilty.

I think I'd like to be hanged to death.

I think our future generations ought to know that even seventy-two years after Bhagat Singh was hanged to death, Indian laws and politics are still skewed against those who, in their patriotic zest, dare to tread the extra mile for the country. Personally, I know I have a clear conscience.

I think what we did saved hundreds of lives.

I'm not sure whether my yearning for death has something to do with the bleakness I've felt ever since Sharad died. I do feel an irresistible urge to be reunited with him, wherever he is, and in whatever form. I feel a yearning to undertake another journey with him – one that will be less encumbered by the need for definition.

This drastic turn of events has left me with an unanswered query – Had Krishna always wanted the Mahabharat to happen and did Draupadi knowingly play along? The question, notwithstanding, I'm convinced that of all the men who came into my life, Sharad was my true soulmate.

❖

My reverie is broken with the guard's announcement that someone has come to see me. Oh, it's Rhea. My daughter, Rhea. Are you surprised to hear me call her 'daughter'? Isn't the child of your soulmate supposed to be like your own?

Rhea has come to visit me often. After the death of her father she has had no one to share her grief with. I am the only other who mourns his passing as deeply as she does. So far we have never discussed her future. Today she surprises me when she tells me that she has decided to enter politics and take Sharad's legacy forward. She says she can only do this with me by her side. She has engaged the country's top-most lawyer to fight my case. Should the High Court verdict go against us, she says, we will challenge it and take it to the Supreme Court.

I embrace her. With her by my side, I feel my strength and optimism return. It's as if Sharad's life force is with me again. We end up taking some important decisions. We decide we will form our own party and name it the Nationalist League (Sharad) We will contest all the Lok Sabha seats in the next elections.

I say to Rhea, 'It is a gargantuan task. We may not win enough to form the next government, but we will have sent the message loud and clear – India needs a million Sharad Malviyas to fight the menace of divisive politics.'

Rhea smiles gently and takes my hand. 'No,' she says. 'India only needs one Shruti Ranjan to keep alive the courage of her convictions.'

ACKNOWLEDGEMENTS

I wish to thank Nandita Aggarwal, Publishing Director at Hachette India, for once again believing in an unconventional subject like *The Edge of Desire*. I'm as grateful to Thomas Abraham and the entire team at Hachette. They have been wonderful to work with.

I'm grateful to my wife Ramyani for diligently reading up the manuscript even while it was being written and providing me her inputs at all stages.

Last but not the least, I remain indebted to my readers whose unflinching support keeps the maverick in me alive.

PRAISE FOR *OF LOVE AND POLITICS*

'Indeed, in today's age of monosyllabic phrases and grammatically horrifying SMS-lingo, it is commendable to have a writer like Sinha who can so adeptly weave Shakespearean phrases... with Shashi Tharoor-esque aplomb in his work.' – *The Hindu*

'The book throws up well-researched and lesser-known trivia about Indian political history that is very illuminating. Tuhin represents a breed of young Indian authors who are conscious of their roots and who keep an eye on their political surroundings.' – *Deccan Herald*

'...the book delves into... the connect between one's personal beliefs and his/her political ideology... the book celebrates democracy.' – **Ravi Shankar Prasad, senior politician**

'The best part about the book is that it provides a distinct perspective on almost every important political event of the last century.' – **Piyush Jha, filmmaker**

'Politics makes strange bed-fellows and this book aptly proves it.' – **Abhijit Bhaduri, author**

'Thought-provoking, easy flowing yet deep. Not only does it raise questions about the flaws in our multi-party democracy but also makes an attempt at offering solutions.' – **Gul Panag, actress**

PRAISE FOR *THAT THING CALLED LOVE*

'A journey of discovery through disparate spectrums, Tuhin waxes eloquent on the choices that lie before the typical urban Indian male and in an odd way strikes a chord that is unmistakable.' – ***The Sunday Indian***

'...the book touches several social issues and deals with them in a manner that has hitherto not been dealt with before.' – ***Screen***

'A subject, currently explored in films, coupled with flowing language and generous use of the first person, makes this book an exciting read.' – ***Afternoon Dispatch and Courier*, Mumbai**

'Set at a good pace, debutant novelist and scriptwriter Tuhin A. Sinha weaves a contemporary story of a bunch of well-etched-out characters exploring expectations, disillusionments and fragility in relationships.' – **Indiantelevision.com**